A VERY TIDY DEATH

A VERY TIDY DEATH

LILY ROCK MYSTERY
BOOK 6

BONNIE HARDY

ON THE OTHER HAND BOOKS

Copyright

Copyright @ 2023 On the Other Hand Books

By Bonnie Hardy

All right reserved.

Cover Design by Ebook Launch

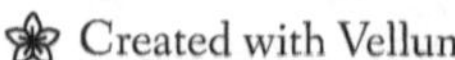 Created with Vellum

GET A FREE SHORT STORY

Join my VIP newsletter to get the latest news of Lily Rock along with contests, discounts, events, and giveaways! I'll also send you *Meadow's Hat*, a Lily Rock Mystery short story.

Sign up on bonniehardywrites.com/newsletter

"Cleanliness is next to Godliness."
John Wesley
1703-1791

Friday

"Would you stop staring out the window and come sit down?" Michael called from the kitchen table. Olivia felt his eyes on her back. Instead of turning, she explained over her shoulder.

"I'm staring at our new neighbor's front door. Do you think he'll invite himself for coffee again today?"

She heard Michael chuckle and his chair scrape against the wood planking. Then she felt his arms reach around her waist, pulling her back into his chest. His lips caressed her neck as he mumbled, "It's okay with me if Jeff doesn't show up every morning. I like sharing our morning just the two of us."

She turned in his arms, reaching her hands up to clasp behind his neck. "We had a lengthy opportunity to be alone last night. Now we must use our coffee time to plot out Sage's future."

Michael bent closer to brush his lips against her neck. "Since when is matchmaking your deal?" He took her by the hand, guiding her to the kitchen table where he'd left a steaming cup of coffee. "My new blend," he explained. "I'm calling it In the Deep Midwinter. Hints of chocolate and a slight touch of cherry. Maybe someday I'll actually like coffee."

She pulled out her chair and sat down. Picking up the mug, she took a sniff. "Smells amazing. Did Cookie invent a signature baked good to go with your blend?"

"He's working on it. I tried to talk to him the other day, but he kept jabbering on about baby Star. 'She's so smart. Look at those eyes. Love her smooth skin.' You'd think he'd never seen a baby before."

"Our niece is pretty special. No wonder he's enthralled." Olivia took her first sip of coffee, relishing the warmth on her tongue and the slight tang of cherry. She put the mug down. "This is delicious. Well done. I'm thinking Cookie will come up with something along the line of Cherry Chocolate Cookies. I'd love that for sure. You two make the best business partners."

"I'll pass your suggestion along." Michael patted her hand. "But what about your matchmaking idea? I didn't realize how serious you were about Sage and Jeff."

Olivia sighed. "Sage only has eyes for Star right now. I suppose a new baby is enough company for any single mom. But I'm beginning to worry."

Michael looked interested, so she kept talking.

"Are all new moms like this? Sage adapts every waking moment to Star's schedule. The baby gets up and sleeps whenever she wants. Sage has expressed no interest in the band getting back together. Sweet Four O'Clock needs to practice and settle gigs for spring and summer. I'm starting to feel antsy, like we may never perform again."

Michael cleared his throat, but Olivia wasn't finished talking.

"But the real problem is that I don't want to move out and leave her alone with a three-month-old baby." This time she stopped talking, sitting back in her chair.

Michael asked, "So playing matchmaker will make it easier for us to move. Is that what you're thinking?"

Olivia had a solution to her problem. "Jeff. He could really help. If he moves in after we move out, then Sage won't be alone. I'll feel so much better."

Michael cocked his head to one side, his eyes following her lips as she spoke. Once she stopped for another sip of coffee, he said, "So I'm hearing two problems. One is about Sweet Four O'Clock and the other is about our moving. You could look at this another way. A short hiatus from Sweet Four O'Clock might free up more time to pack. As for Sage being preoccupied with Star? That's a bit trickier."

He looked at her hopefully. Since he'd started building their new home he'd had that same look. One of expectation. Olivia knew that the latest Bellemare creation was his masterpiece, as least until the next project.

Being partnered with a famous architect and builder had its perks. Even she had to admit that. If it weren't for the problem with Sage, she'd be all in for the move.

A familiar scratch came at the kitchen door.

"Sounds like Mayor Maguire wants his breakfast." Michael stood, making his way to the back door. Once opened, a rush of cold wind accompanied by a handsome brown labradoodle blew past. The dog rushed toward Olivia, bumping into her knees.

"Bork," he said in greeting. He sat at her feet, his eyes lively with anticipation.

She patted him on the head. "Good morning to you too."

Then she heard Michael speak to someone else at the door. "Hey, Jeff," he greeted. A tall man stepped into the kitchen. Jeff Grossman wore a puffy jacket and a black woolen cap. Tall and lean, he grinned and came inside. Michael quickly closed the door behind him.

"Hey yourself." Jeff slapped his gloved hands together. "Cold out there. You guys up for company? I smell coffee."

"We're testing Michael's new blend. Go ahead and find your own mug," Olivia offered, pointing to the cupboard over the counter.

Michael raised his eyebrows at Olivia, who grinned back at him. *Plan on. We just have to figure out how to keep Jeff here until Sage wakes up.*

"How about breakfast?" she asked Jeff. "I'm sure you want to stay and say good morning to Sage and Star. The baby will be up soon. I'll start the kettle for Sage's tea." Olivia glanced over at Michael, who looked amused. *Was I too obvious? Maybe I made too big of a deal about Sage and breakfast.*

Jeff sat down at the table, balancing a full mug of coffee in one hand. Olivia smiled faintly at him, still immersed in her matchmaking plot. *So Sage wakes up and wanders in for coffee. He'll be sitting there all warm and hunky and Sage will say to herself, "Oh hello, big fella. Where have you been hiding?"*

Feeling a pull at her heart, Olivia knew why Sage having a partner mattered so much to her. It was because of her own mom. Growing up, Mona had told Olivia how being a single parent was the hardest thing she'd ever done.

Olivia realized that as their move came closer, she felt

sad. Her usual upbeat attitude had been scraped away, giving rise to a sense of anxiety. *I don't want to abandon Sage and Star in this big house.* Now every time Michael brought up the potential move, she felt a pang of misgiving. But she didn't want to tell him, for fear he'd think she was ungrateful and not all in.

While Michael and Jeff huddled in deep conversation, Olivia walked to the cupboard. She pulled down three plates and then took forks out of the drawer underneath the counter, keeping her ear tuned to the other room for the first sound of her niece awakening.

Placing a homemade loaf of sourdough onto the cutting board, she bent over to inhale the yeasty goodness. The tangy smell of freshly baked bread improved her mood right away. For several months she'd made a habit of buying a fresh loaf every week from Thyme Out.

As she sliced she once again marveled at how well Cookie and Michael had started their small business. Sometimes people just fit. And even more than people, Cookie's bakery just fit. If you asked anyone in town, they'd tell you Thyme Out had been open forever. Probably because no one could remember when Lily Rock didn't enjoy his signature baked goods.

Olivia glanced toward the doorway. *Baby must be sleeping in.* With a balanced but firm grip on the handle of the knife, she deftly finished slicing the last pieces of bread from the loaf. *Perfect for toast. I have Meadow's homemade raspberry jam and butter. A dozen eggs. That should keep Jeff here, at least for a while longer.*

And then the now familiar wail of a baby came from the other side of the house. "Star is up," Olivia announced right away. Jeff glanced over, but then his head turned back as he kept talking to Michael.

Men. No clue. If it weren't for me, Jeff and Sage would never get together.

Olivia grabbed the handle of the half-full coffeepot. Edging closer to the table, she leaned over to fill Jeff's mug. Before she could replace the pot, Jeff's phone buzzed. He picked it up.

"What? Slow down." The hair on Olivia's neck rose at the sound of alarm in his voice. "I'm here with Mike and Olivia. Deep breath. Now tell me again. Honey, stop crying. Do you want me to come over? I can be right there."

After a few moments of listening, he pocketed his cell and stood. "I guess I'll have to have breakfast another time. That's Roxy, my sister. She's crying and very upset."

As he headed to the door he continued to explain, "Roxy's found a dead body. In the bathroom. Where she's working." His clipped sentences only emphasized the alarmed expression on his face.

Michael looked to Olivia and they both nodded. She put the coffeepot down, returning to stand in front of Jeff. "We'll go with you. I'll put the eggs back in the refrigerator and grab my coat."

"Jeff and I will meet you out front," Michael added. He nodded to the back door. As the baby continued to wail in the background, Mayor Maguire followed Olivia, nosing against the back of her knee. She turned to explain. "I'll feed you very soon," she promised. "Or maybe you're ready for a car ride?"

"Bork," he replied. But then he glanced toward the pantry as if he'd changed his mind.

"Food later," she promised.

When she didn't make an attempt to open the pantry, Mayor Maguire gave up and ran ahead of her through the doorway.

Olivia made her way to the front door and opened it to let Mayor Maguire out first. "Bork," the mayor called out, running down the driveway just as Jeff's truck pulled around the corner.

Michael hopped out of the passenger seat. He opened the back door and then explained, "I thought you and the mayor would want to sit together in back."

"Sounds good," she said as the dog jumped in first. Once she'd settled herself into the seat and attached her seat belt, Michael closed the door and got back into the passenger seat.

"Where is Roxy staying?" Olivia asked as Jeff bumped down the driveway toward the main road.

"Up by the Lily Rock trail. That big house owned by Whitney Zimmer. Roxy was hired to cater some retreat for a bunch of tidy influencers. I've never heard of that Whitney woman, but Roxy tells me she's kind of a big deal."

"I think I've heard of her," Olivia said.

Jeff continued. "She owns Time to Tidy. She sells books and runs a popular website on how to curate and clean household clutter. She sets up her retreats in Lily Rock, but I've never met her face-to-face."

Olivia swallowed hard. "Is it..." Her voice faltered. "Is it Whitney that your sister found dead?" She couldn't disguise the dread in her voice.

"I really don't know. Roxy was so upset she didn't say." Jeff looked forward, intent on the road.

Michael glanced toward the back seat. "Looks like you may have another case to solve." He shrugged and then explained to Jeff. "Olivia has a gift. You may not be aware, but she helped the constabulary solve that last case about Beats Malone. People love to confess to her. Once she starts singing, they just spill their guts to anyone who will listen. Lately she doesn't even have to sing."

Jeff's truck accelerated up the winding road toward the top of the hill. He gave no indication that he'd heard Michael's words.

Olivia wasn't surprised. *I bet he's worried about his sister. So traumatic to discover a dead body. I remember my first time.*

She reached over to wrap both arms around Mayor Maguire's warm, comforting body, laying her face against his fur for comfort.

CHAPTER TWO

As Jeff navigated his truck over the winding road, Olivia shared the view with Mayor Maguire from the back seat. It always helped to calm her nerves, the view of the pines along the mountain road. She could imagine their scent even with the window closed. When Jeff accelerated, her head jerked backward.

A blasting horn brought her hands to her ears. Olivia frantically searched the road for the vehicle.

A black Mercedes SUV tailgated behind Jeff's truck. Olivia gasped as the Mercedes jerked into the opposite lane to pass. Engine rumbling, the black vehicle pulled alongside Jeff's truck. Then in a whoosh it sped ahead, honking as if to have the last word.

That was close. She dropped her hands and then gasped again. Another truck, driving full speed, bore down from the opposite lane. The SUV had barely avoided a crash. *One more second and we would have been caught in a collision.*

Jeff lifted his foot off the accelerator. Olivia watched as the SUV disappeared around the bend of the curving road.

She gripped the side of her seat while Mayor Maguire barked.

"It's okay, buddy," she murmured, moving her fingers up his neck to give him a reassuring scratch behind his ear.

"That was close," Olivia said, voice shaking. Michael looked around, his face full of worry.

Both of Jeff's hands gripped the steering wheel. He pressed down his foot, gaining more speed. "Stupid idiot, trying to pass me on this narrow road. That other truck was headed right at him. We could have been sideswiped, maybe killed."

"You okay?" Michael reached out with his hand to pat Olivia's knee.

"Just fine," she commented dryly. "Not my first terrorist tailgater on this road."

The corner of his mouth twitched as he turned back with a chuckle. "You may not know this," he told Jeff, "but Olivia and I met on this very road. It was a really foggy morning and she had her headlights on."

"I thought more light would help me see the road," Olivia admitted.

"And I was following her to make sure she was safe," Michael added.

Olivia interjected. "When he tells this story he always fails to mention that he was tailgating me. In a big truck, much bigger than my Ford, making me even more nervous."

Jeff nodded. "Good story." Then he slowed the truck down to make a quick right turn onto a gravel road. "This is the place." He nodded toward the wood-sided two-story house in the clearing. The wide expanse of porch was flanked by two large pine trees. They'd been carefully trimmed to look identical.

"I know that house," Michael said at once. "Constructed

right when I arrived in Lily Rock. I heard a corporation bought it." *Ever since Michael moved to Lily Rock from Chicago, he's kept up on all of the construction projects in the area.*

"That would be Whitney Zimmer's company," Jeff said. "Like I said, she brings people to Lily Rock for her Time to Tidy retreat and contests. People compete. They win a cash prize and she invites the winner to her Tidy Team."

He pulled the truck to a stop a few feet away from the front door. "Roxy tells me that Whitney is very exacting with her brand. Kind of a tyrant." He shut down the engine.

Olivia stepped out of the truck onto the gravel. Mayor Maguire hopped down behind her. Instead of following Michael and Jeff, he ran around the truck straight into the woods.

So I guess M&M just wanted a ride...

As they approached the house, the front door flung open. Standing on the threshold was a man wearing a pair of pressed blue jeans and a chambray button-up shirt. A couple of inches under six feet, he held his back ramrod straight.

As soon as they drew closer he began issuing directions from the door. "We can introduce ourselves in a minute. Right now I want you to enter the house quietly. Take off your shoes. Line them up alongside this wall in the entry.

Once inside the house, Olivia looked around. Several doors led off the hallway. The one to the left appeared to be a great room entrance. A bathroom door stood ajar at the end of the hall. On the right was a door that Olivia assumed was the kitchen.

She bent over to remove her boots. *At least I wore my best socks.* The man continued to give orders in a firm voice.

Olivia placed the toes of her boots against the wall next

to a tall pair of Uggs. Nearly everyone in Lily Rock wore them. Yet this particular pair looked a little out of place. The shearling fur, folded over at the top, appeared fresh, not matted like most of the boots seen around town. *They're new. Maybe they belong to a tourist.*

She glanced at the man to see if he was going to give more directions. When he glared, she smiled and shrugged off her jacket. Pulling down the sleeve of her sweater, she shuddered. *Kinda cold in here.*

"Hang it on an empty peg," the man told her.

Olivia followed his direction. Lifting her jacket to the peg rack above the boots, she hesitated. A brown leather coat with a fur collar had been draped against the wall, dangling from its designer tag on the inside of its collar.

She inhaled a smoky leather scent, appreciating the smell of fine leather. Tempted to reach over and rub her fingers against the expensive coat, she stopped. *He's still watching me. I can just feel it.* Instead, Olivia hooked her black quilted jacket two pegs down, hiding her smile. *My old jacket doesn't deserve to associate with such richness.*

She glanced back at her scuffed leather boots. *Maybe I need to upgrade my winter wardrobe and get a new jacket and some new boots. Since winter is nearly over, I can take advantage of a sale.*

Olivia had the money to buy clothes since inheriting from Marla; she just didn't want to take the time. She'd been involved with Sage's pregnancy for the past several months. And then the birth. She hadn't made time for herself.

Jeff tossed his sneakers next to Olivia's boots. Then he spun around to face the gruff man. "I'm Jeff Grossman. I'm here to see Roxy, my sister." He waved his hand to dismiss the box of foot coverings.

With a quick glance at Jeff's socks, the man sniffed. Then he reached down to pick up Jeff's shoes, holding them at arm's length. Bending again, he placed them with toes facing the wall, then stepped back.

Wanting to avoid any more discomfort, Olivia spoke up. "I'm Olivia Greer. This is Michael Bellemare. We have clean socks. Just got them out of the dryer this morning," *Does he actually think we need to cover our socks?* When the man didn't offer a name nor a smile, she added, "I can vouch for Michael's socks and mine, of course. We won't need shoe coverings."

The man exhaled a loud humph. He put his arm down, the box next to his thigh.

Well he's a bit much. And he's still not introduced himself.

Michael stepped forward, his hand extended. "Like she said, I'm Michael Bellemare. We were with Jeff when his sister called about the body." He paused to add, "And I'll make sure my shoes line up."

Now an ingratiating smile came over the man's face as he warmed up to Michael. "I appreciate your concern for the orderliness of this house." His eyes narrowed. "Now for my introduction. I am Stanley 'the Wiz' Weyland, Whitney Zimmer's executive assistant." When he waited after giving his name, Olivia wondered, *Am I supposed to know him or something?*

"Such a dreadful circumstance." Stanley waved them forward, closing the door behind him. He jingled what Olivia assumed were car keys in his pocket.

"I've called the police," he continued, sounding slightly breathless. "They're on their way. I don't suppose they'll be here any time soon. Rather a nasty person answered the phone. She acted like I was inconveniencing her, not like a real policewoman."

Olivia shrugged. *I bet that was Janis. She is an acquired taste.* "I've never known the constabulary to delay an emergency," she defended her friend.

Stanley's eyes narrowed, looking doubtful, but he didn't bother to reply.

"Excuse me," Jeff asked, "where is my sister?"

Olivia heard someone crying, coming from up the stairs.

Stanley pointed to the stairway.

CHAPTER THREE

Olivia watched as Jeff took the carpeted steps two at a time. Up until now she'd been occupied with the introductions and taking off her jacket and boots. But now she smelled something very strong lingering in the air. Her nostrils flared; her throat felt thick. She coughed, struggling to clear her throat.

Wondering at the source of the smell, she stared at Stanley Weyland. *Maybe he bleaches his shirts.*

He smiled at her and then discreetly, with an outstretched finger, swiped at his nose. Then he opened the door and nodded for her to step into the next room.

When he didn't offer an explanation about the smell, Olivia looked around the great room. Finally she asked, "Are you smelling the bleach?" Stanley looked bemused but did not agree. So she turned to Michael.

He nodded. "I do. Smells really clean in here."

It was the intensity of the bleach odor that surprised her. She walked from the mud room through the doorway to investigate. She found an oversized sofa and two matching leather chairs at the center of the room. But the smell had intensified.

Glancing behind her back, she noted the sparkling front windows facing the driveway. *They've been recently washed. But people don't usually spray bleach to clean glass windows.*

Still scanning, her eyes stopped at the stairway where Jeff had already disappeared. Upstairs, she thought.

Jeff leaned over the half wall from the second floor. "I found her," he announced. "Come on up."

"Roxanne is in the hallway outside. As far as I know she hasn't moved since discovering the body." Stanley spoke calmly and precisely.

Olivia wanted to scream. *Is he always this withholding? What about that smell, and by the way, who's dead?*

Michael gestured with his head for Olivia to follow him upstairs. She lingered for a moment to talk to Stanley. Now that she knew he would withhold obvious information, she butted right in.

"How many people were in the house when the body was discovered?" Olivia stared at Stanley. She deliberately made her voice sound demanding. *Better get used to answering questions, buddy. Officer Janis Jets won't stand for any of this nonsense.*

Stanley, seemingly unperturbed, didn't even flinch. Nor did he answer her question directly. "You're that Olivia Greer. The one who helps the constabulary as a consultant. I've heard about you. When I first came up to Lily Rock, some kid in the hardware store was going on about your crime-solving abilities."

"Must have been Brad May," she commented dryly. "He does tend to exaggerate."

The corner of Stanley's mouth quirked. He leaned

forward as if to take a closer look at her. "Somehow I think you're being too modest. But no matter."

She glared at him, and then to her satisfaction, he finally explained. "There were the six of us involved in the competition. Whitney, her three newest contestants, me, and of course, Roxanne. The caterer."

Then he shrugged and changed the subject. "How about I start coffee and arrange a few pastries? I've never been at a murder scene but I've heard the police like that kind of thing. Do you want to help me in the kitchen?" He pointed over his shoulder.

His voice sounded inviting and Olivia felt tempted. She'd seen more than her share of dead bodies since moving to Lily Rock. Plus she wanted to stay out of the way until Janis Jets made her initial visit to the crime scene. And a lot of information can be shared while preparing food. *Maybe Stanley will spill something important.*

But then she changed her mind. "Thanks, but I can be helpful to Roxanne. Keep her company until Officer Jets arrives."

"I see," Stanley commented dryly. He frowned, obviously not happy with her refusal.

"Did Roxy say anything to you earlier?" Olivia asked.

His mouth tightened. "She admits that she's probably the one to blame. One of her adjunct job duties was to set up all the cleaning supplies the night before. She obviously mislabeled them. I warn people all the time. You need to be so careful with cleaning chemicals." He shrugged. "Roxanne is a wonderful young woman, but a bit flighty." He turned to walk down the hallway. She'd have to follow him if she had any more questions.

As Stanley disappeared through the doorway, Olivia made her way to the stairs. Stopping on the landing, she heard soft crying more distinctly. Followed by a deep inhale and the constriction of her throat. *Bleach.* She identified the odor. *And getting stronger.* She made a left turn at the top of the steps. Then she heard a man's low voice along with the cries.

"I am so sorry," came a woman's wailing voice. "I didn't mean to hurt her." Accompanying tears rose in Olivia's eyes. She often felt other people's emotions. Sometimes it was difficult to distinguish between her feelings and someone else's. Her mother told her when she was young that she was an empath. "You'll have to be careful. That's a gift and a curse," Mona had warned.

It had only been recently that Olivia remembered Mona's warning. How she'd feel other people's emotions in her body. She rarely admitted it to herself in so many words. But when she teared up like that, with Roxanne's distress, she knew why.

Olivia inched closer, not wanting to cause any undue attention to her approach. A young woman, knees to her chest, huddled on the floor. White-blonde hair draped both sides of her face, which she buried in her hands. She looked up. Olivia noted her pale heart-shaped face, along with red swollen eyes.

Jeff sat next to her, his back braced against the wall. He placed a hand on the woman's shoulder, looking up at Olivia. Her glance found Michael, who stood a few steps back. His eyes pleaded, *Do something.*

I'm going to sit down next to Roxy and just be quiet. She came closer, trying to catch Jeff's eye. She pointed to the space on the other side of his sister. He nodded, so she braced her back against the wall and slid into a sitting position. She crossed her legs underneath her body, folding her hands in her lap.

Opening her mouth to introduce herself, she changed her mind and closed it again. From her seated position, she caught sight of a metal object. Located directly across from the bathroom, it had been lodged between the edge of the carpet and the half wall of the stairway.

A kitchen knife...

She took a deep breath. *Don't mention it. At least not yet.*

Since the woman next to her kept steadily crying, Olivia inhaled deeply, then exhaled slowly. Ignoring the smell and the constriction in her throat, she knew her steady intentional breath would help Roxanne. *I just hope she feels my support and doesn't think I'm her enemy.*

A few seconds later Roxanne rubbed her hand across her eyes. She looked over but didn't seem surprised at Olivia's presence. She leaned to her left and lifted her hand as if to touch Olivia's knee. But then she withdrew her hand and placed it in her lap. Clearing her throat, she spoke in a low voice.

"Who are you?"

"I'm a friend of your brother's. My name is Olivia Greer. You're Roxy, right?"

"That's right. Jeff told me about you. But nothing is going to help me." Her voice grew more intense. "I killed her. It was an accident. I must have mislabeled the bottles last night."

Olivia spoke in a deliberately measured tone. "The police will want to hear your testimony. But you don't have to talk about it right now. In fact the first thing they will do is warn you about your rights. Sometimes people jump to conclusions about how things happened, especially if they are in shock."

Roxanne objected. "But there's no question who did

this. I hate it was me. Maddie would never mix bleach and vinegar. She was the expert about kitchen chemicals. Her brand was about using everyday products to clean your house. She was well aware that vinegar and bleach combined could be toxic."

So that's the other smell. A tinge of vinegar along with the bleach.

"Maddie?" Olivia questioned.

"Yes, Maddox Hall. We called her Maddie. She's the tidy influencer of 'Little Things Every Day.' Have you heard of her?"

"Like I said, you'd better wait to talk about all of this."

Roxy pointed her finger toward the half wall. "I dropped the knife over there. I knocked on the bathroom door. When she didn't answer, I tried to open the door but it was locked. Then I grabbed a knife from the kitchen and used it to get inside. If the door had been unlocked, I might have saved her. But it was too late."

Olivia looked over Roxanne's head at Jeff. His face had a sallow tone. One hand picked at a hangnail where blood had begun to ooze.

He mouthed the words to Olivia: "I tried too."

Olivia reached out to pat the girl's knee. *I guess she's not going to stop confessing.*

"If I'm not mistaken, I hear a siren outside. I bet that's Officer Jets on her way. She'll help figure all of this out. Until then I'll stay with you." Olivia slid back up the wall, standing on both feet. Jeff did the same.

Roxy looked small still sitting on the carpet, her legs crossed underneath her body.

Jeff nodded toward Michael. He took a step closer to the half wall, looking down into the great room. Olivia moved out of Roxanne's hearing range, gesturing for Jeff to follow.

Down the hall, closer to Michael, Jeff said, "I didn't know what to say to Roxy, but you're a natural. I never thought about her rights. She'll need an attorney."

Michael came closer to join their conversation. "Maybe you'd like to call someone right now. If you don't know anyone, I have a few suggestions."

"She's in no shape to be making any calls herself," Jeff acknowledged. He reached into his pocket, pulling out his cell phone. At that moment the doorbell rang, followed by a dog's loud bark.

Mayor Maguire must be outside.

Olivia was never sure where the dog would turn up. Yet the thought of his close proximity made her feel less tense. She heard the door open and then a familiar voice.

"Lily Rock police. Where's the body?" came Janis Jets's gruff inquiry.

"We're up here," Olivia called out.

Jets rounded the top step and stood in the hallway, her mouth tight. Her no-nonsense hair was pulled into a bun at the back of her head, and she wore a blue blazer with tan-colored slacks.

Olivia waited.

"I might have known you'd already be here," Jets said sharply. "Now where's the body?"

CHAPTER FOUR

Olivia braced herself for Janis's usual reproach. When it didn't come, she felt a tinge of disappointment. *That's our thing that we do. She gets mad that I'm here, while I nod my head. Okay then...*

As if anticipating her unspoken comment, Jets said, "I'm not gonna chew you out. That ship has sailed. On the one hand you really annoy me, but on the other hand? It's been a bit since we worked a case."

"Does that mean you missed me?" Olivia's voice sounded hopeful.

"Don't be ridiculous." Jets clamped her mouth shut. She looked down at Roxy and then back up at Olivia, then toward the door to the bathroom. "I presume the body is in there?"

"I didn't look," Olivia admitted. "Didn't want to get reprimanded for disturbing your crime scene." Then she added quickly, "The smell is really strong even downstairs. I assume it's coming from in there." She pointed to the closed door. "And then have a look at that knife. Someone must have used it to get inside the bathroom." She made sure not to sound too positive. Those details were up to Janis, her team, and forensics to figure out.

Jets walked closer. She bent to look at the knife. "I'll let my team bag and tag this as evidence." Then she turned back to Olivia. "The knife may be a clue, but only the experts can make an official decision." Jets inhaled, sniffing loudly. "Sure smells clean in here."

"It does." Olivia nodded. "Even the closed doors can't keep the smell away." She nodded toward the bathroom.

Jets, glancing toward the wall where Roxy sat, said, "I presume she's the main suspect."

"That's Roxy," Olivia said.

Jets spun to look at the bathroom again. "So we have a bathroom with a closed door. A knife that may have been used to unlock the door from the outside." She looked at Olivia.

"Roxanne confessed to you right away?"

"I warned her not to," Olivia protested.

"You and your superpower. Makes me sick." Jets scowled and turned away.

CHAPTER FIVE

Janis Jets pulled on latex gloves and then took hold of the doorknob. She hesitated and pulled her hand away. Instead of looking in the room where the body was located, she took a minute to think. Then she lifted the N95 mask around her neck, covering her nose and mouth. She changed her mind again and paused to remove the mask.

Facing the onlookers, she growled, "Step back, everyone. My gut and my nose tell me this may be a toxic situation, which would contaminate the hallway when I open the door. Once I have a good look in the bathroom, I'll make an initial report to authorities, and then my team will collect any evidence. They'll be here shortly to assist."

She looked around and then added, "In the meanwhile, prepare yourselves. I'll be asking for your name and contacts." Her eye fell on Stanley Weyland, who lurked down the hall. She called out, "And you are?"

He stepped closer to Jets. "I'm Stanley 'the Wiz' Weyland, Miss Zimmer's personal assistant." He sounded self-assured and dignified.

Up until he spoke, Olivia had not been aware that he'd followed Jets upstairs.

"Zimmer. She's the tidy guru, right?" Jets stared him down.

"Some call her a mentor, others an organizing genius." He nodded.

"Okay, personal assistant called Stanley. Where the hell is your boss?" Jets looked around, as if the woman in question could be conjured. "And since you're the big coordinator, what about the other contestants for this tidy fest? Where are they, pray tell?"

Elevating his nose slightly, Stanley glared imperiously at Jets. Even after she stopped talking, he waited a bit longer. Then he waited a little longer. Olivia fidgeted because the silence had become uncomfortable. Finally he cleared his throat.

"Miss Zimmer hosts the Time to Tidy contest twice a year. She left earlier, putting me in charge. The other two contestants, Miss Serenity 'Cleanliness is Next to Godliness' McFee, along with Mr. Bruce 'The Tool' Ward are on assignment. They left early this morning."

"What kind of assignment?" Jets barked.

"Every year the contestants receive challenges and are sent to separate locations. They've been at work since six o'clock."

"That still doesn't explain why your boss isn't here. Does she know about the dead body?"

Stanley cleared his throat again. "As for Miss Zimmer." His nose came down an inch as he stared at Jets. "She is not required to tell me her whereabouts. But according to her calendar, she's," he raised his hands to air quote, "in meetings all day."

Olivia held back her grin, suppressing a chuckle.

I'm enjoying this, how Weyland isn't ruffled by Janis.

Janis Jets stared at Stanley Weyland as if she were at the zoo looking at a chimpanzee who'd accidentally been trapped in the polar bear enclosure. Jets sniffed, then narrowed her eyes.

Olivia watched as Janis's hand made its way around her back to rest near her belt, close to the bulge under her jacket. Olivia knew that underneath the bulge was a weapon concealed at her waist. She also knew that the familiar gesture meant that Janis was irritated, even if she looked calm.

Jets patted the bump. Then a slight smile crossed her lips. "Well isn't that a nice accounting. You are certainly living up to your job description, all patronizing and superior. But I think that's for show, the part about your boss." Jets smiled and continued to assess.

"I don't suppose you realize that deflecting any of my inquires may result in me holding you as an accessory after the fact. Obstructing justice is a real thing, Wiz." She sounded friendly.

But the Wiz didn't seem remotely ruffled. He lowered his nose again and blinked, taking the warning without comments.

Jets continued. "So if what you say is true, the one and only queen of Time to Tidy has fled the scene. And you aren't certain if she knew about the dead contestant in her upstairs bathroom." Jets scowled.

By this time perspiration had formed on Stanley's forehead. He reached into his pocket, pulling out a folded white handkerchief, and dabbed at the moisture, smiling but obviously nervous.

Jets kept talking. "We have a woman who claims that cleanliness is next to godliness and there's a guy called

The Tool? You tidy-uppers are already getting on my nerves."

Finally Jets looked up and closed her iPad, turning to Jeff. "Take your sister downstairs. Make sure she's offered a drink of water. Get some tissues. And be the big brother.

"Then call the Lily Rock doc. Olivia has his number if you don't. I want Martinez to check your sister over. She may have been exposed to the toxins when she discovered the dead woman."

Jets pointed to Roxanne. "Stop sniveling and get up. Everyone is hanging out in the hall because you refuse to move. You're endangering them by staying here. Just follow your brother."

Jeff extended a hand toward Roxy. She took hold of his fingers and he pulled her to her feet. Keeping her hand in his, he led her toward the stairs. That left the Wiz, Michael, and Olivia in the hallway. All eyes were on Janis Jets.

She slipped her mask back in place. Covering her nose and mouth, she reached for the doorknob, giving it a twist. Pushing the door open with her other gloved hand, she stepped inside and quickly closed the door behind her.

An acid smell poured out from the bathroom, as if waiting to make an escape. The smell made Olivia's nostrils and throat sting.

"Maybe we'd better do as Janis suggests and get away from here."

Not liking the smell or the congestion in her lungs, Olivia made her way to the stairway. Michael and the Wiz followed. When she reached the bottom step, the doorbell rang.

Standing to the side, she gave way to Michael, who

hurried and opened the front door. Two people in police uniforms bustled into the room. The taller man flashed his badge. "I'm Officer Warren. Jets called us to a crime scene..."

"Jets is upstairs," Michael said. The other man didn't bother to introduce himself. Both rushed past Michael, heading toward the stairway.

"Bork," called Mayor Maguire. He stood behind a living room chair. Sauntering closer to Michael, his tail waved a greeting. He looked over at Olivia and headed past her toward the sofa. Stopping to sit down, M&M had another look around.

His eyes became haunted when he saw Roxy, sitting on the sofa. He rose to all four paws and padded his way toward her, his nails clicking against the wood floor.

She looked at the dog with a puzzled expression.

Sitting down on his haunches, he sniffed her knee. His nose traveled down her leg to sniff her shoe. Then he raised his head abruptly, glancing quickly at Olivia before turning to Roxy again.

Mayor Maguire lifted his right paw in the air as if introducing himself.

Rubbing her hand over her eyes, Roxy stared at his extended leg as if she wasn't sure what to do. When Mayor Maguire did not lower his paw, she finally reached a trembling hand forward. "Hello," she said quietly.

Mayor Maguire smiled as she pumped his leg up and down. Then he dropped his paw and rested his chin on her knee. His eyes looked up at her face.

Olivia knew that Maguire had his own way of being with people. He'd chosen to befriend Roxy for his own reasons. In the past he'd befriended guilty people in jail and innocent strangers in Lily Rock. It was as if he sensed the most vulnerable person and took them on as his project. Mayor Maguire didn't play the usual favorites.

Roxy scratched her finger behind his ear. He came closer to curl up on top of her feet. His nose rested on her shoe; he closed his eyes. She patted his head. Olivia saw her tentative smile. *M&M has worked his magic. He's a natural companion for those in distress.*

Satisfied that Roxy was in good company, Olivia spoke up. "While we're waiting for Officer Jets, does anyone want a glass of water, or maybe some coffee?"

"Thanks." Jeff was the first to answer. "If you get the water and coffee, I can go look for those tissues. Then I'll call the doc and maybe Roxy's attorney."

"I'll stay with Roxy," Michael offered from across the room.

Taking her hand away from the dog, Roxy leaned back into the sofa cushion. She closed her eyes without a word.

CHAPTER SIX

The kitchen looked orderly. Two appliances on the counter announced their importance. Not because they were unusual—a coffeepot and an electric tea kettle—but because they were chosen.

And should there be any doubt as to the purpose of their use, a sign labeled Beverage Station had been hung on the backsplash nearby. Olivia sighed. *What's up with the cute signs that state the obvious.*

Dismissing that thought, Olivia continued to assess the kitchen, looking for possible clues about the owner of the house. Her eyes rested on the stately high-end refrigerator humming softly across the room. It looked clean, shiny, and efficient with water and ice dispensers on the door and no sign of fingerprints on the stainless steel surface.

Taking note of the refrigerator's side-by-side doors, with two accessible drawers underneath, she remembered a conversation with Michael. "It's time to pick out the kitchen appliances for our new home," he'd said.

But did I? I don't remember if I ever followed through with that request.

The refrigerator held no magnets or Post-it notes. She could see her reflection in the surface. Running her hand over the quartz counters, she not only saw but felt the cool austerity.

This kitchen could pass in an upscale showroom. It tells me that Whitney Zimmer runs her main house with efficiency. Not surprising for a cleaning influencer with over forty million followers.

Olivia walked closer to the kitchen island. Stools without backs nestled underneath the expansive quartz counter. She thought of her own kitchen. The one she'd inherited unexpectedly. The one Michael had designed for Marla before they met. And before Marla passed away.

Ours feels lived in. Mayor Maguire's footprints. Spills of coffee on the counter. Herbs growing on my window sill. We're tidy but not like this. Another glance at the island confirmed her observation. *No table mats or condiments. Not even a speck or crumb.* She turned away.

Her reflection showed in the stainless steel double oven, alongside the six-burner gas range. *I've never seen a cleaner kitchen, that's for sure. Oh, to find a sprinkle of stray corn-flakes or at least a few coffee grinds. Kinda sad.*

Remembering why she'd come to the kitchen, she stepped closer to the filtered water dispenser on the refrigerator. *If I find coffee, I'll make a big pot.* Scanning for where the glasses might be stored, her eyes caught sight of two doors on the far wall. Built to the same proportions and painted with a slick coat of white enamel, they looked more like fraternal twins.

The one to the left had an etched glass front with the word Pantry written across the glass. The other door had no glass insert. Instead there was a raised wood panel, painted to match the shiny white trim.

Intrigued again, Olivia edged closer to the glass-front door. The knob moved easily in her hand. Peeking inside, the smell of rosemary and garlic hit her nostrils, making her sniff.

I may be able to find coffee in here. She stepped inside and flicked on an overhead light. Then she looked around. *This is no ordinary pantry.*

The space was large enough to be a small bedroom.

A butcher block counter extended across the entire back wall, accented by a white subway tile backsplash. Underneath were drawers. Above the counter a line of cupboards rose to the ceiling, looking uniform and efficient. The cabinets gleamed with stark white paint, contrasting with the oiled wood of the counter.

Feeling her fascination grow, Olivia admired an array of containers lined up against the backsplash. Small, medium, and large acrylic storage, each had a red vacuum-sealed lid. The clear plastic made the contents of each unit easy to identify.

A variety of pasta, from spaghetti to bow tie, each with their own vessel. Her stomach growled when she sighted her favorite candy. *Peanut M&Ms. Yum.* Like the pasta, they'd also been sorted by color.

She flung open a cupboard, revealing more plastic containers, the eye-level shelf filled with varieties of rice. Not just brown and white, but basmati, jasmine, and arbo-rio. Above the rice were other containers, the contents bringing a smile. *Coffee. Finally.* She withdrew the container labeled Breakfast Blend, opening the compression top to savor the aroma.

Olivia stepped back, pushing the cupboard door closed. She felt slightly uneasy. *Did Whitney Zimmer stock this pantry...or did one of her personal assistants?*

She glanced at a clock on the wall, aware that she'd lost track of time. *People must be wondering where I've gone. It's only been ten minutes. But it feels a lot longer.*

With the pantry door closed behind her, she stepped closer to the cupboards, opening them one by one. Finally she discovered drinking glasses, organized from tallest to shortest. She also found a glass pitcher.

Feeling like the butler in an old movie, Olivia made her way back to the great room with a tray of glasses and a filled pitcher. The doorbell rang as she set the tray on the coffee table, situated in front of the oversized leather sofa. She turned to find Michael opening the door to a familiar face.

Luis Martinez stepped inside, his dazzling smile the first thing she noticed. Michael slapped him on the back.

Dr. Martinez nodded at Olivia, but his eyes found Roxy, with Mayor Maguire huddled on the floor close by. "You must be Roxanne Grossman," he said by way of a greeting. "Officer Jets suggested that I come over. I hear this has been a very disturbing morning."

Mayor Maguire, as if dismissed, stood up. Walking to the other side of the room, he curled up in a ball, his head dropping to his paws. Dr. Martinez drew closer, his eyes resting on Jeff.

"Jeff, right? If you don't mind, I'd like to speak to my patient alone. It won't take long."

Jeff blustered, "I'm staying with Roxy."

Dr. Martinez smiled gently. "I understand your protectiveness. Especially in this case. But I really have to insist."

Before Jeff could protest further, Olivia pointed to the glasses on the coffee table. "Here's some water for anyone who's thirsty. We'll be in the kitchen. Call us when you're finished." She nodded at Jeff, who stood.

Maybe Jeff was disarmed by Olivia's calm attitude, or

maybe he just didn't want to argue anymore. He turned to Roxy. "All you have to do is call out and I'll be back. I'm right on the other side of that door."

On their way to the kitchen, Olivia heard the creak of hinges and footsteps. The Wiz stepped into the house wearing a thick coat. He explained, "I went to check on the other contestants." He closed the door, taking one arm out of his jacket.

"Dr. Martinez wants to interview his patient alone," Olivia informed him. "Why don't you come with us?" Aware that she gave directions to the man in charge, she expected pushback. When none came, she felt relief.

Seated at the island in the kitchen, Jeff and Michael simply watched as Olivia made her way toward the sink. "Now that we're here, I'll make some coffee." She headed for the carafe.

<h1 style="text-align:center">CHAPTER SEVEN</h1>

The familiar aroma of coffee filled the kitchen.

"This has been quite the morning," Michael said as Olivia sat down on the stool next to him.

Jeff reached for his water glass, emptying it in one gulp. "Tastes better with lemon," he muttered.

Olivia eyed him cautiously. *If this were any other day, I'd push back with my usual 'and do you also want a pony on your birthday' remark. But of course this isn't a normal day. Not by a long shot. He's worried about his sister and there's a dead body upstairs. At least I think it's still there.*

"I could use some tea. And breakfast," Michael said. "Do you want me to scrounge around to see if I can find any food?"

And that, dear friends, is a man who's cracked the code on his entitlement. Her heart filled with warmth as she reached over to pat his knee. "I'd be happy to scrounge, as you saw. Hardly a difficult task with such a well-appointed kitchen. That's what took me so long, but the way, I was nosing my way around." She looked at Michael.

Olivia felt him take her hand under the counter. He squeezed her cold fingers.

"I'm going to look for eggs and bread right now." And then she added, "And a toaster." She pointed across the room. "That's the only door I haven't opened."

As she stood and walked across the room, she thought, *I wonder what's behind door number two?*

Ignoring the door labeled Pantry, she stuck her head inside the paneled door. Her throat, still raw from coughing earlier, instantly constricted. The intense smell of bleach invaded her nostrils. It wasn't until Olivia took the next quick breath that she noticed something else. A second tangy smell. *That's vinegar!* She held her hand over her mouth.

I don't think this is dangerous or anything. But it is a powerful combination.

She flung the door wide open. Holding her breath, she stepped inside. With the light flipped on, she stopped to assess the room. Exhaling slowly, she cautiously took in another breath. *No throat constriction. That's better.*

The first glance revealed a door located on the far wall. She stepped over quickly to turn the handle. The cool rush of welcome outdoor air caused her to inhale more deeply.

Propping the door open, she stopped. Keenly aware that Maddie may have been poisoned by some toxic blend of household products, she cautioned herself.

Give the room a chance to air out.

While she waited, she texted Michael.

Got distracted. Surprised? Be there shortly.
Still looking for that toaster.

After exchanging a heart emoji and a smiley face with Michael, she put her phone back in her pocket.

At first glance the room looked nearly identical to the other pantry. A similar butcher block counter. Extra glossy, very white cupboards and drawer fronts. But instead of containers with candies and pasta, spray bottles had been lined up against a tiled backsplash.

Some were empty, with the sprayers balanced and unscrewed at the top. Some were filled with liquid, the sprayers screwed in, and those had labels adhered to the front.

So this pantry isn't for food, she concluded. *I feel like I've been dropped into some kind of deluxe janitor's closet.*

She rubbed her tongue across the roof of her mouth, aware of the aftertaste and tang of vinegar in her throat and nostrils. *They must use a lot of vinegar for disinfecting.*

A quick sniff reactivated her fear for how the woman upstairs had been murdered: *Not so much bleach as vinegar now.* She admired the tidy line of plastic spray bottles once again. *A mostly sterile feel in here, like an operating room or a doctor's office.* She picked up a spray bottle to look more closely.

The label clearly marked the contents as vinegar. She put down the bottle to pay closer attention to a nearby stack of plastic totes. Positioned at the end of the counter, one held four spray bottles, all with sprayers screwed in securely, but none with labels. Olivia checked each one by unscrewing and screwing them back in. The other totes were empty.

Opening the cupboard overhead, she saw a row of gallon-sized containers labeled bleach, vinegar, detergent, degreaser, abrasive, some with specific brand names. A label maker, stuck in the corner, was the only thing that looked out of place. *Michael gave me one of those for Christmas.*

Using my tidy obsession for good, he told me. She smiled at the memory.

Before she could pick up the label maker for a closer look, she heard the door from behind open quickly. Expecting it might be Michael coming to look for her, she was surprised when the hair on her neck rose. She whirled around.

CHAPTER EIGHT

"I see you're making yourself at home," Stanley "the Wiz" Weyland commented dryly.

"I didn't realize you were back already," she said. "I'm looking for bread to make toast. Looking for the toaster," she added clumsily.

"I see," he said, obviously not seeing at all.

"We're all pretty hungry. No time for breakfast at home." Her cheeks flushed.

Lifting his head higher, he said with authority, "This is the janitor's pantry. You won't find food items in here. Just cleaning products. The frying pan would be located in the pull-out shelf under the range. The toaster is on the first shelf. Why don't I gather the bread from the *food* pantry?" He emphasized *food* as if explaining to a toddler. "We're well stocked since we planned to feed everyone for the entire retreat. Roxanne made a list of necessary groceries well ahead of time." He blinked and then glared.

"That would help." Olivia felt her embarrassment keenly. But instead of apologizing, she knew Janis would change the power dynamic in the situation by asking a question. "Any chance Whitney Zimmer has been located?"

"Not a chance," the Wiz replied sharply. "If you knew Ms. Zimmer, you wouldn't be surprised. It's common behavior for her to disappear and then reappear unexpectedly. That's why she hired me. I am the one to make sense of her every move. I decode what Whitney Zimmer says and does. It's part of my job description."

Olivia knew that the Wiz liked to be in charge. Pivoting on her tactic, she considered, *Instead of pushing him like Janis, I can disarm him. Maybe connect with him on a more personal level. I'll use my embarrassment at being caught snooping to my advantage.*

"I've had any number of temp jobs and been in your position," she said with a smile. "I've made sense of the wildest of bosses over the years. I may have a small idea of what you're talking about."

The Wiz looked her over suspiciously. "Thank you for sharing." He sounded sarcastic. "I hope that in your career as a temp, you knew how to cook. As for myself, I draw the line at eating eggs." His nose wrinkled up. "They disgust me."

Olivia felt a glimmer of connection. Choosing not to be offended at his tone, she said playfully, "I've got you covered. We'll make lots of toast." She closed the open cupboard.

"Come with me," the Wiz ordered, holding the inside door open for her. On her way past she caught sight of a row of small appliances lined up on a shelf by the door. *Toaster!* Sliding it toward her, she tucked it under her arm and walked past the Wiz into the main kitchen.

"I'll have breakfast ready in a jiffy," she told the men.

Michael nodded as Jeff continued to talk.

After plugging in the toaster, Olivia investigated the

refrigerator. Three cartons of eggs were stacked on the top shelf. She removed the top one, taking it to the counter. In a minute a dozen eggs sizzled in the frying pan, along with a generous tablespoon of melted butter. Olivia used a wooden spoon to stir the eggs in the frying pan.

The Wiz, standing close by, cleared his throat. "Serenity will be here shortly." He looked at his phone. "And then Bruce soon after. They've both completed their morning assignment and will return to the main house for lunch."

Olivia focused on her eggs. Once they'd been cooked, she lifted the pan and piled them on a nearby platter. Michael, having joined Olivia at the counter, leaned over and lined up slices of buttered toast around the edge. He picked up the platter, placing it in the middle of the island counter.

Olivia watched as Jeff scooped up a large portion. Michael sat down and filled his plate. Then Jeff spoke. "Can I have more, or are you saving these for other people?"

"Do you think Roxy will be hungry?" *The interview with Dr. Martinez must be over.*

When Jeff didn't answer, she went on. "Go ahead and finish what's there. I'll make a few more eggs just in case." She called from the stove to the Wiz. "Anything else you'd like that doesn't include eggs or toast? You must be hungry."

"I will eat toast when everyone else is finished," he stated calmly. "I need to check in with the remaining contestants after Officer Jets completes her interview and arrests Roxanne. There will be time then."

Jeff looked up, sending the Wiz a glare. "She's not arrested yet."

Before Olivia could agree, a voice called out. "I'll take a plate of eggs and toast." Janis Jets didn't waste a minute. She strode into the room.

"Where's your boss?" she said, standing in front of the Wiz.

He glowered. "She cannot be located. I've tried the usual places but no one's seen her."

Janis dismissed him with a quick up and down assessment. Then she shrugged and turned her back, loading eggs and toast onto a plate.

Thinking Janis was done talking, Olivia turned back to the stove.

"And who are you?" Jets asked in an even louder voice.

Olivia swung back around. An unfamiliar woman stepped out of the janitor's closet.

"The door was open, so I just came inside." Ducking her chin as if shy, she introduced herself. "I'm Serenity McFee. I'm supposed to meet with the Wiz. I came back as soon as I finished my morning tasks." She looked around nervously, her eyes returning to Janis.

Olivia switched off the exhaust fan in order to hear the conversation more clearly.

Jeff spoke up first. "Have a seat here," he offered. "Want some eggs or a piece of toast?"

"She's not here for breakfast," Janis stated. "Or playing footsie with you." Making her way closer to Serenity, she extended a hand. "Let me introduce myself. I'm Officer Janis Jets, and you're a person of interest in the death of Maddox Hall."

Serenity's face drained of color. She quickly sat down on the stool. "I'm not that hungry," she explained. "I didn't know Maddie very well."

Jets moved to the end of the counter. "On the one hand, whether you two were long-lost BFFs or mere acquaintances matters to me. But on the other hand, people kill impulsively. Sometimes random strangers. Let me tell you—and I warn you, you'd better not lie again—I've already heard that you and Maddox were pretty tight."

Olivia felt her heart quicken. Listening over her shoulder to the questioning with great interest as she scrambled more eggs.

"I knew Maddie pretty well," Serenity began again. "We went out to lunch at several of the Time to Tidy conferences. In fact, we hoped we would both be selected for the Tidy Team competition this year. I told her I'd pray for her, and it worked out." Her voice faded away.

Finished with the eggs, Olivia turned off the burner. She filled the empty platter, which Michael had already prepared with more thick slices of buttered toast. She felt him touch her elbow. He leaned over to ask, "Do you want to sit down?"

"Sure, I could use a bite to eat. And how about some more coffee and hot water for tea..."

"On it." He gave her a quick smile.

Olivia took the platter to the table, along with a large serving spoon. "Here's some fresh eggs and toast." She offered the platter to Serenity first, taking that minute to look at her more closely. Dressed in jeans and a T-shirt, white athletic shoes tucked behind the legs of the stool, Serenity had a no-nonsense appearance.

She may have a soft voice, but her body and demeanor are all business. I can easily see this woman reorganizing and cleaning houses.

"I'm Olivia," she told her with a nod.

"Are you the new caterer?" she asked.

"What makes you think there's a new caterer?" Jets interrupted. She shoved another forkful of eggs into her mouth.

"Stanley told me you'd arrested Roxanne. I don't suppose it's a secret."

"I haven't arrested Roxanne, actually. She's right in the next room waiting for the doctor to finish up." Jets's lips drew a straight line. "I suggest that you ask me questions about this investigation before jumping to conclusions."

Then Jets pivoted toward Stanley, who'd been standing out of the way in front of the pantry. "And that goes for you too. You have one job, to find Whitney Zimmer. That does not include telling everyone else what you think is going on with my investigation. Are we clear?"

"Perfectly clear," he said calmly.

Jets turned back to Serenity. Apparently forgiving the woman's initial lie, she used a calm tone of voice. "Why don't you have some eggs and tell me what you know about the victim. I'm all ears."

Janis snatched another piece of toast, propping an elbow on the counter. "Tell me everything, even about your business. What's it called? Cleanliness is Next to Godliness? That's some tag line. Are you religious or just stealing the old saying for your brand?"

Olivia knew this Janis Jets tactic. Annoy people and then sit back and watch them scramble. Serenity immediately took offense and started to explain.

"I have a highly successful online organizing business. It's taken me five years to build it up. I make a decent profit and have over a million followers. Maddie and I were competitors, but we also supported each other. In fact, we'd planned on combining our businesses and opening a new one together, after the competition."

Stanley looked alarmed. His eyebrows raised.

That must have been news to him.

"Did Whitney know of your plan?" Stanley demanded.

"Not yet, but now that you've heard, Whitney will know soon enough." Serenity shrugged. "I guess it doesn't matter. Maddie is gone. All that planning for nothing."

Olivia took a moment to consider Serenity. *She's obviously disappointed. She planned on collaborating with Maddie in a new business venture. But why would she bump off a future business partner? Makes no sense.*

Olivia glanced at Janis. "More eggs," she offered.

"Had enough," Jets muttered. "But you?" She pointed at Serenity. "Do you have an alibi for the time of the murder? I assume your pal Stanley told you all the details before you got here."

"I'm not a killer." Serenity's soft voice grew more breathy. "Plus Bruce must have seen me at the site. I took several trips to my car for cleaning supplies. He could be my alibi, if he wants to be."

"So explain more about why winning this competition is so important to all of you," Jets said, shifting the topic once again.

"The prize money is good. But we are mostly competing for name recognition. Whitney gives the winner a lot of social media exposure. Which we can share on our own platforms. Her acknowledgement will boost our sales and bring more followers who would eventually sign up for my seminars and buy products from my online shop. It's just that simple."

Olivia interrupted. "Winning the contest would help. I get that. But what confused me is your business name—how having a clean house results in being more spiritual." Olivia knew the connection herself. Her mother had taught her a similar wisdom. But she watched to see Serenity's response, playing not exactly dumb but at the least unaware.

Instead of answering her question, Serenity asked, "Do you follow me?"

"I don't, but my sister Sage does. She's shown me how you sell tidy journals, along with group classes, and one-on-one spiritual consulting especially. There's a waiting list."

"That's correct. I'm considered the most spiritual of all the tidy influencers. That's because my brand focus is not only on products but on process. The path to a spiritual life begins with tidying up the space you live in. That's how I lead my followers to be better people and divinely connected."

Jets retorted, "Cleanliness is Next to Godliness—give me a break."

Olivia walked to the sink. She began to rinse dishes, making certain to keep listening over her shoulder. Even though Janis had dismissed Serenity's explanation, Olivia knew differently.

She realized that Serenity spoke a universal truth. A tidy environment could evoke a sense of calm. And it was in the calm one could hear a still small voice within. She'd experienced the same process herself.

CHAPTER NINE

"Olivia, stop doing dishes," Jets commanded. "We have to talk about what Roxanne told you earlier. Her confession."

Olivia dried her hands and turned. She could tell that Janis's words had caught the Wiz and Serenity by surprise. Unaccustomed to Jets's particular form of interrogation, they may not have expected to be dismissed for the sake of the inquiry.

Jets explained to the room as if she were the teacher. But her words were directed toward Olivia. "On the one hand, Roxanne didn't confess to me directly. She confessed to you instead. Because of your superpower, of course. I'm surprised you didn't sing her a lullaby. Did you?" Jets questioned.

Olivia shook her head. *Is she deliberately giving a warning to the others? What's her purpose in telling people about my supposed superpower...*

Jets turned to Jeff to explain. "Have you heard about her gift? All she has to do is pull out that autoharp and sing an old ditty and people leap up to talk about the weirdest things—confessing to her, spilling their guts with all the secrets."

"I didn't sing to Roxanne," Olivia objected.

"Oh please, everyone knows it's not the song that gets people to spill. It's the way you are, all open and accepting. Makes me sick." Jets shook her head. "Like I was saying, I may get that confession after reading Roxanne her rights. I can salvage my reputation as an honorable cop who doesn't rely on mumbo jumbo from her consultant."

Mumbo jumbo. Really. I just sit there and listen. Hardly a trick.

Jets kept talking. "At first I was frustrated that Roxanne's attorney can't make it up the hill until tomorrow. But now I think it might be in my favor." Her glance fell between Jeff, still sitting at the island, and Olivia, back against the sink.

"So for now why don't you and Jeff go check on the number one suspect. Just so you know, the doc called in a prescription to the pharmacy. In a few minutes I'll get someone to pick it up. Then I'll talk to her."

Jets tapped her fingers on the island countertop. "Even though Roxy's inadmissible confession may only confuse things, she's still the most obvious candidate in my mind. She did discover the dead woman. And she admits that she filled the cleaning spray bottles and may have made a mistake."

"Don't forget, she had to break into the room before she found the body," Olivia added. "That's just weird, don't you think?" Jets did not acknowledge her remark because the Wiz chimed in.

"I'd be happy to pick up the prescription."

"You are handy," Jets commented dryly. "That would be appreciated."

She turned to face Olivia. "As much as I'd like to get an official testimony from Roxy, I can't until her attorney shows up, because she's asked for one."

"I see," Olivia said quietly.

"I do want to interview Bruce Ward." Jets looked back at Stanley. "Did you call him and tell him the Lily Rock police want to talk?"

Stanley beamed. "Bruce just texted. He'll be here in ten minutes."

Jets scowled. "Do I have to ask again? What about Whitney Zimmer?"

"She's still not replying to my texts," Stanley explained. "And her phone sends me to voicemail."

"So I'm curious," Jets drawled. "Where does Whitney Zimmer usually hang out when she's in Lily Rock?"

"The hotel bar at the Refuge. Just up the road," he stated matter-of-factly.

"I know that one." Jets looked thoughtful. "Doesn't she sleep here when she's in town?"

"No, this is her conference house. She commutes from Palm Springs in her helicopter. If she needs to spend a night, she takes a late flight back to the desert."

"Of course she does!" Sarcasm dripped from Janis's voice. "So she's giving me a bad impression right off. Like she's too important to participate in a police inquiry. But she's also making herself scarce, which makes me think she's hiding something. What's the address of her home in the desert?"

"Since you do not have a warrant, I cannot divulge any personal information about my employer until she gives me permission to do so. She uses a PO box, by the way." The Wiz cast his eyes toward the ceiling as if repressing his impatience. Or to avoid Janis's piercing glare. Olivia couldn't decide which.

"That's okay. I have ways of getting her address. So, hotshot assistant, it's your job to protect and advise the boss and get her here for an interview. If you know what's good for you!"

Olivia had heard enough—Janis enjoyed sparring with the Wiz and he seemed to appreciate her saucy attitude. *What is this, some kind of love fest?*

"I will move forward with that goal in mind," the Wiz said. "In the meantime I will check up on Bruce Ward."

During the conversation between Janis and the Wiz, Serenity fidgeted with a stray hair that fell beside her cheek. Olivia couldn't tell if she was pretending not to listen or may have felt impatient to get back to work.

When Janis and the Wiz were finished talking, Serenity glanced quickly at Olivia. *I suspect after Janis's warning about my superpower, she may be nervous around me.* Olivia's heart went out to the shy young woman. Before she could come closer to reassure Serenity, the Wiz interrupted.

"Serenity, now that you've finished your interview with Officer Jets..." He paused to look at Janis for confirmation. When she nodded, he continued, "It's time to prepare for our initial audit of your business.

"Remember, I am looking into all aspects of your work, beginning with an accurate accounting of the number of your followers and the revenue you received in the last fiscal year. I'd also like a list of your affiliate marketing partners, other brand partnerships, official network monetization programs, merchandising revenue, and direct merchandising accounts."

Olivia's eyes grew wide. *He certainly sounds like he knows his stuff.*

Serenity answered at once. "I have all of that and more. I'll bring my laptop for the meeting."

Jets glared at Serenity. "If you go upstairs to your room, stay away from my crime scene. Use the restroom on the first floor until we clear the area."

Serenity sighed. "I paid a lot to attend this conference, and I hope there will be a refund for my inconvenience."

Stanley glanced at his phone. He typed a message while he spoke. "We'll work out something." He continued texting as he spoke to her. "No refunds, understand. But something. In the meanwhile, follow Officer Jets's orders."

Did he just smirk at Janis?

"Yah, follow my orders," Jets mumbled.

"I have a few questions," Jeff Grossman announced.

"Not now," Jets snapped. "Check in on your sister. And take Olivia with you."

Michael came closer, leaning into Olivia.

"I've got my marching orders. Would you mind finishing the clean up?" Olivia said, glancing at the stack of dishes waiting to be rinsed.

"I've got this," he said. "Better for me to look busy. If I sit here, Janis will be giving me orders too. Once I'm done I'll duck out the back. Since neither of us drove here, I'll call one of my guys at the work site to pick me up."

"I might need a ride later," she said.

"And I'll drop off your car and leave the key. One of the guys will help," he assured her. "See you tonight." He leaned over to kiss the top of her head. Then he turned to plunge his hands into the soapy water.

CHAPTER TEN

Away from the kitchen, Olivia lingered in the dining room. She took a moment for a deep breath. *That was a lot. The interview felt oddly disjointed with everyone standing around listening in. Was Janis showing off for the Wiz? I wouldn't put it past her. She's been known to like an audience.*

Hearing murmuring coming from the great room, Olivia looked over. Jeff sat close to Roxy. He spoke to her calmly as she waited on the sofa with Mayor Maguire. Brother and sister. Olivia became aware of a sinking sense of fatigue. With another breath she could feel sadness. Mostly for Roxy, but also for Jeff, who loved his sister.

Laying her open palm across her chest, she focused on the feeling, which grew more intense. Only a few years ago she would not have been able to identify the source of her feelings. They would have confused her. That was before she'd realized she had her own sister, Sage. Personal experience changed everything.

In the past Olivia would wonder what it felt like to have a sibling. Watching brothers and sisters at school, she'd envy how they stood up for each other. At least some of them. She'd also wonder why some siblings never got along. But the envy persisted even when siblings seemed at cross purposes.

There were the twins, Sam and Sue, in high school. Not identical but in the same classes. At least until Sam was held back a grade and Sue spurted ahead. After that they never seemed to get along. Olivia never knew what went on at their home, but she always felt a twinge of envy. *At least they had each other.*

Now when she looked at Jeff and Roxy, she knew that they both felt apprehensive and afraid. She felt what they felt. *That's because I have Sage. Now I have a sibling.* She removed her hand as her heart warmed. Identifying the feeling always helped.

Olivia walked through the dining area toward the great room. She smiled watching Mayor Maguire snuggle next to Roxy on the sofa, his head resting in her lap. Roxy scratched behind his ears, looking absentmindedly toward the large window at the front of the house.

Jeff nodded to Olivia, his face drawn with worry.

Roxanne turned to face her, eyes puffy from crying.

"Are you okay? Can I get you anything?" Olivia asked.

"You mean me?" she asked in a soft voice. "Okay, I guess. Maybe Jeff wants something." She looked toward her brother.

"No thanks, I'm fine," Jeff said.

Once Olivia got Roxy to answer, Jeff came closer. He sat down in the nearby chair while Olivia sat on the edge of the sofa cushion. She reached over to pat Mayor Maguire's side, digging her fingers into his curly coat.

I want to talk to Roxy but I'm afraid she'll start confessing again. Maybe some small talk...

"Did you like Dr. Martinez?" Olivia asked, keeping her voice casual. "He's well respected in town, considering he's only been here a few months."

"I never met him before. He is rather good-looking. Nice to have around." Roxanne smiled slightly before dipping her nose into Mayor Maguire's fur.

"He's single, you know. He was my sister Sage's doctor during her pregnancy."

At the sound of Sage's name, Jeff's eyes brightened. "Has Martinez been over since the baby was born? You know, to see Sage?"

Roxanne turned to her brother. "You like Sage McCloud, don't you!" Her voice assumed a teasing lilt.

Jeff's cheeks turned slightly pink. "I do like Sage," he finally admitted. "As a friend."

Roxy gently poked him again. "So you say. But I remember that voice you have. It's the one you used when you talked about your last serious girlfriend. Like you were awestruck. That's how Mom knew you had a crush on her. What was her name?"

"Linda Sue Argot," he said with a smile. "I think you're confused though. My heart belongs to Star. She's a beautiful baby."

"You don't fool me. You've got that starry-eyed look. You're interested and that's not about a baby."

Olivia repressed a smile. *Roxanne did all the work for me. Jeff's crush on Sage is now an open topic of conversation. Can't wait to tell Michael.* Before she could tease Jeff herself, a knock came from the front door.

When no one leaped up to answer, a tall blonde man stuck his head inside. "I'm ready for my interview," he told them. Walking in, he pulled the door closed behind him.

He wore jeans and a bold blue T-shirt, and his short

hair was cut close. The front of the tee read: Follow Bruce "The Tool" Ward *@FromTidytoMighty*. His outfit was accessorized by a leather tool belt that dangled from his waist.

"I'm Bruce 'The Tool' Ward," he announced in a loud voice. "The Wiz called me to come over for an interview with the police." The tools on his belt bounced as he came closer, looking curiously at Roxanne. He reached his hand out toward Olivia, the muscle in his right arm rippling.

Olivia suppressed a grin. She stood and shook his hand. Then she pointed to the kitchen. "Officer Jets is waiting for your interview. The Wiz must have already told you about Maddie. That she was found dead just upstairs in the bathroom."

Bruce's grin deflated. Hi frown was so exaggerated, it looked almost comical. "The Wiz told me. So sad. Maddie was a worthy competitor."

I guess Maddie is only important in relation to him. Interesting.

Before Olivia could introduce herself, another brisk knock.

The Tool took charge, stepping closer to open the door.

Two men dressed in paramedic uniforms stood outside. Both wore identification badges on their shirts.

"We're here for the body," the taller guy announced.

Bruce made room for them to walk past.

Janis must have heard them arrive from the kitchen because she bustled through the doorway. "Upstairs and to the left," she told them.

The men lifted a stretcher. They walked toward the stairway together, their boots thudding across the wooden flooring.

Olivia felt a stab of worry. *Wearing shoes inside. What will the Wiz say?*

When they disappeared up the stairway, she turned to Bruce. "By the way, I didn't get to tell you. My name is Olivia Greer." Unfortunately Bruce had already directed his attention to Janis Jets.

Bruce began his introduction again, this time for Janis's benefit. "I am Bruce 'The Tool' Ward; I assume you're the officer in charge. Wiz called me just half an hour ago. He told me Maddie was found dead in the bathroom and to come over to make a statement. I can't imagine what I would have to say that would help your investigation."

"You're a person of interest." Jets's eyes narrowed. "Did the Wiz tell you that part? Anyone here for the weekend, even people not in the house when the body was found, are people of interest. Time of death has not yet been officially established. And since you're here now, why don't you come into the kitchen and we'll have a little chat."

Bruce gripped his tool belt with both hands, his jaw tightened. He looked toward Roxanne, who watched with fascination. His eyes shifted past Olivia to Janis once again.

"Okay, I'll chat with you. Just so you know, time is money. I'm a contestant and I have a lot to do today." He took a breath. "Plus I have an interview with the Wiz coming up in an hour. So let's get this over with." He stepped toward the kitchen, his tools bobbing against his thighs, disappearing through the doorway.

"Olivia," Jets's voice prompted. "Come with me. I want you to be my second pair of ears." She didn't wait for Olivia to agree as she followed Bruce back to the kitchen.

Olivia sighed. She sat back down on the sofa to pat Mayor Maguire. He opened his eyes and yawned in her direction. Then he turned his head to sniff Roxanne's hand.

Apparently satisfied that she smelled okay, he shook himself from nose to tail. Trotting toward the front door, he halted and then pawed the wood. Then he glanced back toward Olivia.

"Okay, M&M. I'll let you out. Don't go too far." She stood, walked closer, and then opened the door. The dog scampered outside. "Bork," he called out before taking off running toward the woods.

By the time she closed the door and turned around, Jeff sat next to Roxy on the sofa. She rested her head on his shoulder as he smoothed her hair with his hand. "I'll see you two later," Olivia told them. Neither said a word as she headed toward the kitchen.

Olivia found Jets and Bruce sitting next to each other at the end of the island. With her iPad open, Jets was ready to take notes.

Olivia sat on an empty stool next to Bruce.

Janis Jets began with a question. "Why would a guy like you be interested in a Time to Tidy conference?" She looked into Bruce's eyes, as if she could read his thoughts.

Just to make him squirm.

"I'm not the only macho tidier," The Tool explained. "I come from generations of janitors. My grandfather and my dad. They taught me all their tricks."

Jets nodded but then asked a different question. "Tell me how your morning went, no detail is unimportant. Did you talk to Roxanne in the morning? That would be a good place to begin."

"I didn't have time to chat with anyone." The Tool's eyes shifted to his right then back to Janis. "As soon as the Wiz said go, I drove up to my cabin to start cleaning. The place was a mess."

"So I heard," Jets said. "But no contact with Maddox.

Okay, then did you stop to talk to Serenity once you got to the house?"

"Like I said, no time for chitchat." He scratched his head. "But I did see Serenity briefly, going out to get her mop. Then she disappeared back into the house."

Jets made a note on her iPad. When neither Olivia nor Bruce spoke, she asked another question. "How well did you know Maddox?"

"I saw her at other conferences. But I didn't really talk to her. She was okay, I guess. Not my type."

Jets looked him over and then shut down her iPad. "So you were basically at work during the time of the murder. I'll ask Serenity if she saw you. That's enough for now. I know where to find you should there be any more questions." She dismissed him with a nod of her head.

"I'll take the back door." Bruce stood and made his way toward the janitor's pantry, disappearing through the door, which he left open. Olivia heard the outside door slam shut.

Janis stood. "So what do you think of The Tool?"

"He seems nervous," she said at once. "He kept looking around and over my head. I noticed that when you first addressed him in the living room."

"Yah, I got that too. I expected him to chat with you while I was taking notes. But when he clammed up, I decided to cut things short. I'll talk to him later when he's not so prepared." She looked at Olivia intently. "Okay, so see you later. I'll text if anything comes up."

Janis disappeared back into the dining room. Olivia assumed she'd be talking more to Roxanne.

Left alone in the kitchen, she realized it was time to check and see if Michael had dropped off her car. But first she needed to retrieve her boots and jacket.

To her surprise Stanley Weyland waited for her at front

the door. He held out her boots with a slight smile. "I took a minute to give the leather and soles a good brushing. I thought it was the least I could do, considering all of your help today."

"They're old but I love them," she admitted. "Thanks." She bent over to pull her left boot on, then her right. The jacket came last.

"See you later," she told the Wiz.

Once outdoors she spotted her car. Michael had parked it under the shade of a cedar tree. With no sight of Mayor Maguire, Olivia was on her own. It was time to let go of the investigation and connect with the rest of her life.

It wasn't until she hit the main road that despite her good intentions, she realized her thoughts still lingered over the latest events. *Things are looking bad for Roxy. So far everyone has an alibi, except Whitney Zimmer.*

CHAPTER ELEVEN

As the evening sky closed around them, Michael and Olivia huddled close to the firepit. She held a mug of peppermint tea with both hands, while he took a sip of beer. "So how did the interview with Janis go?" He placed the bottle on the wide arm of the Adirondack chair. Reaching out, he took one of her hands in his. "Tell me everything."

"Janis only had a couple of questions for The Tool," she said.

"That's not his real name, is it?" Michael looked at her with raised eyebrows.

"His real name is Bruce Ward. I researched him and found his accounts. He has over a million followers. I can show you." Olivia reached for her phone.

Michael held up his hand in protest. "Not for me. All those hacks and shortcuts. No matter how easy it looks to a camera, I'm not convinced. In my experience the hacks rarely work."

"It's like you already know The Tool," she laughed. "I think his ideas about quick cleaning may just be a come-on. Once he shows people how to do a job he moves to selling merchandise. He convinces people that they need his special brand of tool, which he sells to his followers from his shop on Instagram. You can also buy them on Amazon, but for a little more money.

"He has a unique high-powered drill, costs a fortune," she continued. "He's obsessed with the attachments. So for example, to clean the grout in your shower, you use his handy-dandy extension with a steel brush that hooks into the end of the drill. You spray his brand of cleaning solution on it first. His brand is better than anything you can buy elsewhere. Or so he says. Of course his name and face are on the front of every bottle and tool. He guarantees no grout stains once you've used his product, or a full refund."

"And no grout either," mumbled Michael. "You dig into grout with a steel brush like that, you'll be replacing it every couple of years. Plus there's the chance of chipping the tile. Just use a plain old bristle brush in your hand and the cleaner of your choice. Preferably with bleach. If you do that two or three times a year, the grout stays pretty clean."

"I didn't know you were also a household cleaning expert," Olivia teased him.

"People complain to me all the time about how their builders messed up. How hard it is to keep their bathroom and kitchen tile clean. They call it 'builder's grade' workmanship and materials. A lot of the problem is not because of the builder or the quality of the products. It's the maintenance after installation. Of course, some guy on the internet steps in and tells them it's not their fault and people blame other people for shoddy workmanship." He sighed.

"Want to start your own Instagram account?" Olivia smirked. "We could brand you. Let me think..." Olivia put down her mug of tea. "I've got it. Mighty Mike's Magical Cleaning Solutions. Yep. I can see the T-shirt right now."

"Better not," he growled. Then he leaned closer. "But I do like the mighty part. Is that how you think of me? Any chance I could, you know, prove my worth tonight?"

Olivia squeezed his hand. "Tonight would be a wonderful time to maintain your brand. But honestly, you should consider becoming a social media presence. I'm sure The Tool would advise you—for the right price, of course."

He guffawed. "I am so private. The very thought of posting online makes me cringe." He tugged on her hand. "Come on then. I feel my mightiness already. Afterward we'll have dinner."

They lay side by side in bed, warmed in the cocoon of their realized love. Olivia squeezed his hand, enveloped by the familiar sense of sanctuary. Closed curtains for privacy, only a candle lit the darkness.

Michael cleared his throat. "That was fun."

"It surely was." She snugged her face into his shoulder. The faint smell of lavender from the candle floated over the bed, adding to her contentment.

"So you didn't finish telling me. The interview with Bruce sounds very different than the first group thing. Did you learn anything new?" Michael asked.

Olivia blinked, reluctant to step out of her lovemaking reverie. And maybe she wasn't sure where to begin explaining. He was right. Both interviews were decidedly different. She squeezed his hand again and rolled onto her back. Eyes closed, she focused on his question.

"Janis did her thing; didn't get much new information," Olivia said. "I did learn more about the Time to Tidy competition. From the interviews and what I could gather online, each of the contestants is assigned their own house to clean. Whitney inspects their work, does interviews in between, and then announces her favorite at the end. She invites them to join her Tidy Team."

"And what do they get for being selected?"

"There's a cash prize. But that's not the real draw. Whitney gives them a lot of social media time. Which they can share with their followers on their website and other platforms like Instagram. She also sells their branded items in her online store. A lucrative crossover for the winner."

"All of that for free?"

"Oh no, Time to Tidy is not free. Each entry form is accompanied by a three hundred dollar fee. Not refundable, by the way. Hundreds of people apply. Then if they are selected, they pay ten grand to attend the competition. Whitney makes it such a big deal, people are begging to give their money away to be involved with her."

"So ol' Whitney pockets all of the application fees plus thirty thousand from three people. Pretty slick. Can't wait to meet her."

"Whitney is still missing," Olivia mused. "She's elusive, and her assistant, the Wiz, is very protective."

Michael pulled her closer. "The Wiz and The Tool. Okay then, sounds like you have a hunch about this Whitney woman."

"I think Janis may also be taking a close look at her, getting cozy with the Wiz. They have a way of talking back and forth that borders on flirting. Anyway..."

He leaned up on an elbow to stare her in the face. "Do I need to warn Cookie?" Then he lay back down. "Janis and the Wiz. Kind of has a ring. But from what you say, this Wiz character isn't going to give up anything about his employer, especially to the police."

"I see Janis kind of testing him. She agreed to let him

help out right away, by having him pick up Roxy's prescription. Plus she does that thing where she asks pointed questions, then steps back and watches him squirm. After the first few times I got the feeling that he was rather enjoying the process. He wasn't even annoyed by Janis's attitude."

Michael turned his head on the pillow to face her. "Interesting."

She lifted his hand to wind her fingers between his. "My turn for the post-coital questions. How's the house coming along?"

"A couple of months, tops," he said, a hint of pride in his voice. "Then we can move in. Of course there will be a lot of tweaking after that, but it will be basically done."

She rested her chin on his shoulder. "So I have two months to get Sage and Jeff together. Roxanne moved things along today. She asked Jeff right out if he liked Sage. That's good news, right?"

"I suppose," he said softly into her ear. She heard his breath deepen and then grow soft.

"Don't go to sleep. We haven't had dinner yet." She shoved his shoulder playfully. When he didn't respond, she dropped his hand and rolled over. Feet on the floor, she looked back at the man in her bed. Michael's eyes had closed, his lips slightly parted. She could hear the steady rhythm of his breath as he slept.

I'll start dinner and give him a chance to snooze. He has a lot on his mind on the construction of the house.

It wasn't until she stood at the kitchen sink that she acknowledged a sense of unease. It lay right underneath her conscious thoughts. She swallowed. For the second time that day she spread her palm over her chest.

What is it? Why am I feeling this way...

She felt a trickle of fear poking at her heart. Then it

came. The rush of words to accompany her feeling of unease.

I only wish I was half as excited as Michael about the move.

Olivia blinked, realizing what she'd actually known for some time.

I'm not ready to move.

CHAPTER TWELVE

On Saturday Olivia patted the warm spot on the sheets left by Michael. The sound of water splashing in the shower told her everything she needed to know. *He got up early.* Relieved that he'd not already left for work, she sighed.

For the first time since they'd gotten together, she felt insecure about their relationship. The realization last night still unsettled her.

Will he be hurt if he finds out I'm dragging my feet about this move?

Olivia had always wrestled with her thoughts and her sensitivities. For as long as she could remember her mother helped her sort out what was real and what was her imagination. Even as a child she'd been derailed on more than one occasion, worrying about the worst. Visions of knives and falls from great heights chased her for years. Pushing away intrusive thoughts took an iron will.

Mona would remind her, "You have the power to turn away negative thoughts." And she'd learned that part. But then in adolescence she'd learned her lesson too well. Shoving down unwanted emotions led to a lack of awareness of what she really felt. At that point Mona intervened again. "Visions and emotions require a different response. Distinguish between the two and then you'll know what to do next."

That's when she'd learned to spread her open palm over her chest to focus on a feeling. Sometimes the feeling just disappeared on its own. But sometimes, like last night, the feeling lingered and became a vision. *Silly groundhog.* She groaned, covering her eyes with her arm.

Olivia knew better than to ignore the words that came after. They'd been released like some kind of mythical kraken. From groundhog to beast, she'd have to deal with her feelings and the situation to achieve any sense of peace.

And that's why she lay in bed wondering how to tell Michael that she wasn't ready to move.

She stretched her body full length, reaching her arms over her head. She pointed her toes, appreciating the tug of resisting muscles in her calves. A deep sigh emitted from her chest.

Maybe I'll talk to Sage and see if she's interested in Jeff.

The shower shut off. A few minutes later Michael appeared at her side of the bed, a towel wrapped around his waist. He nodded toward the closed bedroom door.

"If we hurry we can catch up with Jeff over coffee," he suggested. She could feel drops of water on her arm as he stood near the bed grinning down at her.

She lifted herself on an elbow. "That's just what I was thinking."

He smiled, looking happy with himself. "I had this idea. What about a double date with Jeff and Sage. Maybe up to the Refuge. It's been a while since we were there. I could use an under-grilled steak and a bottle of outrageously priced wine."

"Great idea, master matchmaker. I'll meet you in the kitchen as soon as I'm dressed." She lifted herself from the covers, swinging her feet to the floor as he headed back to the bathroom to shave. "Once you're done I'll take a quick shower," she called after him.

He turned around. She continued to explain, "My plan is to make lots of noise going upstairs. Maybe the baby will hear and wake up earlier. Then Sage will come to the kitchen and run into Jeff. You realize I'm a grown man playing matchmaker." He smiled conspiratorially.

Olivia's heart tugged. *He's such a sweetie.*

"We found each other, that's why you've conspired to matchmake. Don't you want everyone else to feel like we do?"

"Change of plans. Let's forget getting dressed and start making noises right away." He abandoned his towel. With quick steps he landed on top of her.

"That would mean derailing our morning plan." She closed her eyes inhaling the scent of woodsy aftershave. "But it would be a shame to miss this opportunity."

His lips brushed hers. "We can multitask. Make love and make enough noise to wake the baby."

Running her fingers up his back, she gripped his hair. She spoke in his ear. "I think it is our duty as aunt and uncle to wake that baby. It's time to get her on a dependable schedule."

It was eight o'clock by the time Michael and Olivia sat down at the kitchen table. She raised her coffee mug and he held up his. They clinked them together before taking a sip. "The blend is good," he admitted. "But I'm still not a coffee drinker."

"I know," she answered.

Then both looked down at their cell phones.

"Why don't you text Jeff and invite him over?" Olivia asked.

"Good idea," Michael said.

She put down her phone and made her way to the kitchen sink to look out the window. Her eyes traveled past the picket fence and through the vegetable garden. Jeff's truck wasn't parked in its usual place in the driveway. She turned around.

"I think he's gone out this morning."

Michael put down his cell phone. "He isn't answering. I bet you're right. But what about our plan?"

"I guess we'll have to implement it later. He does have a sister who's suspected of murder. He could be getting some breakfast for her."

"A good excuse to ignore his love life, I suppose."

"A murder didn't stop you," Olivia reminded him.

"Just to make one thing clear? Murder or no murder, I never doubted my feelings for you, from the first moment I saw you. Actually maybe even before."

She walked closer to the table. "Before we met on the road?"

"Actually I saw you the Christmas before that," he explained. "I had this kind of premonition thing happen. I've never told anyone because it sounds lame. But Marla brought it on. She kept talking about her friend Olivia from high school. Every time she said your name I'd feel funny, in my gut.

"And then when I asked to see a photo of you, I actually felt my chest get all warm. Craziest damn thing. It never happened to me before. Just the photo of you took my breath away. I never told her, but just seeing you hit me hard, like you were important."

Olivia thought back, considering his new revelation. "I wish that happened to me. Unfortunately the first time I saw you I felt furious."

"And did I let that stop me?" The corner of his mouth lifted.

"You made a real pest of yourself," she admitted.

"And that's why I am not Jeff. Wild horses couldn't have stopped me from getting close to you."

Olivia chuckled. "Relationships are like artichokes."

"What do you mean?" His eyebrows raised.

"We keep revealing ourselves to each other. Like tugging at an artichoke one leaf at a time."

"Getting to the heart," he added. "I like that."

She glanced into her empty mug, raising her head with a pout. "Someone forgot to refill my coffee mug," she said playfully.

Michael's cell phone rang. He held it to his ear. "It's Mike," he said into the receiver. "Okay. That explains it. I'll tell Olivia. I understand. We've got your back."

He placed his phone on the table. "That was Jeff. Janis arrested Roxy late last night. She's in a cell."

"I was afraid of that!" Olivia felt her heart wrench.

"He probably won't be here for breakfast. At least not until the situation with his sister is resolved."

A tone of nonchalance in Michael's voice caught Olivia's attention. She felt more connected to their neighbor than he did, that was obvious. Even though Michael wasn't being one bit critical, she felt a connection she hadn't recognized before. *We both have sisters. I get how Jeff's probably feeling right now.*

Olivia tried to explain. "I'm feeling discouraged. Not

just about the matchmaking. I figured Janis would arrest Roxy. But when you said the words, I was still shocked. She's not a murderer. I know in my gut she's not the type."

"Anyone can make a mistake," Michael countered. "Mixing up those cleaners isn't that improbable. Don't forget that some mistakes lead to awful consequences, like traffic accidents, for example. Dead is dead."

"But that's it, Michael. I don't think that Roxanne is the type to carelessly mix chemicals. She strikes me as someone who is especially careful."

"Apparently Janis is not of that opinion," he remarked dryly.

"If she arrested Roxy, she must think she's the number one suspect."

Michael shrugged. "I told Jeff that we have his back. That could mean anything from morning coffee to..."

"Finding the real killer..." Olivia added.

"To getting knee-deep into his love life." Michael smiled. "That all seems kind of trivial now that Roxy's in jail. I guess we'll have to leave our matchmaking plan until later."

A baby's wail came from the other side of the house, and Olivia glanced at the wall clock. "Okay, it's nine thirty. Even if it's not about Jeff and Sage, it wouldn't hurt to get Star on some kind of schedule. She's sleeping in later and later. How does Sage deal with all of that and plan her own day too?"

"Some mothers let the baby make the schedule," Michael said knowingly. "Good parenting comes in all shapes and sizes."

"I suppose." Olivia wasn't convinced. *But he's had a kid and I haven't, don't forget.*

A soft look came over Michael's eyes. "My son was on a

schedule. His mom and I couldn't do it any other way since we both worked."

Startled at his confession, Olivia nodded. Michael rarely brought up Daniel. "I forget that you're an experienced dad. Maybe you could have a chat with Sage."

"Oh no way!" He held his open palms in front of his chest. "I wouldn't presume to tell a new mother how to feed a baby. I'd have to hand in my man-card and maybe..." he looked around the kitchen, "move out sooner than we planned. Matchmaking is one thing, but the care and feeding of an infant. That's so out of my league."

She heard the sadness in his voice, lurking behind his words. *And maybe that's why he wants to move. Star is reminding him of Daniel and his loss.*

CHAPTER THIRTEEN

The pine trees moaned in the wind, making Olivia shiver. She stood to lean over the rail, looking more deeply into the woods. A squirrel ran up the trunk of an old oak, chattering to a friend two branches away.

The sky peeked through the trees, as blue as a first-prize ribbon. Mayor Maguire sat next to her, his nose between two horizontal rails, staring at the squirrels.

Michael had left for the construction site, giving Olivia time to appreciate her Saturday morning. Despite the chill in the air, Olivia liked sitting outside this time of year. "Good things are ready to happen," her mother used to tell her when she was small.

Turning from the railing, she sat back down, thinking back on her conversation with Michael about Roxy's innocence. *If only Whitney Zimmer had been interviewed right away, I bet Janis may have come to a different conclusion. Zimmer's definitely hiding something.*

Olivia fidgeted in her chair, realizing that she had some time with nothing else to do. *The Wiz mentioned that Whitney lives in the desert and commutes by helicopter to the hill. I can check the private airstrip up by the tram to see if there's a record of her last trip. The flight manifest would have details.* She flexed her fingers, aware that they tingled with excitement. *The airstrip must be open on Saturday. A lot of people come up the hill for a weekend getaway.*

Mayor Maguire, having given up his squirrel surveillance, lay folded into a ball on Michael's chair. The dog's lips quivered as he slept. Stretching out her hand, she fluffed the fur behind his ears.

He lifted his head.

"Get up, sleepy doggo. We have work to do."

By the time she grabbed a jacket and put on her boots, Mayor Maguire waited by the front door. He trotted outside as she turned to lock up the house, then they got in the car.

"We need to turn up our investigation of Whitney Zimmer," she explained to Maguire, once they hit the main road. Glancing over at him, she smiled. "We haven't done this for a while, just the two of us."

Mayor Maguire turned his head, and then he turned back to the passenger-side window, his nose pressed against the glass.

"I suppose this isn't exactly of interest to you right now. You'd rather be at the constabulary with Roxanne. You two seem to be good friends."

The dog turned back to stare at her.

"Go ahead. Admit it. You love to help people in trouble."

He moved his head to look out the front windshield, as if he didn't hear her. But Olivia knew differently. She sensed that Mayor Maguire understood everything she said. She just wasn't sure how.

Driving the winding path, she accelerated into the curve. When she left the house, she'd fully intended to drive to the airstrip. Someone there would probably know more about Whitney Zimmer. But as she drove, she felt her mind pull away from the original plan. With Mayor Maguire by her side, she found herself open to other possibilities. And then the idea came. This one floated past, so unobtrusive she nearly ignored it. *Go see Cayenne.* Such a simple idea but definitely unexpected.

Olivia reached over to pat the dog. "Let's go say hello to Cay. We haven't spoken to her in ages."

Mayor Maguire's tongue hung out the side of his mouth. He turned toward the side window again, his furry back to Olivia.

Instead of making a right turn toward the airstrip, Olivia made a left, following the sign to the labyrinth and chapel. Heading up a narrow side road, she thought about the first time she'd encountered Cayenne Perez. Arlo, Cay's partner, had told her where she was most afternoons. "Walking the labyrinth," he'd said.

At the time Olivia didn't know anything about labyrinths. Once she drove to the location she saw Cayenne, who explained. Constructed under a cathedral of pines, rocks and small boulders formed a circular path. Wide enough for one person to walk. That day Olivia watched Cayenne's tall form taking slow steps. When she reached the labyrinth center she stopped, raising both arms to the sun. After several minutes Cayenne turned and took slow steps back to the entrance, retracing her steps.

That first time Olivia knew instinctively that walking a labyrinth was more than just following a path. She also knew with certainty that she wanted to learn more.

After talking to Cayenne, she learned that each stone in the labyrinth had been placed intentionally, a project that Cay had taken on when she was going through a challenging time in her personal life. The Native woman attributed the healing of her marriage to constructing and walking the labyrinth. As a result she often acted as an unofficial hostess to visitors who came to make their own journeys.

That first experience at the labyrinth, Olivia had felt an instant kinship with Cayenne. Over time she grew to appreciate her sense of presence. The Two-Spirit shared an inner calm with her that rarely required words. After sharing silence they would talk. About life and then deeper things.

As she drove the dirt path toward her destination, the tall chapel steeple caught her eye first. A beacon to many, it was the first worship space in Lily Rock. Olivia's eyes scanned the lot. "There she is," Olivia announced to Maguire. She could see Cay's tall form near the chapel entrance.

As she drove over the gravel, Cay turned to greet Olivia with a wave.

Olivia pulled her car onto a paved area, next to another vehicle with a business name painted in bold letters: Two-Spirit Cleaning. *Cayenne changed the name of her company.*

Olivia turned off the ignition and got out of the car. She opened the passenger door to release Mayor Maguire. He ran to greet Cayenne, shoving his nose into her outstretched palms. Then he spun around and bounded toward the woods, barking as he went.

As Olivia drew closer, she smiled.

"Olivia Greer. What brings you today?"

Before she could respond Mayor Maguire shot back out of the woods. He yipped with joy, running toward them. Circling Cayenne's body, he ran around and around, dirt clods rising from his back paws.

Cayenne smiled but ignored the dog's antics.

Mayor Maguire ran slower and then finally stopped to

sit in the dirt. Only then did Cayenne lean over to pat his head. "Good to see you too, Mayor."

She turned back to Olivia. "Would you like to come sit down? I have a thermos of tea. Peppermint, as it happens. I believe that's your favorite."

"You remembered," Olivia smiled.

"I had a feeling I might see you today," Cay admitted. "Come ahead." She gestured with her hand. Olivia took note of Cay's weathered skin and her long dark hair, Since they met the strands had become streaked with gray. It lay in a braid down her back, a rubber band at the end.

Once they sat down, Cayenne poured hot tea into the lid of her thermos. She handed it to Olivia and waited for her to take the first sip.

"Perfect," Olivia said calmly. She handed the cup back to Cayenne. "Your turn."

Cayenne took the cup in both hands and then sipped. She handed it back to Olivia again. For a few minutes they sat in silence, passing the cup back and forth, no one needing to explain.

"That's what I like about you, Olivia." Cayenne took the empty cup, tapping it on the side of the bench to remove excess moisture. Then she screwed it back on the thermos. "You understand the importance of ritual. Back and forth, sipping the warmth, no words necessary."

In Cayenne's presence Olivia felt she could relax. She didn't need to protect her heart or her openness from this woman. In the time they'd spent together, she knew that Cayenne had a way of wrapping her spirit around hers, giving Olivia a chance to be herself, without feeling fear or anxiety.

"I heard about the death," Cay stated calmly. "Word gets around."

"Do you know about Time to Tidy? I thought since you are an owner of a cleaning business that you may have heard of Whitney Zimmer."

"I've heard of her." Cay nodded. "But I don't use social media to promote my cleaning business. I only go online to promote Native issues."

"So you've never met Whitney Zimmer?"

"She doesn't exist, at least for me."

Olivia felt a finality in Cayenne's answer. "I admire your ability to ignore certain people. I'd like to be more like that."

"You are very open. It shows in your face, your body, your eyes. I don't think the essential nature of a person can be altered. You are curious and people feel at ease with you. That is well known."

With Cayenne's words, Olivia felt the warmth in her chest increase, as if her heart were expanding. Cayenne's eyes sparkled. "I see you are already feeling better."

"I feel transformed in your presence," she admitted.

"That's my gift to share. I've transformed myself and now I can transform others. From confusion to clarity. Not unlike how you share your gifts. Everyone who comes into contact with you feels the warmth of your spirit. They aren't afraid to speak the truth in your presence. So I'm asking today. How can I help you, Olivia Greer?"

Olivia took a quick breath. *It's so good to be seen that clearly.*

"I actually have specific questions," she said at once. "Not of a spiritual nature but about your day job as a cleaner. Some combination of household chemicals may have killed the woman called Maddox Hall."

Cayenne answered, "If people are not aware that combining common elements can create a toxic gas, they can get into real trouble. Things get mixed. Like bleach with ammonia, for example. When combined it creates chloramine gas, which can make you sick and damage your airways.

"Mixing vinegar with bleach is also very dangerous. The combination creates chlorine gas, which can lead to respiratory distress. Unchecked it can cause death. There are more toxic combinations. I can tell you if you want to know."

"You may have already explained," Olivia said. "You see, I smelled vinegar and bleach the minute I walked into the house yesterday. The smell only got stronger as I went closer to the bathroom. That's where she died. Locked inside, most likely no ventilation." Olivia bit her bottom lip.

"No window or exhaust fan for air?" Cayenne asked.

"I didn't see inside the room. Janis Jets kept everyone except her team from getting any closer."

Cayenne looked away as if considering what to say. Then she turned back to Olivia. "You would be wise to leave the evidence to the police. This particular piece is most likely not yours to solve. But there must be something else you are concerned about that you can help with."

"Janis has arrested the most likely suspect. Her name is Roxanne Grossman. But I don't think Roxanne poisoned Maddox, either on purpose or by mistake."

Cayenne remained silent, creating a space for Olivia to assess her own feelings.

That's why I appreciate talking to her. She never questions my intuition. She accepts me. She trusts that I'm a reliable source. And she gives me space to figure things out.

A shiver came up her spine. *I'm really worried about Roxy, that she'll be held responsible for poisoning Maddox. I'm afraid for her now that she's confessed. Maybe I'm not meant to help Janis. I'm here for Roxy.*

"Do you know who else might have killed the woman?" Cay finally spoke.

Olivia shook her head. "There are a few suspects. Officer Jets has interviewed everyone at least once. Everyone except the company CEO, Whitney Zimmer. She can't be found, even by her very capable administrative assistant."

Cayenne tilted her head to the side as if waiting for her to keep talking.

"I wanted to learn more about cleaning products. That's your business. I can't trust everything I research on the internet. Just last night Michael and I were talking about cleaning and organizing influencers, and some of the negative consequences of following bad advice."

"Probably TikTok." Cay smiled at Olivia's surprised look. "Natives have their own influencer presence on social media. Our children communicate through social media just like everyone else."

Olivia brushed her jeans with the palms of her hands and stood. "Roxy is on my mind. She's the one I want to help."

"Then that's a good place to focus your attention. At least for now." Cayenne took a long look at Olivia.

When Olivia didn't keep talking, Cayenne rose to her feet. "Before you go, let's walk the labyrinth. I will follow from behind. I think it will help clear your mind as you consider what's important."

Mayor Maguire, who lay at Olivia's feet, rose up on all fours. He walked toward the labyrinth path. Olivia followed, with Cayenne coming last. Then the dog looked into the woods, sprinting into a bank of pine trees. "See you later," Olivia called after him. She made her way toward the entrance to the circular rock path.

Pausing to fold her hands in front of her body, she closed her eyes. "Thank you," she said aloud, as Cayenne had taught her years ago. Thrusting one foot forward she paused to balance and then lift the other foot. Both feet side by side she paused again. Thoughts jumbled her mind. *Not now.* Then she took the next step, this time listening to her heart. Cayenne's spirit lingered, Olivia only felt calm.

Taking each step slowly, Olivia stopped, now aware of a crow flying overhead. It cawed into the vast sky. She inhaled and took one more step. This time she could feel the soft loam under her shoe give way, lifting the earthy smell of damp dirt. Her foot sank in as she balanced on one foot and then brought forth the other.

Pine-scented air filled her nostrils. Wood smoke from a nearby fireplace tinged her senses. *Go on,* her inner voice urged. So she took the next step...

Moving at a slow pace, Olivia became aware of Cayenne walking slowly behind her. Far enough away so as not to disturb, but close enough for Olivia to feel her peaceful and steady presence.

Nearly to the center of the labyrinth, Olivia became aware of a word, like the caw of the crow, the same word repeating. Roxanne. Roxanne. Roxanne. The name of the only one who confessed to the murder.

CHAPTER FOURTEEN

Mayor Maguire waited next to the back bumper of her parked car. "Find any squirrels?" Olivia called to him. He turned around and wagged his tail.

After settling him into the passenger seat, she shivered and shut the door with a thud. The sun had begun its descent, and she felt the chill in the air.

With the driver's door closed she turned on the ignition and pushed the button for the heat. The dog pressed his back against the seat, staring forward through the windshield. She shifted to reverse and backed out of her parking place.

On the main road, she leaned to turn the heat up to the highest notch. *My feet are cold. Darn boots. Need to get new ones.*

As usual the winding road and the quiet companionship of Mayor Maguire helped Olivia's mind to wander. She'd bid Cayenne goodbye feeling open and clear-headed after the labyrinth walk. With the information about the toxicity of mixed cleaning chemicals, she knew she was on the right track. Plus the confirmation was all she needed from Cay to now focus on Roxanne. *Which means I need to find the real killer.*

In the past, Olivia, like Roxanne, had been the first to take more than her share of the blame when it came to mistakes. She'd spent eight years in a relationship with a man who was more than happy to tell her, "You're too sensitive. This is your fault," every time she'd try to bring up something that bothered her.

As the sun set behind the mountains, Olivia turned on her headlights. A sense of isolation came over her as she drove the darkening road. Her fingers tapped anxiously against the steering wheel.

In the rearview mirror she could see the long curving highway that sliced through the bank of trees. A tingle of apprehension traveled up her spine. She'd gotten better at driving the mountain roads but she still dreaded the dark when she was the only one on the road.

Instead of focusing on her feelings, she decided to shift her attention. Familiar rock formations along with signage told her she'd be home in a few minutes. Planning her dinner menu kept her from focusing on her feelings, and thinking about reheating the white chili made her stomach growl.

The two-lanes divided into four. Vehicles moving more slowly changed to the furthest right hand lane. Faster moving vehicles passed on the left, right before the lanes narrowed back to two.

Olivia lifted her foot from the accelerator, easing up on her speed to steer into the right lane. A flash in her rearview mirror drew her eyes upward. *What's going on!* Her stomach lurched to her throat as the driver began a series of loud honks.

The lights on the black SUV flashed. Followed by the

sound of an engine accelerating. The vehicle began a pass on her left. Panic rose in her chest as she watched the SUV linger alongside her car, long enough for the driver to stare at her.

Unfortunately the tinted windows made identifying the SUV driver impossible.

Headlights from a truck traveling in the opposite direction came over the bluff. The SUV accelerated hard, pulling ahead of Olivia and swinging sharply back into the right lane to avoid a head-on collision. Olivia gasped. They'd barely missed her front bumper.

The truck from the opposite lane streamed by, honking as if to say, *You damn fool!*

Olivia leaned over her steering wheel, eyes peeled. She hoped to get the license plate number this time. To her frustration the SUV sped ahead, preventing her from reading the license plate. A shiver crept down her spine.

Looking over, she patted Mayor Maguire's side for reassurance.

As soon as she looked up, she slammed her foot on the brake. Red lights blinked on the vehicle ahead. The SUV again. She looked down at her dashboard, registering the thirty miles per hour speed.

She'd barely avoided a collision.

Her heart beat faster. Olivia bent over the steering wheel again. The license plate holder was empty. *It must be a new vehicle.* Her eyes traveled to the back window. A white slip of paper had been taped to the corner, but she couldn't see the number in the dark from this distance.

The vehicle ahead slowed down again. She braked to stop from tailgating, her car crawling to a near halt. Her eyes narrowed. Finally she'd had enough. "Hang on, Mayor. We're taking a little detour." Twisting the steering wheel to the right, she drove onto a narrow dirt road, her car bumping forward.

Teeth chattering as she made her way over uneven dirt, Olivia kept moving. Finally she looked into the rearview mirror, exhaling with relief. The SUV had not circled back to follow her.

Mayor Maguire stared at her and then nosed her hand. She knew the gesture meant only one thing. "You'll have to wait until we get home," she explained.

Ready to turn back around, she found a wide area of the road. Her headlights shone on a sizable ditch, which she avoided by directing her car around and then forward.

Back on the main road, she pulled out into the far right lane. It wasn't until later that evening, when she had a chance to settle her nerves, that she realized—*I've seen that SUV before.*

CHAPTER FIFTEEN

By the time Olivia came through the door, she found Sage sitting at the kitchen table. The smell of thyme and tomatoes made Olivia's stomach growl. "That soup smells fantastic," she said.

Sage turned around revealing baby Star, asleep in the crook of one arm. She held her finger to her lips.

"Hey you," Olivia said softly. She didn't want to be the one to wake the baby.

Sage dipped her rounded spoon into the soup. Slurping at the edge, she lowered the spoon to whisper, "You've been busy. Helping Janis out with the investigation?"

"Kind of." Olivia kept her voice low. "I'll feed M&M first and then join you."

The dog stood at Sage's elbow, right next to Star. Sage admonished him with a shake of her head. "Don't you dare lick the baby. It will wake her up."

Mayor Maguire's ears drooped.

"Dinner," Olivia leaned over to announce in his ear. She stood away from Star and then shook the kibble in the dog food dish. Maguire rose to his feet, trotting to his usual place near the pantry.

Olivia put the dish in front of him. "Okay," she said softly.

Forgetting about the soup, Olivia knew it was her chance to talk with Sage. She sat down at the table, leaning over to gently touch Star's cheek with her forefinger. "Gosh, she's pretty when she sleeps."

Sage slowly spooned soup into her own mouth. The gentle repetition of her actions and the sight of sleeping Star made Olivia smile. *They're beautiful together. A real team. If only Jeff would join them. How do I tell her that he's enamored with both of them? It would be just perfect.*

Olivia cleared her throat. But Sage spoke first.

"I hear Janis arrested Roxanne for the murder of that woman. What's her name?"

"Maddox Hall. They called her Maddie." At the mention of the dead woman, everything else on Olivia's mind evaporated.

"Why did Janis arrest Roxanne?" Sage asked. She'd finished the last bite of soup and was using a more normal tone of voice. Olivia glanced anxiously at Star. When the baby didn't open her eyes, she went along, dropping her whisper for a low speaking voice.

"Actually Roxanne confessed before Janis arrived. She's convinced that she'd inadvertently mixed toxic cleaning chemicals and that she poisoned Maddie by mistake." Olivia frowned.

"So I'm wondering why Maddie didn't just open the door and run for help," Sage said.

"That's another thing." Olivia warmed to the topic of her investigation. "The door was locked from the inside."

Sage placed her spoon against the empty soup bowl.

When she didn't ask another question about the investigation, Olivia's intention to talk about Jeff returned.

Okay, now I can move this conversation in my direction. "How did you hear about Roxy's arrest—did Jeff talk to you?"

She looked hopefully at Sage, trying to gauge her sister's reaction when she brought up Jeff's name. Sage looked down at Star. Then glanced at Olivia. "Why are you staring at me?" she whispered crossly. "Do I have soup on my chin?"

"You're fine," Olivia said quietly.

Sage's eyes narrowed. "In answer to your question, I spoke to Luis Martinez about Roxanne. He happened to mention that he'd been up to the house to see her and that Janis arrested her, that's how I knew something was up."

Olivia kept a straight face, pushing back a sharp thrust of irritation. *I can't believe a doctor would talk to Sage about a patient. Isn't that some sort of ethical conduct violation? Those two must be closer than I thought.* Olivia rose, picking up the soup bowl and spoon, and walked to the sink.

"Dr. Martinez seems like a nice guy," she said over her shoulder. "I've heard that he's quite popular." *But I like Jeff Grossman better. He's not as arrogant for one.*

"He's fun," Sage admitted. "In fact I wanted to know if you could look after Star this Saturday. He's asked me out for dinner. I'll use the breast pump ahead. She takes the bottle pretty well. Would that be okay?"

Olivia turned from the sink. It didn't take a genius to hear the fatigue in her sister's voice. *She hasn't been out of the house for as long as I can remember.*

"I'd love to watch Star," she said immediately.

"Thanks." Sage looked down at Star, lifting her gently to her shoulder. "If you don't mind I'll try to put her down. I may close my eyes for a bit too. Love you." Sage stood, Star perched on her shoulder.

Facing the sink once again, Olivia looked out into the darkness toward Jeff Grossman's cabin. Staring into the backyard gave her time to think. She'd started that habit when Michael lived in the cabin. That was before he moved in with her and then started construction on their new home.

I wonder if Jeff's home or at the constabulary with his sister...

Leaning over, she finished rinsing the soup bowl and spoon. Then she put the dishes in the dishwasher, compartmentalizing her matchmaking plan to consider the investigation.

It's time to check out that flight manifest up at the helicopter field. I've only been there that one time before. She shuddered remembering how she'd gone undercover at the Lily Rock music academy for Janis Jets. *My one ride on a helicopter and I was nearly shoved out.*

As she leaned over to put soap in the dishwasher she heard Sage speaking to someone from the other room. *Probably on her phone. I bet she's talking to Luis. Telling him they're on for dinner Saturday night.*

Olivia flipped scrambled eggs onto Michael's plate.

"Heard from Jeff?" he asked, fork poised over the plate.

Olivia turned just as two slices of toast popped up, looking brown and crispy. "I think we may be on the wrong track. Sage asked me to look after Star this Saturday."

She turned back around to watch his reaction.

"And..." His eyebrow quirked.

"She's having dinner with Luis Martinez."

"Oh." He frowned. "That is not our plan. Martinez is okay but..."

"I don't think he's live-in partner material," Olivia sighed. "Oh sure, he can't keep his eyes off of Sage. Even when she was pregnant and on bed rest he'd come over a lot more than a regular doctor. I didn't think doctors made house calls until he showed up."

Olivia frowned. "I wanted to talk to her more, you know, feel her out about Jeff and Luis, but she's excited to be going out, so I bit my tongue."

Michael held up a forkful of eggs. "So now I see that being a matchmaker has its challenges. I had no idea. When

I think about it, minding my own business is a full-time job." He winked at her. "So let's change the subject. How did your search for Whitney Zimmer go?"

"I'm headed up the hill toward the helipad later this afternoon."

Turning to retrieve the toast, she shuddered, remembering the scene, the aggressive driver and the SUV on the dark winding road. For a moment she wondered, *Did I overreact?* Olivia of all people knew from experience that driving the mountain roads could be hazardous, even in the best of times.

But she'd also seen drivers take curves at breakneck speeds. Passing slower-moving vehicles was, for some, a kind of sport. They liked to see how far they could drive in the opposite lane before shifting away from oncoming traffic.

Tourists especially thought playing chicken was fun. Despite her feelings, she suspected that the SUV was most likely not directly threatening her in a personal way. Which meant she didn't need to tell Michael.

Shaking that thought from her mind, she brought a plate of buttered toast to the table. Sitting across from him, she said, "I went to visit Cay. She filled me in on the properties of cleaning chemicals; mostly the dangers of mixing them together. By the way, she's bought a new van and renamed her company."

"Sounds like business is good," Michael said.

"She's calling her business Two-Spirit Cleaning."

"Nice. It says everything about her personally along with her work. Branding can be tricky. I think she nailed it." Michael swallowed his last bite of egg. "You know Cay is in the same business as the social media cleaners. But she's so different."

"No online presence for her business. I asked her," Olivia added. "I didn't get a chance to ask why the change. You know Cay. She keeps things close until she's ready to talk, so I figured I'd wait. Anyway, she was so helpful. I walked the labyrinth after we talked..." Stopping mid sentence, Olivia felt tempted to share her fears about the drive home once again. For some reason she couldn't let it go.

"Everything okay?" He leaned forward, concern on his face.

Brushing aside the incident, she offered him the last piece of toast. "Everything's fine. I'm going to check the flight manifest to see if Zimmer's name comes up. Then I'll report to Janis."

"I'm getting the feeling that you think Whitney Zimmer may have murdered Maddie." Michael looked thoughtful. "If you can't talk to her face-to-face, how can you decide if she's the murdering type? Her alibi is based on the Wiz's word. He's definitely an expert at protecting his boss."

She stood. "Yes he is," she commented distractedly. Stepping over to the sink, she glanced toward Jeff's cabin. "I was kind of hoping Jeff would stop by and that we'd get a firsthand report of how things are going down at the constabulary. I didn't see him yesterday. Figured he was with Roxy."

"I'm headed to do some errands. I'll give him a call once I hit the road. See what I can find out," Michael suggested.

She came back to the table and leaned over to kiss him on the cheek. "That would be fantastic. I'm heading out too."

He cleared his throat. "So later, maybe at dinner, I'd like to talk about our up-and-coming move."

She inhaled quickly, feeling a tug in her gut, then forced

a smile. "How about I call the packing place and order some boxes today?"

"Great idea. That would make me feel like we're heading in the right direction. I've spent over a year on this project and can't wait for us to move in."

She came closer, wrapping her arms around his shoulders from behind. "I can't wait to be in our own place," she whispered in his ear. But the words, meant to be encouraging, sounded hollow to her ears. *Fake it till you make it, Olivia.*

A deep sigh escaped her lips. She pulled her arms away, hoping he wouldn't hear her ambivalence.

It wasn't until she drove up the hill that she revisited the conversation with Michael and her feelings of doubt. She knew Michael's house was a tremendous gift of love. Something he was famous for, and for him, the house was his way of saying, "I'm all in."

Up until now she thought she was also all in. But since Sage's baby... Lying to Michael, even by omission, made her feel conflicted and, if she had to admit, trapped.

Once she'd parked at the heliport, she got out of the car to focus on her surroundings. The scent of evergreen and earthy soil filled her nostrils. Unlike LAX, her usual city airport, the small heliport had been built among the pines, giving it an outdoorsy feeling. No hustle-bustle here. Nor any large planes. Spotting a sign that read Office, she walked toward the building.

Olivia could see beyond the low-lying structure to a landing pad. Located to the side and behind the office, a helicopter hovered over the pavement looking poised and ready to take off. Smiling at the resemblance of the helicopter to an oversized cricket waiting to jump, she glanced at the words printed on the side in bold red letters: River-side Fire Department.

To the left of the helipad, a large outbuilding stood open. Industrial-sized trash bins stood near each side of the opening. She squinted to see a small helicopter housed inside.

Surprised that no one was around to greet her, she turned to walk toward the office. Olivia felt confident that a place that seemed this organized probably kept equally accurate records of who flew in and out.

Opening the door, she was greeted by a thin young woman standing behind a counter. Tattoos along her neck, she sported a nose piercing and a scowl. Her short dark hair had been brushed back into a ponytail, making her look somewhere in her late twenties.

"Hello. What can I do for you?" The young woman's words sounded inviting, but more like something she'd been told to say, not anything she felt.

Approaching the counter, Olivia's eyes fell on an array of trifold brochures. Each had a photo of Lily Rock on the front, advertising tourist adventures. Tempted to pick one up, she stopped and instead spoke to the young woman behind the counter. "Officer Jets asked me to have a look at your flight manifest. She'd like to know the names for the past two weeks."

The woman shrugged. "Do you have a warrant? I don't want to get in trouble."

"Unfortunately not at this time," Olivia admitted.

"How about an identification badge. You do have that?"

Realizing that the young woman's strict adherence to the rules may make getting the manifest impossible, Olivia tried another tactic. "Maybe we could dispense with all the formality. It will take less time. I'm looking for the flight information on one particular woman. Maybe you remember her. Did a Whitney Zimmer land here in the past two weeks?"

Olivia looked at the woman's jeans jacket, hoping to find a name tag.

Perhaps sensing the scrutiny, she took a step back and responded in a clipped voice. "Sorry, I don't recall. But I do know that we don't keep an official record of who comes and goes. We're private up here." At that moment the door behind Olivia squeaked. The young woman's eyes looked past her to see who was coming inside.

Olivia turned, unable to disguise her surprise. "It's you!"

Stanley Weyland walked inside.

"How can I help you?" the woman asked in her disinterested tone.

Instead of acknowledging the woman's greeting, he reached out his hand to Olivia and she took it. "Hello there. Fancy meeting you here. I'm just dropping by. I hoped to pick up Whitney. She was supposed to arrive about now." He let go of Olivia's hand.

Unlike the day of the murder, the Wiz looked more rested. He wore a tucked-in light blue Oxford shirt. His slight paunch edged over perfectly creased tan slacks, and his brown Oxford shoes had been freshly polished.

"Why are you here?" he asked Olivia.

"I'm also wondering if Whitney Zimmer is flying in today," she said dryly.

"Oh, Whitney won't see you without an appointment. Have you tried messaging her?" he said with authority.

Olivia felt a flush of anger. His words reminded her of his shoes, well polished without a scuff. "Officer Jets wants an interview with Zimmer," she reminded him.

Unfortunately her words came out sounding empty

because unlike the Wiz, she was just the messenger. Not a paid employee of the constabulary.

The Wiz assumed an air of dismissal. He brushed his finger over his ear.

Olivia glared.

The Wiz cleared his throat. This time he sounded less confident. "Whitney texted me this morning. I told her the police were hoping to schedule an interview as soon as possible. She said she needed to finish her weekly podcast first." Stanley's eyes narrowed. "Interviewing Whitney is a constabulary concern. Are you here on behalf of Officer Jets?"

"I'm helping out with the investigation," Olivia explained.

A look of amusement came over his face. "When I first came to Lily Rock, someone told me how a woman named Olivia Greer assisted the constabulary with their interviews."

Olivia's eyes dropped down to stare at her scuffed boots. She felt a tingle up her spine, suspecting that he was trying to trap her into admitting she'd overstepped her role.

"Janis Jets asks me to help out on occasion," she explained, trying to make her half truth sound firm and convincing.

"You get people to confess to you. At least that's what I heard." He sounded interested. "The town thinks you're quite gifted, as a matter of fact. Almost magical."

"I think that rumor is greatly exaggerated. I just happen to have the kind of face that disarms people."

"I can see that." He nodded. "You're very open and friendly. No wonder people bare their souls."

Uncomfortable with the scrutiny, Olivia shifted the

topic. "So is your boss coming soon? I'd love to make an appointment for her to talk to Janis."

He looked at his watch and then back to Olivia. "It looks like she's been waylaid, but I can speak to her," he said. "Then I'll let you know when she's available."

"I do have one more question," she said. "Why isn't Whitney here in Lily Rock to check in on her contestants? After finding a dead body you'd think she'd want to be present herself."

"Whitney has me," he told her calmly. "The dead body is up to the police. We must make certain that the competition goes on despite the death—the participants have invested a lot of money in this opportunity. Our job today is to evaluate their progress at the cabins."

Olivia's jaw tightened. She couldn't help but question the callousness of the competition continuing, despite his logical explanation. "What cabins?"

"Whitney owns three side-by-side A-frames that she rents to weekend visitors. The contestants are assigned one cabin each."

"So they clean up for Whitney?"

"They know what's expected before they sign a contract," he insisted.

"I guess people will do anything to get her endorsement for their online business."

"That's right. Her endorsement can bring in thousands of new followers. Nearly everyone on the Tidy Team have given up their day jobs after they get that endorsement. They double their profits within six months." His cheeks flushed as he explained. She assumed because he was talking about his boss. When he glanced at his phone again she watched with curiosity.

"I have a text from Whitney. Came in just now." He scrolled with his thumb, turned his back to Olivia.

Olivia resisted the urge to move closer to look over his shoulder. "Oh, I didn't hear an alert. What does she have to say?"

"Looks like she won't be traveling to Lily Rock as planned." He clicked his phone off and turned back to her.

"Figures," Olivia muttered.

"I have an idea," the Wiz offered. "Can I buy you lunch in town? I heard the diner has good food."

Olivia knew when she was being deliberately distracted. Not wanting to talk about Whitney Zimmer any further, the Wiz made the lunch offer. This only convinced her that she was on the right track and that she somehow needed to help track down the elusive woman.

"Thanks, maybe another time. I've got to check in at the constabulary and then make a few calls. We're moving in a month and I haven't even started to pack."

"You're moving to a new house. That's right. I guess I also heard about that in town. Maybe when this competition is over, I can have a look at the new construction. I knew Michael Bellemare's name sounded familiar when you introduced him the other day. You must be very excited about the move."

Determined not to get involved in talking about the move, she pulled out her cell. "Why don't I get your contact information. Then you can tell me when Whitney arrives." She took out her phone and opened her contacts list.

He took it from her hand to tap his number into her contacts. Then he handed it back. "I'll look forward to seeing you and your boyfriend and getting to know you better. Lily Rock is growing on me more and more." When she only glared at him, he nodded toward the door. "Are you ready to go?"

She dropped the phone in her purse. "I'll be going now," she said to the young woman behind the counter.

"Sorry I couldn't help." She shrugged.

The Wiz accompanied Olivia to her car. He took a casual look inside the passenger window. "Where's the labradoodle? I expected to see him in the front seat. He's so cute the way he sits next to you like he's a kid on the way to school."

"Oh, he's not just any labradoodle," Olivia explained. "You must know that Mayor Maguire is a politically appointed Lily Rock legend. He's also free range—a goes-where-he-wants-to-go kinda dog. Apparently I was not on his to-do list this morning."

As she drove away she felt uneasy, aware that the Wiz had shifted his conversation to more personal topics. She wasn't sure if it was how he picked up gossip about her in town, or the surprising lunch invitation, or even his sudden interest in Mayor Maguire. The one thing she knew for certain was that the Wiz was covering up.

CHAPTER SEVENTEEN

Olivia arrived in town aware that her emotions were in a jumble. Once out of her car she made her way across the street. Glancing in the library window, she hoped to catch sight of Meadow McCloud.

In all of her worrying about Sage and the move with Michael, she'd not thought to consult with Meadow. As Sage's mother she might have some feelings about her daughter being left alone with her baby.

Stepping inside the library, Olivia sniffed. Bibliosmia, or the familiar smell of old books, hit her senses, accompanied by a quiet hum. Not quite silent but very close as people went about their business without talking.

A large seven-foot-long sofa in the middle of the room held two teens. One poked the other, showing her friend a page. Both giggled holding their hands over their mouths. Behind them the row of community computers was filled. People sat with their backs to the sofa, their eyes to the screen.

Her eyes drifted to the tall stacks filled with books. Two women stood together. One reached to the top shelf, taking down a book and showing it to the woman standing next to her. Then she closed the book and returned it to the shelf. So far there was no sight of Meadow.

Olivia's eyes drifted to the back shelves lined up against the far wall. She recognized Meadow at once. Wearing her customary denim jumper, without her customary braid, her fluffy gray hair in a disarray of curls dancing down her back. Meadow reached to the top shelf to pull down one book. She ran her hand over the spine and then slid it between two other books on the shelf below.

Next to Meadow's knee, Olivia smiled at a familiar sight. Sitting politely near Meadow, Mayor Maguire also faced the bookshelf. She watched as he sniffed one book, then another. Intently focused, he kept sniffing each book in the row.

Olivia quietly approached Meadow and Mayor Maguire. Drawing closer, she politely cleared her throat. Meadow turned and smiled. "Hello, dear," she said in a stage whisper. One that most librarians adapted. "I've been thinking about you." She placed the book in her hand on a shelf.

"Do you have time to talk about Sage and Star?" Olivia imitated the librarian's tone of voice.

Meadow's face lit up. "Of course I do, dear. A big change is coming very soon for you and Michael."

"And for Sage and Star," she whispered back.

"Let's go to my office. We can talk more freely." She pointed to the glass door located across the room behind the main counter. Olivia headed in that direction, followed by Meadow. Mayor Maguire scooted around the corner, deciding not to follow.

Once inside the office Meadow sat down in the chair facing the door, giving her a view of the front desk. Olivia sat across from Meadow, scooting her chair over to avoid blocking Meadow's view.

Olivia picked up the conversation where they'd left off. "I suppose there will be lots of changes for us," she admitted. "But mostly I'm worried about Sage and Star being alone in that big house."

"I assumed that might be a problem." Meadow nodded. "Especially for you."

Olivia felt a pang of discomfort. Why would Meadow assume she'd have problems? Was it that obvious...

Meadow continued. "You and Michael are the ones moving into your first house together. None of the distractions of a roommate. Now that's a couple's dream." A gentle smile came to her lips. "But it's also a challenge. I've never lived with a man in my home, but I can only imagine there will be obstacles, at least at first."

A niggle of annoyance caused Olivia to pull back. She wanted to disagree with Meadow and get the conversation back to Sage and Star. Her jaw tightened.

Yet Meadow looked so loving and calm, sitting at her desk, her eyes warm with affection. Words of retort, at the very least denial, settled on the tip of her tongue. She took a deep breath, not wanting to sound defensive.

Leave it to Meadow. Olivia knew that she didn't mean to upset her. But Meadow echoed her worst fears. That a move with Michael wasn't the fairy tale she'd hoped for. It came with complications. And once expressed, the move might turn out to be more than she could handle.

As Meadow waited for Olivia to reply, the pause in the conversation only grew more awkward. She could see Meadow's motherly concern in her eyes and half smile. Olivia knew she usually reserved that look for Sage.

She thought of Mona. How she'd react when Olivia got

defensive. Then she smiled. Like most good mothers, Meadow was not unfamiliar to a daughter's resistance. Her calm patience stated clearly that no matter how long it took, she wasn't going anywhere.

"I suppose we are the ones who will be making the biggest change," Olivia finally admitted.

Once she acknowledged the change with words, Meadow's expression shifted. The practical librarian, with a look of concentration, returned. "I have a couple of excellent books that I can recommend about how to negotiate moving in with a mate.

"One in particular," she continued, "is about the demands and challenges of moving into a new construction. Lots of practical ideas." She turned to her desk computer, lowering the glasses on her nose. "I'll research and have them waiting for you behind the circulation desk the next time you drop in."

The conversation felt over. She said, "Thanks," and stood. She opened the door with a small wave at Meadow, whose eyes were on the computer screen.

Once outside the library, Olivia stepped onto the boardwalk, then headed left toward the constabulary. Pushing the uncomfortable conversation with Meadow out of her mind, she focused on the up-and-coming conversation with Janis.

She wanted to fill her in on her recent chat with the Wiz. And of course, the disappearing act of Whitney Zimmer. Olivia admitted to herself that she wouldn't necessarily recognize Zimmer if she passed her by on the boardwalk. *I have no idea what she looks like.*

Olivia reached to open the constabulary door. Once inside she called out, "Hey, Brad, how's it going?"

Brad swiveled from his computer to face her. "Hey, Olivia. The boss has been ranting and raving all morning.

And in case you haven't heard, we have a prisoner in the back," he commented dryly.

Brad swiveled again and rolled his chair around to slap a card key on the pad next to the inner door. "See you later then." She walked past his desk to step through the doorway into the hall. From down the hall she could hear Janis Jets's bellow.

"Don't tell me she was poisoned. I know she was poisoned. Do you think I'm stupid! Nobody could breathe in that bathroom, even two hours after she died. That's right. The coroner gave me a two-hour time frame. From 6 a.m. to 8 a.m. Just call me back and tell me something new already. I've got the confessed killer in a cell, I just need some evidence. She probably just made a mistake with those cleaning chemicals. Once I interview her again, we can wrap this up."

Olivia waited outside Jets's office door, hiding from view. She'd rather listen than interrupt an irate Janis Jets.

Then the voice shifted from yelling to more compliant. "Yes, sir. No, sir. Won't happen again, sir. Got it. Motive. Will call later with more information." The conversation stopped.

Taking her cue, Olivia walked around the corner, her brightest smile illuminating Janis Jets's scowl. "Want to have lunch?" she asked brightly.

Jets's eyes narrowed. "Lunch, is it? That's what you have on your mind? I'm in the middle of an investigation." She glared at Olivia. "So you've left me alone for a couple of days. A good thing. I'm busy. But you look off. Don't tell me you've been investigating behind my back. Now I'm beginning to think you've been up to no good."

Olivia feigned a look of shock.

"That's it, Nancy Drew. I know that face. What have you been doing since the last time I saw you?"

"Let's have lunch and chat," Olivia suggested again.

"On the one hand I have better things to do than a girly lunch with the likes of you." Jets tapped her desk with the tips of her fingers. "But on the other hand, Brad could bring us lunch and we could sit right here. I know what's gonna happen. I can read you like a book. You're going to take my perfectly simple arrest, with a confession, and turn it into something complex and ridiculous. I hate that!"

As Olivia took a chair across the desk, Jets picked up her phone. "Brad. Two burgers. Two orders of fries. More coffee." She glared at Olivia, sliding her phone back on the desk.

"Go on. Spill it. You know you have things you want to tell me." Jets's scowl grew more intense.

In moments like this Olivia wondered if Janis was capable of leaning over her desk and giving her a good shake with those strong police hands. She inhaled to steady herself and then placed her hands in her lap with a smile. The wide expanse of desktop between them not withstanding, she hoped to calm Janis down with her report.

CHAPTER EIGHTEEN

By the time Brad returned with the food, Olivia had finished explaining to Janis about her conversation with Cayenne and then the Wiz. He stood next to Janis's desk waiting for a pause in the conversation.

"The Wiz got a text from Whitney when I was standing there with him. She canceled her trip to Lily Rock," Olivia explained.

Brad put the paper sack on the desk.

"Get outta here," she told him. As the office door closed behind him she looked into the paper sack and removed two wax paper-wrapped burgers. She slid a burger across the desk toward Olivia, placing the sack of fries between them.

"So let me get this straight," Jets began. "You talked to Cay and got pretty near the same explanation I got from forensics down the hill. Not surprising. Not much gets past her when it comes to cleaning." She unwrapped her burger and took a big bite.

"I also took a good look around the heliport." Olivia reached for a fry.

"The fire department often parks a vehicle up there," Jets said, taking another bite of burger.

"They don't keep manifests," Olivia explained.

"Could have told you that and saved you the trip." Jets nodded. "That'll teach you for going rogue."

Olivia ignored her to ask, "How's Roxanne doing?"

"She's gone very quiet. Her attorney showed up and her brother's been here a lot. She's reading a book about mindfulness."

"Have you changed your mind about her culpability in the murder?"

Jets crumpled the empty burger wrapper in her hand and tossed it into the metal trash can. "Once I thought about her confession, I had to admit it was very fast. Plus even if she was the one to mix up the chemicals, there's the locked door and the knife." Jets looked over at Olivia.

"I did a deep dive into the victim's social media accounts. Maddox 'Maddie' Hall comes up in a lot of searches. She owned a company called Little Things Every Day. You'd think she'd at least show a cute photo of her dog in some ridiculous sweater in one of those postings. I mean, that's what people do, right?"

"Not everyone," Olivia explained. "Some influencers choose to keep their personal photos on a separate account that's only visible to friends. What about this? Maybe we could talk to Roxanne again about her relationship with Maddie. We'd learn more about both of them."

"We could do that," Jets nodded. "I'll have to call in the attorney so she's legally represented. It can be arranged."

Jets ate another fry, her eyes growing distant. When she focused back on Olivia her voice sounded thoughtful. "So Roxanne's confession kind of kicked the investigation sideways from the start. I may have," she glared at Olivia, "gotten off course. Not sayin' I did, of course."

Realizing that Jets had just admitted she may have jumped to conclusions, Olivia felt a sense of relief. "I didn't fully realize how confusing an early confession might be."

"Yep, Nancy Drew. You're not a professional. Just sayin'. But...I think you're on to something. I like your idea about talking to Roxanne. Now that we've eaten, let's move her to the break room. Before that I'll contact her attorney and tell her I just want to chat her client up a bit. Keep it informal. Not on the record." Jets reached for her cell.

She held the phone to her ear and then put it down. "I know I'm not supposed to interview a suspect if she's invoked her right to an attorney. But I'll make it clear that we're talking just to help the investigation and that it will help her client in the long run. Plus the attorney knows me. If she agrees, then let's make this chat all cozy. Kind of makes me sick just hearing those words coming out of my mouth, but I can get Brad to pick up some cookies at Thyme Out and we can make a big pot of coffee. We can sit down the three of us and begin by swapping boyfriend stories. Like girlfriends." Jets smirked.

"I'm invited then?" Olivia asked.

"Oh yah. I could use you to make her feel all safe. That's who you are. There's no way I could pull off that part. People tend to clam up when I interview them. I wonder why?" Jets smirked again.

"Because you're the bad cop," Olivia explained.

"Pathetic cliché," Jets said brightly, obviously not disappointed with Olivia's assessment. "I have my own style of getting confessions. I admit that." She sat back with a look of great satisfaction. "First the attorney, then the cookies. You just sit tight and finish off those fries." She picked up her cell.

A few minutes later Brad stuck his head in the door. "Anything else I can do for you ladies? I'm taking a break and going to the hardware store."

"You can stop calling me a lady," Jets barked. "How many times do I have to tell you?"

"Yes, sir, I mean ma'am, I mean boss." Brad glanced at Olivia and rolled his eyes.

"Doesn't anyone take me seriously around here!" Jets bounced up from her chair, her voice getting louder. "On your way for a meetup with your nut and bolt buddies, stop by Thyme Out and get a dozen cookies. Tell my boyfriend to put it on my tab. It's lemon ricotta cookie day. Make that two dozen. Now get out of here!"

As the door closed Olivia glanced at Janis. "So how are things with you and Cookie?" Her eyebrows raised as if asking Janis to dish. She hoped to make her laugh with a more obvious personal question.

But Jets surprised her. Leaning over the desk, she spoke seriously. "Cookie wants to have a baby."

Olivia was shocked. Her eyes widened as Janis laughed aloud.

"Look at your shocked face. I think that's the way I looked when he brought it up. I mean, me? With a baby?"

Olivia cleared her throat, trying to wrap her mind around Jets's confession. "Okay, so you're both very good with Star. I've seen you and Cookie play with her. That's in your favor," she added hopefully. "You would make an interesting mother."

"Interesting? That's all you've got?" Jets sounded indignant.

"How old are you?" Olivia asked.

"Early forties," Jets mumbled. "Okay, more middle forties."

"Maybe a surrogate? Sage's doula told me all about surrogacy when Sage was on bedrest. It's a thing. Can you afford that?"

"On my salary? And remember Cookie owns a bakery. Unless he can trade his ricotta cheese cookie recipe for some cold hard cash, there's not a chance we can afford a surrogate."

Someone tapped on the door. Brad walked in. He sat on the edge of the desk as if ready to chat. "Cookie—the snack, not the guy—won't be out of the oven for another ten minutes. Apparently your boyfriend wants you to have them fresh and warm."

"I'll give him fresh and warm," mumbled Jets. But the corner of her mouth lifted.

"They have to cool before he packs them up," continued Brad. "I'll go back and get 'em for you." He stood. "I'm outta here."

The door closed, but then he poked his head back inside. "Boss. That's what I forgot to say. I'm outta here, boss." After that he made a quick retreat.

When Jets picked up her phone again, Olivia mulled over Janis's confession about having a baby. *Maybe she doesn't want to think about motherhood anymore. I get that.*

Once Jets put the phone down, Olivia spoke. "Our personal life is a bit overwhelming. How about we solve a murder instead?"

"Oh thank God!" Jets sighed. "Me with a baby and you moving in with your boyfriend. Please. That's for ordinary women." She paused, then went back to the original topic. "So I agree with you about not recognizing Zimmer. I might run over her in a crosswalk and not have a clue." She reached into a bottom drawer, bringing out an ordinary manila folder.

"I'll share what I've found out when I was doing those social media searches. Zimmer posts on Instagram at least three times before noon. But just like Maddox, she never posts her face. She jibber jabbers and hashtags about her expensive supplies and online coaching. Then there are the organizers and planners. Notebooks with nifty tidy ideas. I have to admit I kept clicking and scrolling, and I don't give a damn about dust bunnies under my bed. But social media makes everything feel personal, like they can fix whatever ails me. So I just keep looking for solutions to problems I don't have."

Olivia nodded in complete agreement. "Me too. I can spend so much time on my cell phone looking for the next best thing. I never used to be that way."

"So I shut down Zimmer's posts and went old school. I did get something when I checked the Department of Motor Vehicles. Whitney Zimmer's name popped up because she just registered a new vehicle."

Olivia felt the hair raise on her neck. "Did you also find the make and model of her new vehicle?"

"Yes, I did. Along with an address in the desert. Give me a minute." Jets opened her folder. She removed a paper.

"A brand-new black Mercedes SUV," Jets read and then slapped the folder on her desk closed.

Olivia felt her heart quicken. "I know that vehicle!" And then she began to explain.

CHAPTER NINETEEN

Olivia reached for a fragrant lemon ricotta cookie as Janis sat down in her chair and Roxanne looked nervously at her folded hands. She sank her teeth into the first bite and closed her eyes to appreciate the soft texture and the sugary goodness. A slight lemon flavor coated her tongue. "Lemon is my favorite," she mumbled, taking another bite.

"I like the chocolate chip pecan." Jets nodded. "But these are a close second."

"They are also amazing," Olivia agreed. Aware that the cookie small talk may help set a conversational mood, she looked over at Roxy. Brad had escorted her to the break room a few minutes earlier. Jets's plan for an informal conversation was set to begin.

Roxanne looked calm She'd brushed her hair back into a ponytail. Her skin, devoid of makeup, still looked pale and slightly translucent. But her previously red-rimmed eyes were no longer puffy. In fact the faraway gaze of her light gray eyes brought a wave of warmth over Olivia's heart. She wanted to take her under her wing and offer comfort.

Roxy longs to be understood. I can just feel it.

Jets cleared her throat. "Have a cookie." She slid the plate closer to Roxanne. "Olivia will get us some coffee." She darted a side-eye at Olivia as if to say, *why didn't you think of that already?* Olivia stood, the lasting taste of lemon ricotta goodness lingering on her tongue.

She brought three mugs and the carafe back to the table. "Want some?" she asked Roxy.

"No thank you," the woman said quietly. "Maybe some water?"

Jets shoved her mug closer. Olivia filled it to the brim. Then she filled her own and walked the carafe back to the counter. She returned with a fresh glass of water, which Roxy accepted immediately.

Once Olivia was seated again, she took another cookie for herself. "These are amazing," she told Jets.

"Go ahead and try one. You won't be sorry." Jets nodded to Roxy.

"Okay." She lifted a cookie to her lips. Taking one small bite, then another, she said, "These are delicious."

"I know," Jets replied. "My boyfriend owns Thyme Out, the bakery in town. His cookies are his superpower." She nodded to Olivia. "Olivia over here, her superpower is to liberate people from their secrets."

Roxy's eyes grew wide. "Is that what you call it—liberation?"

Jets insisted. "Yep, that's how I see it. Because you might not realize, but anything you can tell me about that morning would help with the investigation. Even stuff that seems unimportant.

"This conversation is not on the record, by the way," Jets added. "I checked with your attorney. She agreed with me that an informal chat might reveal important facts that may have gotten overlooked in light of that early confession." Jets patted the top of her closed laptop to emphasize her point. "See, no reports or taping."

"But I've told you everything. I just made a horrible mistake. I can't take it back. You might as well punish me." Roxy's eyes filled with tears.

Olivia's gut twisted. The conviction of guilt was in her voice. No one could ignore that.

"That's the thing." Olivia spoke in her friendliest voice. "I don't think you actually were the one to confuse those cleaning chemicals."

"And since you haven't convinced Olivia, I'm willing to look at things another way," Jets chimed right in.

Olivia added, "So could you tell us more about that morning and your routine? I mean, you were there as a caterer. Meal planning and food would be included in your contract, not keeping track of the cleaning totes and bottles. How did that responsibility become yours?"

Roxy looked thoughtful. Then she spoke in a hesitant voice. "Okay, I see where this is going. I'll do what you said: tell you all the details of that morning—even the small stuff. I've been going over and over it in my head anyway."

Roxy folded her hands on the table. Her cheeks pink, and a crumb of cookie at the corner of her mouth. Olivia resisted brushing it away.

The girl began to speak, using a measured tone. "So this is what I remember…"

CHAPTER TWENTY

"This egg white scramble is to die for." Serenity McFee took another bite. Dressed for the first day of the competition, her bright pink baseball cap covered most of her face. She'd secured her blonde hair in a bun right above the nape of her neck.

She scooped the last bite into her mouth. Roxanne stood to her right, holding the serving platter. She offered another helping.

"It's low in cholesterol, no egg yolks," Roxanne told the woman. "I've worked on this recipe for several months just to get it as healthy as possible without making it dry and tasteless like most egg white-only dishes."

"Avocado." Serenity nodded. "Avocado makes everything more moist and much better. You're a great cook."

Roxanne stood back with the spatula in her hand. "If you want to know, this job was a surprise to me. I was a last-minute hire, but I like it here. And I'm happy that you appreciate my cooking." She turned away from the table, attending to the frying pan on the stove.

A voice came from the doorway. "Do you use butter

with the eggs?" Maddie Hall wore black leggings and a tight-fitting white T-shirt. Little Things Every Day, printed in gold letters, was boldly displayed on the front. She came closer to lean over the frying pan. Roxanne looked up.

"I use butter for more flavor. But if you prefer I can omit the butter. This pan cooks eggs beautifully with very little fat." Roxanne filled another plate with the scramble, handing it to Maddie.

Ambling her way to the kitchen table, Maddie sat down and balanced her fork in her hand, but she didn't eat. Instead she poked the eggs around her plate. Roxanne came closer to observe, a slight frown on her lips. Maddie looked up from her plate. "Do you do all of this? Set up the table and all the cooking?"

"Yes, I do," Roxanne said with a smile. She took a minute to note the difference between the two women competitors. Maddie didn't seem to enjoy her food nearly as much as Serenity. Unlike Serenity's rounded curves, Maddie's body looked more lean. Roxy avoided looking at her chest, basically because her breasts didn't go with the rest of her body. They looked large, firm, and frankly fake.

A squeak from the other side of the room made her look up. The door to the janitor's pantry opened slowly. Bruce Ward stepped into the kitchen, his overly confident grin leading the way.

He wore distressed jeans and a logo T-shirt which read: From Tidy to Mighty. Obviously fit with a trim gut and muscled arms, Roxy couldn't help but smile.

"I was just checking out the totes." Bruce flopped down on a chair, joining Serenity and Maddie. "As soon as I eat I'm heading over to my cabin." He checked his wristwatch and then glanced at the center of the table where the egg platter lay.

"We have totes?" Serenity asked.

"All of them labeled, right in that janitor's pantry behind me. We're supposed to pick them up on the way to our work cabin."

Roxanne held the frying pan aloft with a mitt-covered hand. She'd prepared another dozen eggs. "I set up your totes. Everyone has the same amount of cleanser. The usual stuff—bleach, vinegar, tile and floor cleaner, glass cleaner. All labeled and ready." She pushed a generous helping of the egg scramble from the frying pan onto Bruce's plate.

Stanley sauntered into the kitchen from the living room and looked at his cell phone. When he looked up, Roxanne asked, "Would you like some breakfast too? I've got more eggs."

"I would love some breakfast. Toast will do, and some orange juice. I'll be right back. I need to check in the janitor's pantry first, just to make sure everything is ready." Hurrying across the kitchen, he disappeared into the pantry. A light came on from inside.

When he didn't return right away, Roxanne called, "Everything alright in there? Did I set up the totes correctly?" When he didn't reply she added, "Do you need help?"

Stanley hollered, "I've got this. Keep on serving breakfast." He sounded mildly irritated but then shifted his voice to a milder tone. "I'll be right there."

Roxy called out so that he could hear. "Plus there is bread for toast. And jam, and Irish butter. It's the best kind of butter, at least that what nutritionists say."

CHAPTER TWENTY-ONE

Finished with recollecting, Roxanne swallowed a sip of water.

Jets looked thoughtful. "So Stanley spent some time in the pantry after you had set everything up?"

"That's right," Roxy confirmed.

"Okay, I didn't hear that the first time you told your story. That means he had the opportunity to rearrange the cleaning bottles, as the rest of you were busy eating breakfast."

Roxanne's eyes grew wide. "I never thought of that."

"Before you go back to your cell, there's one more thing. Did you see Whitney Zimmer in the house that morning?" Jets looked intently at Roxanne.

"No one expected to see her. The Wiz told all of us the night before that she kept her distance at the contests to maintain her impartiality. When she offered me the job on email, I did some research."

Jets's eyebrows raised with an unspoken question.

"Everybody does that now. Check on who's hiring them,

especially when it's last-minute. Not everyone is on the up-and-up."

"Another example of Roxanne's attention to detail," Olivia said with a satisfied nod.

Roxy continued, "I did discover that Whitney is quite keen on maintaining boundaries. I wasn't surprised when the Wiz said she didn't micromanage the daily operations, especially with the contestants. And then I found that Whitney runs a six-week seminar on boundaries for those who are interested."

"So she hires a really good administrative assistant. We all know that," Jets said. "From what you say that makes sense. I guess. Sure wish I could have a sit-down with Whitney. She's a person of interest for now, but the longer she stays out of sight, the more chance she'll be added to my list." Jets lifted her phone and hit a button before putting it to her ear. "Come get our prisoner," she snapped.

Olivia flinched. The word "prisoner" did not fit with Roxy and its use made her feel defensive.

Brad arrived within minutes to escort Roxy out of the break room. As they left, Jets opened her laptop. "Before you go, we need to talk about our next move."

"Okay," mumbled Olivia.

"Any other ideas where we might find Whitney Zimmer?"

"So she is a suspect; you sounded less sure when you were talking to Roxy."

Jets kept typing, talking at the same time. "Not a suspect, at least not yet. I am playing it cool with Roxy. She's not privy to all the details of the investigation. Between us, Whitney may not be a suspect, but she's certainly a person of interest. Her avoidance behavior being the first qualifier."

Olivia shrugged.

Jets closed her laptop. "I just made us a reservation at the Refuge for tonight. Four of us."

Olivia was surprised. "Okay then. You might have asked if I'm busy."

"Are you?" Jets stated flatly.

"Not really," Olivia admitted. "What's your big hurry for a couples night? Is there something I should know about?"

"It's part of the investigation, Nancy Drew. You heard the Wiz say that Whitney hangs out at the bar there when she's in town. I know the bartender. Too bad we don't have a description of her," muttered Jets.

"Okay, then a work dinner, with very good company," Olivia said.

"Plus I've been wanting to talk to you about the progress on the castle," Jets smirked.

"Castle?" Olivia asked.

"Michael's building his lady love her own castle. Or didn't you know that's what the folks in Lily Rock are saying?"

"It's not like that." Olivia flushed. "Michael's an architect and a contractor. That's what he does. He builds houses. Kind of like Cookie bakes for you."

Jets scoffed. "A house is much different than a baked good. A lot more permanent for one thing. He might as well put a moat around it so everyone can call you Princess Olivia. Can I call you princess? Please say I can!" Jets's face lit up as if she'd just had the best idea.

Olivia felt her cheeks flush. *People are talking about me?*

"I'm just sayin' you have every right to be nervous. I eat a cookie and it's done. Castles are much more permanent."

Olivia's heart plummeted. It was unnerving when Janis

expressed her fears in one sentence. "See you tonight," she muttered, making her way to the door.

"Here's your table." The Refuge server pointed to a seat near the indoor waterfall. He waited for the four of them to sit down before offering a menu. "Here's our menu. Note that the duck à l'orange is the special tonight. The soup of the day is leek and potato. I'll stop by in a minute to see if you have any questions."

He walked away as Olivia opened her menu. She glanced over the top at Janis, who did not acknowledge her stare. Deciding on the special, she shifted her gaze to the right to get a better view of the bar.

Mirrored glass reflected bottles of Scotch and whiskey. The bartender stood in front of a female patron shaking a cocktail. Her back was to the main dining room, but Olivia could hear her throaty laugh from across the room. Watching the large mirror behind the bar, Olivia tried to catch sight of the woman's face reflected in the mirror, but the array of liquor bottles blocked the view.

The woman's platinum-colored hair, cut in layers, hung in a straight line down her back. Still wearing her puffy coat, Olivia could still see tight-fitting black jeans.

The bartender laughed. Olivia glanced at the woman's back again, taking note of her Ugg boots propped up on the bar stool. *Uggs.* Her eyes shifted back to the jacket. Olivia sniffed. *I can smell the fine leather from here.*

She eyed the empty stool next to the woman but decided against walking to the bar because the guy on the other stool was Spike Rocco, one of Michael's construction crew. Spike hovered over his drink, his shoulders slumped, not looking to the left or to the right. Olivia didn't want to engage him, let alone have him come over to talk shop with Michael. That would derail the apprehension of Whitney Zimmer.

Because now Olivia felt even more certain. Her eyes shifted back to the blonde, recognizing the boots and the jacket. Jets's voice interrupted.

"So Mike, how are you doing on the castle? Got the moat dug and the bridge constructed?"

Olivia felt Michael grow tense. She looked over to see his puzzled expression. A half-hearted grin followed. "We're coming along," he said hesitantly. He eyed Janis carefully. "I didn't think about a moat, but now that you mention it, I could make that work."

Unable to get a rise out of him, Jets tried again. "What I want to know is whether or not Princess Olivia is ready to grow her hair like Rapunzel in that fairy tale."

"Castle and moat. And now my princess. I didn't know you were such an authority on medieval imagery." Olivia heard Michael's deliberate attempt to stay calm in the face of Jets's barbs.

Cookie broke in. "Janis is an authority on a lot of stuff. Don't let her get to you. She's edgy for some reason." He gave her a stare, as if to say *knock it off*.

Janis shrugged. She did an imitation pout by rolling her bottom lip. At that point everyone at the table burst out laughing. Michael, no longer defensive, slipped his hand under the table, laying it on top of Olivia's thigh. "I don't think Olivia would tolerate a castle. She's not that kind of woman." Her turned to her with a teasing voice. "What do you think, Princess?"

Olivia felt herself flush. Feeling trapped in the conversation, Jets hit too close to the truth for her to ignore her feelings. Plus Jets had escalated by involving Michael. This only made her feel more vulnerable. So Olivia dove in, knowing full well she'd regret what she had to say as soon as the words left her mouth.

"I've noticed I'm dragging my feet about packing for the move. It wasn't until Janis brought up the enormity of your gift earlier that I wondered if that had something to do with my reluctance."

Michael moved his hand away. Feeling his disconnect sharply, she stared at the tablecloth.

The waiter arrived at the table, interrupting the silence. "Any questions about the food?" He held up his iPad, waiting for their orders. All talk about the new house and princess were dropped as Michael and Cookie each made selections from the menu.

Janis abruptly pushed her chair back from the table. "We can talk Dungeons and Dragons later. I'm going to the ladies'. Cooks, order me something with a lot of red meat. You know what I like." She leered at her partner and then turned to follow the restroom sign.

"I'm going with her." Olivia rose too. "I'll take the special," she told the waiter. As she walked away she heard the waiter prompt Cookie, "Any questions about the menu?"

She wound her way past tables and chairs toward the bar. Halfway across the dining room Olivia stopped, remembering the blonde woman. *I've seen that leather coat before, and those Uggs too*, she assured herself.

To her surprise the woman still sat at the bar. On her feet as if to go, she appeared taller, probably around six feet. Lifting her hand to slide money across the counter, she made her way to the exit, carefully ducking her head. Olivia couldn't see her face.

Olivia watched as the woman pushed the door open, disappearing as the door closed behind her.

Janis came out of the restroom right as Olivia rushed forward, nearly running her over. "That's Whitney Zimmer," she said breathlessly. "She's heading to the parking lot. I recognized her coat and her boots from the other day."

"So why are we standing here? Lead the way," Jets barked.

"What about the men?" Olivia glanced back. Michael and Cookie were deep in conversation.

"They'll manage," Jets insisted.

Olivia darted to the exit in a half-run. Jets came alongside. Olivia held the door open for Janis, who rushed past. As soon as they stood outside, Jets shuddered. "Really cold out here."

Olivia stomped her boots. Scanning the parking lot, she looked for car lights. When none appeared she looked toward the main road. A familiar SUV waited at the stop sign, red taillights glowing. She pointed to the car as it made a right turn and sped onto the main road.

"That's her," Olivia hollered.

"And you can tell that because..." Jets sounded skeptical.

"I know it's her," Olivia insisted. "Plus the boots and jacket."

"So give it up, my little princess. Anything else. Real evidence, perhaps?" Jets said.

"Because that's the SUV that followed me from the labyrinth yesterday. A new Mercedes. It's black with tinted windows. It has to be hers. You said she registered a new vehicle at the DMV."

Jets nodded. "That's the make and model that came up when I did the internet search. You may be right," she said, not sounding completely convinced.

"That's not the only time I saw the vehicle," Olivia

explained. " Whoever is behind the wheel is aggressive and dangerous, especially on our mountain roads. That's the same SUV. I just know it."

Olivia shuddered, the cold numbing her nose and ears.

"Okay then. You probably are right. Let's talk inside. I'm freezing my you-know-what off out here." She looked longingly toward the restaurant entrance.

They moved quickly through the Refuge's front door. Janis kept talking, her teeth chattering. "This dinner hasn't been a complete loss. We finally got a sighting of the infamous Whitney Zimmer, and I've managed to make Michael Bellemare squirm." Jets took Olivia by the elbow. "Add a thick steak for dinner and my day is complete."

Inside the warm restaurant, Olivia looked toward the bar. Unlike Janis, she didn't feel hungry anymore. Plus she'd felt Michael's anger when he took his hand away from her leg. She didn't want to go there again.

"Before we go back to the table, let's ask the bartender if he knows that woman. We could get confirmation about her name," she told Jets.

Janis needed no more persuasion. She headed right toward the bar. "Hey bartender," she called out, sliding onto a stool.

"What can I get you, Officer Jets?" His name tag read Skip. "You stranded your dates." Then he looked at Olivia. "Have a seat," he offered. "I can put your order on the tab."

Jets flashed a disarming smile. "She doesn't drink and I'm kind of on duty. I was wondering what you could tell me about that blonde who was sitting here when we walked in. Is she a regular?"

Skip pulled a lever to fill a glass with draft beer. He set the foaming glass on a tray. "I can't say she's a regular. But tonight she was really friendly. Gave me her name and number with a sizable tip." He reached into his pocket. Unfolding the napkin, he said, "Whitney Zimmer." Olivia's heart skipped a beat as Skip handed the napkin to Jets.

Jets held the napkin, grinning from ear to ear. "Thanks, this is just what I wanted. Come on, Olivia. I hear dinner calling." On the way back to the table, Jets was already looking at her cell.

As Olivia sat down, Cookie pulled out a chair for Janis. She didn't say a word, her head bent over her phone. When she realized everyone was staring at her she leaned over to give Cookie's cheek a peck. "Hey, sweetie."

"Are you doing some kind of phone search?" asked Olivia.

"I am being a good detective. I've got the woman's name and number from the napkin. But there's a small problem. She gave him the correct name with a fake number. I can do more when I get back to the office." She slipped the phone back into her pocket.

As the waiter approached their table, he announced, "I have the duck à l'orange," and lowered the plate in front of Olivia. "And the T-bone steak, rare." He placed the plate in front of Janis. "Be right back with the gentlemen's food."

Olivia watched as Janis cut into her steak. "Want a bite?" Janis offered to Cookie. She extended her fork as he leaned closer. A quick grin, then he grasped the meat with his teeth. "Delicious," he commented, looking straight into her eyes.

Jets eyed him seductively. She put down her knife to pick up her glass of cabernet. "Now that I've called Michael out, you're next." She looked at Cookie over the rim of her glass. "What's all this about having a baby—at my age? Ridiculous."

Cookie's mouth fell open. She'd caught him off guard.

He shrugged, forcing an uncomfortable laugh. "You got me," he admitted. "I was hoping this was Michael's night to be grilled, but apparently you're after a piece of me too."

Jets picked up her steak knife. "You men need to remember—I play dirty, especially when I have the knife." She grinned, shoving the bite of meat into her mouth.

Olivia had to give her some credit. At least she chewed with her mouth closed.

<h1 style="text-align:center">CHAPTER TWENTY-TWO</h1>

The next morning Olivia stood in the kitchen. Her thoughts wandered over the near apprehension of Whitney Zimmer and the revelation of her moving fears. Holding her mug of coffee, she stared out the window, realizing the sheer perversity of Janis Jets to get to the truth, no matter how messy.

Since they met, Olivia had come to appreciate the hard-edged cop. Especially as Janis included her in her investigations. But when she stepped into her personal life, the appreciation faded to irritation. *I'm not one of her suspects.* She sighed.

Of course when they'd first met, she *was* a suspect. Not even just a person of interest, but the only real suspect, just like Roxy. She didn't confess because she hadn't done anything, unless discovering a dead body counted.

Olivia shuddered remembering how insecure she'd felt that first time being introduced to the Lily Rock constable. *That's when I had no home and no real friends. Before I came to Lily Rock. I didn't even know Michael.*

In the growing friendship with Janis, she'd forgotten

how people walked on eggshells around her, especially when she used her sarcasm like a knife and cut into their soul with a biting observation.

Over time Olivia had come to expect Janis's probing questions and sarcastic remarks. But the whole thing about the castle and the house had surprised even her. And also Michael. When he took his hand away—that upset her a lot. He'd never done that before. Somehow their relationship had been thrown off kilter.

Not because Janis wasn't right, but mostly because Olivia was forced to talk about her feelings when she wasn't ready.

She sighed, remembering that the rest of the night didn't go very well either. They'd driven home in silence. He'd rolled over in bed without the usual goodnight kiss. She lay awake for a long time before she was able to go to sleep.

Back to the present, Olivia looked over at Michael. He sat at the table scrolling on his phone. She moved closer, placing her coffee mug next to his. She knew she had to explain, even if it caused him to withdraw even more. She hated feeling disconnected from him, but she knew it would only get worse. She sat down, pulling the mug closer and opening the conversation.

"Janis was on a roll last night," she tried.

Michael shifted uncomfortably in his seat. He didn't look up right away, his chin dipping further toward his phone. When he finally raised his head, she felt her heart drop at the sad expression on his face. *I did that.*

"She did kinda come after me. But I'm used to her." He looked at her without his usual smile. "But what surprised me is that you didn't disagree about the house being too big of a gift."

Olivia's throat tightened. She knew what she said next

would be very important, so she chose her words carefully. "I was as shocked as you, how she just brought it up and flung it at you right at dinner." She shook her head. "It was a weird day for me. Both Meadow and Janis came at me out of the blue. Meadow was nicer, of course..." Olivia picked up her coffee mug and then put it down with a thump. She watched him closely, gauging his expression.

The tightness at the corner of his mouth had relaxed. To her relief he reached across the table to take her hand. "So you haven't been hiding doubts just to please me?"

"You know, my doubts are confusing me too. I've realized more and more that Sage and Star have occupied my mind completely, so that might be the real issue for me. I told you about that part, remember? I even got you to conspire as a matchmaker." She could tell by his expression that he was considering her words very carefully.

"Yes, you did tell me," he said, "and you enlisted my help." He rolled his eyes toward the ceiling, eliciting a laugh from Olivia. She could see that Michael felt better, but she knew that he wasn't entirely convinced. Something about his voice and his eyes. At that moment a knock came at the back door.

"Maybe that's Jeff," Olivia said. She walked to the door and opened it. Mayor Maguire scampered past, heading to the pantry.

"Good morning," Jeff greeted her.

"You're looking spiffy today," Olivia commented. Standing before her was not the usual scruffy just-out-of-bed Jeff, but a Jeff whose hair had been trimmed and slicked back. He wore a denim button-up shirt, and he smelled like vanilla pachouli. She stretched out her arm to invite him inside.

Making his way to the coffeepot, Jeff reached for a mug

and filled it to the brim. Then he turned, resting his back against the counter. "I'm cleaning up my act. Got a court date for Roxanne comin' up. Have to make a good impression for the judge."

"Have a seat and fill us in. Is there a chance she'll make bail?" Olivia asked, making her way to the pantry. She bent over to grab Mayor Maguire's empty food bowl and then opened the door.

"Why don't you encourage Roxy to stay here in Lily Rock? At least until Jets sorts it out," Michael suggested.

Olivia placed the bowl of kibble in front of Maguire. "Roxy can stay with us."

Jeff shook his head. "Actually we talked about that possibility. Roxy can stay with me. I have a futon in the loft." He looked over at Michael. "You left that when you moved out of the cabin." Then he looked toward Olivia. "So neither of you mind if Roxy hangs out with me? I didn't know how you felt about harboring a person who's under suspicion for murder."

Michael spoke up immediately. "I don't think Roxanne actually murdered Maddie. I don't think Olivia does either." He sounded quite convinced.

"Just yesterday at the constabulary things took a turn in another direction, away from her," Olivia admitted.

"That's what I heard," Jeff said. "As a matter of fact, Roxy called me right after she spoke to you and Officer Jets. That Brad guy snuck her a phone. She sounded so much better. You encouraged her to think that the poisoning may not have been her fault."

Olivia agreed. "As soon as Officer Jets stops focusing on your sister, she will find the real killer. Like Janis always says, 'This is an ongoing inquiry.'" Olivia made her voice sound hard and certain, imitating Jets's style of talking.

Jeff smiled at Olivia. "Roxy and I weren't always close. But she's my sister and I want to be there for her."

In that moment Olivia felt a pang. As if Jeff's words held some kind of truth for her. Reminded of Sage and their newly minted sisterhood, she took a moment to focus on her feelings. "Sage and I just realized we were sisters recently. When I first came to Lily Rock," she said, her voice faltering.

"I see," Jeff said thoughtfully. When he didn't ask her to explain more, she became aware of a flood of emotions. First was concern and insecurity. And then underneath the insecurity was anxiety. The kind that made a knot in her stomach.

She knew fairly soon that having a sister had changed her world. When they moved in together, it felt like a homecoming. And then when her sister had a baby, that only doubled the importance of being a family.

Maybe people who were raised with siblings took this closeness for granted. She looked at Jeff more closely, feeling a fondness for him. It took Jeff telling her about his relationship with Roxy to stir this up. She really had no idea how people acted with their siblings because she'd never had one before.

To her surprise she felt tears filling her eyes. It was about Jeff. She'd grown very fond of him over the past months. Olivia had come to know him better and realized that he was a good person. His attraction to Sage hadn't hurt any, of course. But she also loved that he included Star, though the baby wasn't his main interest.

The idea of family made Olivia emotional. More than she ever anticipated. She stopped to acknowledge this reality. *This is family. Me, Sage, Star and Michael. And maybe even Jeff. We've been formed out of the bits and pieces of what's left over.*

Michael interrupted her thought process. It was his turn to swing back to the investigation. "So we've got the search for Zimmer under control. But what about the morning of the murder? I still have some questions. Mainly is it just me, or does anyone else wonder why the bathroom door was locked from the inside?"

Olivia patted her stinging eyes, following his line of thinking. "Maybe the killer wanted everyone to think that Maddie committed suicide. That she poisoned herself and locked the door to finish herself off."

"I guess that's one way to look at it," Michael commented. "Do you think she was desperate enough to do that?"

Before the conversation could go any further, Sage appeared in the doorway. She tiptoed into the kitchen. Smelling of lavender soap, her hair dripped down her back, wet from the shower. Baby Star, fast asleep, was cradled in the crook of her mother's elbow.

"Any coffee left?" Sage spoke in a low voice. "Oh hi Jeff," she added, still keeping her voice down.

"There's plenty," Olivia said softly. "Want me to hold the baby while you have something to eat?"

Sage came closer, gently dislodging Star from her elbow. She slid the bundle of baby and blanket into Olivia's waiting arms.

Cradling Star close to her body, Olivia bent her head to breathe in the scent of freshly laundered cotton, mingled with the soft scent of baby lotion. Bracing Star's head from behind with one hand, she looked into the sleeping face of her niece.

Closed eyelids hid Star's blue-green eyes. Soft light

brown curls circled her head. Her tiny fists, held in a ball, made Olivia's heart quicken. "You are very beautiful," she whispered to the baby. "You look just like your mom."

Back at the table, Sage sat in the empty chair. She waved a piece of buttered toast in the air. "And she looks like you," she explained, "especially her smile."

"And she looks like our mother," Olivia added. *Star is part of our new family. The new one made from bits and pieces.*

For a reason Olivia couldn't explain, she realized in that moment that planning for an impending move may have unleashed a lot of stored emotions. Especially when it came to family and belonging.

Olivia looked at Jeff and then Sage, sitting at the kitchen table, chatting comfortably in low voices so as not to wake the baby. *They're becoming better friends.* Then she glanced over at Michael. He raised his eyebrows at her, nodding toward the other couple as if to say, *Sage is doing just fine.*

The baby stirred in her arms. Olivia ran her finger over Star's chubby arm, from the elbow to her hand. The tiny fingers grasped and opened and then, to her surprise, they grasped again, this time clinging around her index finger.

She bent closer to brush her lips against the baby's forehead.

Later that morning Olivia stepped out of the shower to the sound of her cell phone ringing. She quickly toweled herself dry before picking up the call. "Hello," she said.

"Jets here."

"Greer here." Olivia mocked Janis's stern voice.

"Why are you calling me?" Jets demanded.

"Stop typing while you're talking to me. You called me. Don't you remember?"

"Oh yeah, I guess I did. Meet me at the house where

Maddox was murdered. I have the forensic report here in my hand. Plus I want to get another interview with the Wiz." The line clicked off.

Olivia dressed hastily. In distressed jeans and a soft blue sweater, she felt ready for the day. She hurried down the hall to the stairway, greeted by a friendly, "Bork." Mayor Maguire stood at the top of the stairs. His tail wagged and he held one of her well-worn boots in his mouth.

"What! You're carrying around my boot yet again?" Feeling rushed and indignant, she ran up the last few steps to snatch the boot from his mouth. Holding it up for inspection, she looked over the worn condition; there were newly added bite marks near the sole. Olivia glared at Mayor Maguire. "My feet are always cold now because of you."

Instead of acting ashamed, the dog barked, assuming a downward dog pose. He was ready to play.

Pointing a finger, she scolded, "You're not supposed to chew shoes. I've talked to you about this. I thought you were done with this puppy nonsense."

"Bork." He jumped up on all four paws, spinning around, then faced her again.

Olivia sighed. *How can he be so naughty and so cute at the same time?* "I can't play right now. Janis wants us for an interview. You want to come along?"

Mayor Maguire ran to the front door. He sat with his back to her, waiting patiently for the door to open. She felt relief at the sight of her other boot, lying where she'd left it the night before.

Pulling the left one over her sock first, she stopped. Fiddling with the lace, she sighed in exasperation. It had been chewed into two pieces, which barely hung together, connected by a thin leather thread. She double knotted the pieces and tried again, then stood up to test the boot. She repeated the process by tying the remaining lace before slipping it on her right foot.

Mayor Maguire leaned over her as if fascinated with the process. He shoved his nose on the sole of the left boot. Olivia pushed his head away. "That's not helping," she told him in a firm voice.

Olivia frowned at Mayor Maguire. "Come on. Let's go, you silly mutt."

On the drive into town Olivia thought about the Wiz. Her curiosity niggled, realizing she found his unwavering loyalty to his boss a bit annoying. She anticipated that Janis would lunge at him with questions. Do her duck and weave, dart in and out with barbed remarks and attacks like an experienced fencer with a sharp sword. *He might spill some important clues.*

Remembering the directions from the first day, she turned off the main road onto the driveway of the Time to Tidy main house. With Mayor Maguire at her side she walked toward the front. Stanley Weyland opened the door as she approached.

"Saw you coming." He looked her over, his eyes dropping to frown at M&M. "I didn't expect to see the dog." He stepped aside for her to enter, holding the door for Mayor Maguire to come inside.

"Bork," the dog responded, and then turned. He ran back out the door toward the woods.

"He probably sensed a squirrel," Olivia explained.

The Wiz sniffed, then shut the door.

Olivia slipped off her boots. She hung her coat on the peg rack. Her first glance told her there were no Uggs or leather jacket. Before commenting about the absences, her eyes fell on Janis Jets's scuffed Doc Martens. Toes against the wall. They stood as a reminder of a solid but worn presence.

A scratch came at the front door. "You might as well let him inside. He'll pester us until you do," Olivia warned the Wiz.

Stanley opened the door. Mayor Maguire trotted past, stopping to sniff the Doc Martens. He moved to sniff Olivia's boots, growling under his breath. "Leave it, Maguire," Olivia commanded. Then a voice came from the living room.

"Just hurry up already. I want to get this interview going," Jets hollered.

Maguire turned away from the boots to stare at the Wiz, who only shrugged, apparently disinterested in the dog's behavior. Then he addressed Olivia. "May I get you a hot beverage?"

"Enough with the butler act. Olivia can get her own drink," Jets hollered again from the great room.

Stanley rolled his eyes at Olivia. He pointed for her to join Janis and then headed in the opposite direction toward the kitchen. Olivia made her way to the living room. She found Jets sitting in an overstuffed chair. Taking her seat on the empty sofa, Olivia waited.

"Give me a minute," Jets muttered, her eyes on her iPad.

Before she was done typing, Stanley returned with a tray containing a teapot and three cups with saucers. There were lemon and sugar in small matching bowls, along with a pitcher of milk. After sliding the tray on the table, he sat at the other end of the sofa. Back straight with his feet on the floor and his shoulders squared. "Would you like me to pour?" he asked, his voice sounding like a stuffy waiter.

"So here's the deal, Mr. Wiz." Jets turned off the iPad.

"I am either Stanley or the Wiz," he corrected her. "All

of our names are a part of our company brand. Whitney and I made that distinction when we first got together; I'd play the role of her assistant and handy-person, while she played the role of entrepreneur and businesswoman."

"So how did you two meet?" Olivia asked, deflecting Jets's look of annoyance. She usually waited for Jets to begin an interview.

"At a tidy convention," the Wiz answered immediately. "They happen all over the world, where social media tidy influencers gather to swap ideas. We were in Seattle at the Hilton. Whitney came up to me and asked if I'd like to have coffee. We met later and right then and there she invited me to join her. Said she'd been observing me for some time. She knew that my attention to detail might be the catalyst to bring her to the next level. Now we're the biggest multimillion dollar organizing and cleaning business on the internet." His eyes grew misty as he told the story. "I was honored to be seen by her, of course."

Then he added, "I listened to her entire pitch and accepted on the spot."

Janis looked thoughtful. She tapped her finger on the iPad cover.

The Wiz brushed his eyes, continuing to speak. "At the time, my small business was making no profit whatsoever. Ms. Zimmer helped me realize the cause of my problem. 'No one wants to see an otherwise unremarkable bald guy clean his house.' That's what Whitney said one night after a few drinks." He smiled, a look of admiration crossing his face. "She persuaded me by using her own enthusiasm mostly, something I couldn't hold a candle to. Plus she's a very handsome woman. With vision," he added as an afterthought. "Such astounding vision."

Jets stopped tapping. "So when was that exactly?"

"Five years ago," he answered promptly. "We've had five beautiful years of branding and creating Time to Tidy." He looked away, as if he were having trouble reeling in his emotions.

"Whitney was right. As the profits would indicate, we've become the most lucrative organizing and cleaning business on the internet. And I don't mean in my opinion. It's well known. That's why we have no trouble getting contestants for our Tidy Team competition."

Janis Jets had enough listening. She cut to the chase. "Are you and Whiney close, you know, as in a couple?"

"That is not an option," he said stoutly. "Whitney and I have a strictly professional relationship." His face turned red as if the mere thought of anything else was impossible. "We are colleagues and business partners. Nothing more," he added.

Olivia looked at Jets. Jets looked at Olivia.

I think he doth protest too much.

Jets nodded as if she'd read Olivia's mind.

23

SERENITY MCFEE

One Day Before the Competition Began

Serenity McFee

Serenity McFee, owner of Cleanliness is Next to Godliness, stepped out of her 2010 Dodge Caravan. Her white sneakers hit the gravel with a crunch. With the push of a button the side door of the vehicle slid open, revealing her tools of the trade. She was an experienced cleaner. Unlike many of her competitors on the internet, she'd actually worked as a housekeeper for several years. That was before she became an internet clean-and-tidy influencer.

Two mops, two buckets, one set red and the other blue, lay on the middle seat. On the floor in front of the cleaning tools were plastic tubs filled with necessary spray bottles to assist her during the Time to Tidy contest. Glancing at her welcome packet one more time, she viewed the instructions: "Check into your room at the main house." *Okay, I did that. Got my keyring with three keys.* They jingled as she dangled them from her forefinger. *One to the house and one to my room. And here's the one to my assigned cabin, right in the middle of the other two. That's good. I can keep my eye on my competitors.*

She lifted the bright rainbow-colored key, holding it between forefinger and thumb. Then she continued to read from the instructions. *Somewhere Over the Rainbow. Very folksy name for a rental cabin.* Glancing at the sign by the door, she confirmed her location. *Yep, this is it!*

Serenity knew to be careful. In situations where she was competing, she'd learned not to ask random questions. Competitors would overhear and assess her weakness. Like that one time when she'd asked if she could use her own cleaning chemicals. Everyone had laughed, making her feel foolish. She hated feeling foolish because that led to being teased and ridiculed.

Serenity learned later that all of the chemicals in tidy competitions were carefully selected and measured beforehand to make the cleaning projects as fair as possible. And it was also true that Serenity, after several glasses of wine, would admit that she did have trust issues.

The flip side of her lack of trust came with the perfected art of watching her back. Having been raised by her single father, in a family with an aggressive brother, she'd experienced manipulation firsthand.

"The trim matches your key," she read aloud from the list of instructions. And because she was very detailed, she read the instructions one more time.

Satisfied that she'd found the right place and located her house, she eyed the other seemingly identical cabins on either side of hers. Situated in the middle of the woods, each looked inviting and what one would expect from a weekend rental.

Shaped as A-frames, all three cabins had quaint front porches. Wood trim around the large expanse of windows emphasized the height and narrow designs. *They remind me of that Candy Land game.*

She unlocked the door to Somewhere Over the Rainbow, taking one last quick look over each shoulder. *You never know who's watching. Trying to catch me doing something wrong so that I'll get disqualified.*

Stepping inside the cabin, her eyes scanned the room from left to right. From the living area to the kitchen with the table and chairs. The open concept floor plan and the vaulted A-frame ceiling gave the small space a more spacious feeling. Her first assessment was that the renters had moved furniture and not put it back. Lamp cords were strung tightly, along with crooked lamp shades. The sofa bed lay open with rumpled sheets. Random chairs had been brought from other rooms.

She placed her backpack on the kitchen table, turning to look at the living room more closely. Whitney Zimmer was known as a stickler for detail. Serenity liked to think they were the same that way. She folded the paper instructions and shoved them into her back pocket, convinced she'd memorized the rules and would not need to ask unnecessary questions.

Each of the contestants had been assigned a bathroom for the first day, so that's where she headed. *Makes sense picking a bathroom. I'll bring my mops and brushes from the van today so that I can get started right at seven o'clock tomorrow. Nobody said staging tools would get me disquali-*

fied. Only if I start the actual cleaning. Then I'd be in trouble.

Yanking the instructions from her back pocket, she consulted them again. Because she'd read the directions so often, the staple in the corner had fallen away, leaving the pages out of order. Once they'd been rearranged she read: "Day one is the bathroom. Day two, the kitchen." She folded them again. *After that it's bedrooms and the living area. The final day will be spent organizing that first floor storage under the stairs.*

Okay, got it. Easy peasy.

In front of the bathroom door she stopped to inhale. Her sense of smell had proved to be a powerful indicator of dirt and grime over the years. One whiff told her she had her work cut out for her. The strong odor of stale sweat and vomit and something equally distasteful filled her nose. She pinched her nostrils with her fingers, breathing through her mouth instead.

Her stomach churned. Not just the smell but anger. She pushed it down by swallowing. *Why can't people just take care of themselves—why do they leave their messes for someone else to clean up!*

Holding her hand over her mouth and nose, she swallowed again. The feeling of anger and nausea were all too familiar. But the sight of the overflowing trash in the bathroom, along with the backed-up sink caked with soap and scum, made her cough.

Forcing back her gag response, she coughed again. The knot in her throat traveled to her churning gut, which rumbled in protest. She swallowed again, forcing back the bile.

Truth be known, she got into the tidy business because she needed the money and because she hated messes. In fact, she'd left her childhood home as soon as she could to avoid the smell and chaos in her own house. Her father and brother were pigs.

If only she'd had the money to support herself and go to community college. But the only thing she knew how to do was to pick up after other people. So she got a job as a cleaner.

It was better to clean houses than to stay there and be chased by her stepbrother, she'd tell herself every morning for nearly five years. And she felt proud that she'd made it on her own without asking for money or returning to her father's house.

Convinced that her stomach was under control, she glanced at the trash and then quickly turned her head for a sharp inhale through her mouth. An empty roll of toilet paper hung over the side. Stuffed with stained tissues and feminine sanitary products, she could smell dried menstrual blood. Shoving the toilet paper inside, she held the receptacle at arm's length, glancing toward the bathtub. *A window. I can open it up to air things out.* She put the trash can back, next to the basin.

Stepping into the tub, she yanked at the slider. When it didn't open she ran her finger along the edge of the metal frame, then the track, searching for a lock. *There you are.* She unscrewed the butterfly-shaped bolt, removing it from the track.

The window slid open this time, but not without some struggling on her part. *I'll use WD-40 on that as part of my cleanup. It will be a small detail that will make this place feel cared for.* Serenity knew from experience that a house can have a cared-for feel, and not just because of careful staging and fancy furniture. People can feel it when everything in the house works efficiently.

She stepped out of the tub. A quick glance told her that the shower curtain liner was part of the problem. Scum and stains had dripped down both sides. The stale pungent odor made her gag again. One look at the hem of the curtain explained. It was stained light red, mildew growing along the bottom.

They never told me this was a long-term rental. It would take a couple of months for this buildup.

Fortunately Serenity carried extra shower curtain liners in her kit because of this very problem. She'd learned over the years about the power of a fresh vinyl shower curtain liner. Despite the chemical odor, people associated that smell with clean. *The smell of vinyl is superior to mildew and old body wash.* Tempted to take the curtain down right away, she remembered, *I have to wait until tomorrow morning. That's what the rules say.*

She inspected the toilet next. She flushed three times. To her horror the water rose as the back of her throat tingled. *The toilet is backed up and needs to be plunged.* Shutting the lid, she turned to eye the full trash again.

The open window was helping. But it still smelled terrible in the bathroom. *I wonder if I can get away with emptying the trash right now? Otherwise it will be waiting for me in the morning.* She gagged and swallowed again, clamping her hand over her face.

Feeling lightheaded, she stepped into the hallway to take a deep breath. Over the years she'd managed her gag reflex with any number of tricks. Managing also took some reasoning and adjusting, but she suspected the gagging may have helped her in the long run.

Conquering her own weakness was something she shared with her followers. She sent out a list of things to do to help other people in similar circumstances. If she were to be honest, sharing her weakness, along with a few stories of past cleaning situations, had only increased her number of followers.

"We can gag together," she'd say, pretending to be happy. Most of Serenity's life had been spent pretending to feel one way when she really felt another.

Her mind immediately went to how she'd reframe this experience and post it on Instagram. *I'll tell the story about how I won the competition. I'll include the transformation of this disgusting bathroom. People will be inspired that I got through it.*

Three years ago, when she started Cleanliness is Next to Godliness, Serenity had no idea how popular the company would become. It only took a few months before it went viral. People reacted favorably to her sharing her journey.

She realized right away that the journey from vulnerable to strong was inspirational to followers. When the number of responses dwindled, she pitched another story about how she'd overcome a particular instance. But when that stopped working, she decided to bring God to her brand. She'd open her chats with, "Cleanliness is next to godliness." The idea appealed to nearly everyone, no matter what religion. Her followers doubled in just a couple of months.

Serenity knew the big money was in selling her brand, making it accessible online. Using everyday household materials, products you'd find right under your own sink, she'd been able to capture people's attention. But that didn't make the money. It was afterward when she began an online class, charging a large sum, that she'd doubled her income. People loved hearing about how a clean house would lead to a clean and tidy mind. "And a clean and tidy spirit," she'd tell them, assuming the role of expert.

It was after six months of selling her online course that she hit a wall. No more new ideas. Her followers and students wanted to know more about being spiritual instead of cleaning their houses. And then things turned upside down. Women began to harass her, claiming she was using her influence to oppress her fellow sisters by glamorizing cleaning.

One woman wrote, "You're just a throwback to times when women were considered chattel to men, only good for making babies and keeping house."

Even though she saw their point, she pushed back. Doubling down on the importance of a clean spirit, she added another online seminar emphasizing the cleaning journey. After that people stopping throwing shade her way. Her online courses became so popular she had year-long waiting lists.

It turned out that spirituality was profitable. When Serenity doubled the cost of her courses, people didn't blink. They just kept coming. *Cha-ching!*

Her followers had no idea that she wasn't religious. Despite what she taught in her online classes, she rarely, if ever, prayed or meditated. The truth was that her mind was an anxious bowl of jelly, constantly quivering and shaking.

She held her breath and walked back inside the bathroom. She bent over to pick up more trash. Tissues. Tampons. Dental floss. A used condom. Stuffing it inside the can, she made a decision. *I'm going to empty that can anyway. Who cares if it's breaking the rules.* She sucked in her breath, holding the trash away from her body, forcing herself not to look at the contents.

Once in the kitchen her eyes rested on the back door.

Hurrying across the room, she unlocked and opened the door. A quick glance to the right showed three plastic bins lined against the side of the cabin. She stepped closer and opened the lid labeled Landfill.

"You must be Serenity McFee," came a voice from behind her back. Neck stiffening, a bolt of fear shot through her. *I've been caught. Whatever you do, don't act guilty.* Refusing to acknowledge the voice, she turned the trash can over as the contents tumbled out. Slamming the lid down, she pushed down her nerves. *Take it easy. Pretend like you don't know you've started too early.* She turned around slowly, planting a smile on her lips.

A tall blonde man wearing a short-sleeved T-shirt and a big grin stared at her. His sunglasses blocked his eyes, but the audacity of his smile told her everything she wanted to know. *Bruce "The Tool" Ward, in the flesh. I swear his muscles are even bigger than last time.* The logo on his T-shirt confirmed her suspicion.

His brand, From Tidy to Mighty, had been printed on the tee across his chest in bold dark green letters. She knew that the color was not by accident. Everything he posted used that same green signature brand.

She looked down at the empty trash can in her hand. "You caught me," she said in a joking voice. *Might as well admit my mistake. Not like I can toss this thing out of sight.*

"No worries," he told her, his voice nonchalant. But Serenity knew she was in trouble. If The Tool reported to the Wiz what he saw, she could easily be eliminated from the competition for breaking the rules. *Time to Tidy will keep my money and I'll be sent home. And be banned from going to their conferences ever again.*

Anger and embarrassment flushed her cheeks, causing her to duck her face. *I don't want him to see how I feel. It will only give him more ammunition to bring me down.* She held down her fear to find him still staring at her, a big smile of amusement on his lips.

She grinned sheepishly. "Okay, so now you know I've broken a rule. Which may be a problem for me. Unless of course I know something about you that you keep as a secret, that I can use to get even..." She made it a point not to sound threatening, even though she knew that was what she was doing. Threatening to reveal something about him that he didn't want exposed.

Bruce's grin vanished. She'd caught him by surprise. It wasn't the first time that someone underestimated her.

Serenity walked back inside the house, locking the door behind her. Once she replaced the trash can in the bathroom, she glanced out the front window. His truck was still parked in front of his cabin.

I think he'll keep quiet. At least he's on the defensive. I have dirt on him and he knows it.

24

BRUCE "THE TOOL" WARD

Bruce "The Tool" Ward

Serenity thinks she can get away with starting ahead of time. Pretty sneaky, checking in early and then emptying the trash beforehand. Every minute of cleaning matters. Maybe I've underestimated ol' Cleanliness is Next to Godliness. She's no slouch and a bit underhanded.

Realizing that his mind was racing, he pulled himself up short. Whenever he felt as if his emotions were running past his logic, he adjusted by shoving out his chest and flexing his sizable biceps. He did this to counteract any tendency of weakness when he felt less than confident. *Don't forget. The Tool knows how to be strong.*

The one thing he was keenly aware of, his real weakness if it could be called that, was that he made a habit of talking to himself in the third person. Not aloud, that would be crazy, but in his own head. He couldn't remember when he'd started doing that. Maybe in his childhood, when his dad lost his temper and smacked him across the head. Making him feel small and weak. Even thinking of his father brought back that sense of inadequacy. *The Tool knows how to be strong.* That was his motto, though inside he felt more like a puppy who only wanted to please.

That's how The Tool rolls, he'd also tell himself whenever he felt remotely vulnerable, which wasn't often. But this time even the inner pep talk didn't make him feel less uneasy. So he flexed his biceps again.

As soon as Bruce arrived he'd caught sight of Serenity's old minivan. Annoyed that she'd gotten ahead of him, he hid in a shadow behind the corner of his cabin. As luck would have it the back door of Somewhere Over the Rainbow opened, revealing Serenity and her overflowing trash can.

Yuck. It stinks even from here.

He knew not to reveal himself until Serenity actually broke the competition rule. Once she'd opened the trash can he stepped around the side of the cabin. But it wasn't until she turned it upside down that he called out. That look of surprise of her face. *Nailed it.*

But his triumph at catching her didn't last long. She'd twisted the power dynamic so that he now felt surprised. *What did she mean when she said, "...to get even?"*

I bet she's background checking all of us, the Wiz included. Or maybe Maddie told her about the last conference when they'd hooked up. Bruce knew that tidbit was bad enough. But there was something worse that he didn't like thinking about.

I was just a kid. Not even eighteen. It was just a frat prank. Nothing really happened.

After the one night, which The Tool spent in jail, the cops couldn't find any proof. It was Bruce then. Just plain

Bruce. None of the charges stuck. *Plus it wasn't even my idea. Greg dropped the drug in her beer, not me. The Tool just happened to be there. A case of wrong place at the wrong time.*

But if Serenity McFee has dug up an old arrest report, then The Tool might be in trouble. She'll tell the Wiz and it will be an excuse not to award The Tool the prize.

He shook his head, dreading any chance that he'd have to admit failure.

For the past few months Bruce had come to the conclusion that the only way to save his brand was to get the endorsement of Time to Tidy, specifically by winning the yearly contest. The win would save his online business from a recent free fall due to a pending lawsuit.

Why did that guy have to be so picky? The Tool's tools are pricey, but they're top of the line when it comes to quality. The drills alone with all the attachments. Plus The Tool's floor cleaners. Truly exceptional.

He'd be okay for an hour or two. Confident, the way everyone perceived him. And then he'd forget something and he'd remember the lawsuit and his insecurity would flood back like a tsunami crashing over his head, leaving him in a cold sweat, shaking. The lawsuit was frivolous in his opinion. *Just because my deluxe drill bit chewed up that guy's kitchen grout. Come on, buddy, step into the twenty-first century. No one has counter tile in the kitchen anymore.*

Bruce yanked a keyring from his pocket. Green. *Nice. Matches my brand. The Tool likes.* He walked around to the front of his cabin, noting the sign, which read Pine Haven. At the front door he stopped to tap his lug-soled boots against the jam before unlocking the door.

The fumes of decaying food hit his nostrils, making him turn his face aside in disgust. He gasped and inhaled quickly, looking around for the source of the stink. An underlying scent of cigar smoke met his nostrils, along with a stale booze smell.

*Renters. They forgot to empty the trash. Users and abusers. They think money buys them the right to leave things a mess. F***ing idiots.* He wanted to use the F bomb, but he stopped himself. He couldn't afford to besmirch his clean image with bad language. So he didn't swear, even in his own head, just in case the wrong word would slip out at some unexpected time, revealing how he really spoke.

The Tool talks clean.

Bruce rubbed his nose with the back of his wrist. *So I get it, why Serenity was putting out the trash. The Tool needs to open the window to this place as soon as he can.*

Bruce eyed the sliding doors leading to the deck outside. He flipped the locks and tugged the door open. *I don't think they can penalize The Tool for opening windows and doors ahead of schedule.* He rubbed his wrist across his nose again, coughing at the back of his throat. He knew other tidy organizers who were gaggers. That wasn't his particular problem. But sometimes the odor was so foul, even he felt the need to swallow down the catch at the back of his throat.

The Tool has to do something. This place smells like a week-old dumpster.

The source of the smell became instantly apparent once he walked into the kitchen. He lifted the lid to the metal trash container to look inside. Chicken skin and a carcass lay on top. Underneath someone had left fish bones with bits of clinging meat on top of brown butcher paper, which lay open. Two fifths of bourbon, the bottles open, lay under the carcass. He dropped the lid and it clanked shut, then put on his latex gloves.

Pulling on a mask over his mouth and nose, he opened

the lid again. Grasping the sides of the plastic liner, he edged the bag out of the can carefully. *This sack of **** better not break open.* He stopped himself. *I mean sack of trash better not bust, or The Tool will have you-know-what over his boots.* He stopped himself from using another swear word.

Cinched at the top, Bruce slid the bag to the back door. He opened it slowly to look outside. *Don't wanna get caught like Serenity. And if Maddox sees me she won't hesitate to report to Whitney.*

Hoisting the bag so that it didn't drag on the ground, he walked closer to the trash cans. He lifted the lid to the one labeled Landfill and in one heave of his right shoulder deposited the bag inside. It exploded as soon as it hit the bottom of the receptacle. Bruce shut the lid quickly, breathing out of his mouth.

Glancing around to make sure no one had noticed, he ripped off his mask. The scent of natural pine and cedar from the woods filled his nostrils. *Not like a deodorizer. Last year that woman got disqualified for using them in every room.*

It was known in the tidy community that fake plug in-style pine deodorizers only covered up odors.

Outdoor fresh air. The Tool was smart to open those windows.

He walked to the front to take a closer look at the two other cabins. No one parked in either driveway. Apparently Serenity had already left. He exhaled with relief. *Nice move, Tool. Arriving the day before. At least the source of the stink is contained. Airing out the place. That isn't against the rules.*

His phone buzzed. He pulled it from his pocket, touching the button as he raised it to his ear. "Yah," he said.

"This is the Wiz," came the voice on the other end.

"I figured," he said in a clipped voice.

Dumbass thinks The Tool doesn't have caller ID? Is ass a swear word? Nah, it's in the Bible for Christ's sake. Oh, that part may be wrong. Nix the Christ.

"Just checking to make sure you found your cabin." The Wiz sounded businesslike.

"Oh yeah, I'm here. Had a nice chat with Serenity McFee too."

The Wiz cleared his throat. "Don't fraternize with the other contestants. Whitney doesn't like that kind of thing. A year ago two of her contestants tried to team up. She got wind of it and made sure they regretted that plan." He paused, giving Bruce a minute to digest the warning, and then continued.

"I want to reiterate our plan and make sure you are following our agreement. Whitney will ask for a report on her favorite contestant and I want to have nothing but good news." The Wiz paused and then added, "You know there's no guarantee, right? Your contract doesn't say she will necessarily pick you."

"But I paid for the win," Bruce protested.

"No, you paid for Whitney's extra attention. She'll favor you, that's all. So stay on your toes."

"You can tell Whitney that I've got this. I'm her man. That's why I paid the extra ten grand. So don't worry."

"Goodbye, Bruce," the Wiz said calmly. The phone clicked.

Holding his cell in his palm, Bruce fumed. "The Tool knows what he's doing," he mumbled under his breath. Then he pulled himself up short. Once he pocketed his phone, he opened the back door and stepped inside again. The lingering odor from the trash still assaulted his nostrils.

Walking to the sink, he leaned over to unlatch and tug open the window above it.

To his surprise a dog stood outside, his paws on the sill, staring him in the face. "Bork," he said in greeting.

"Bork yourself. Get away, you mutt." The Tool banged his palm against the glass to startle him.

"Bork," came the reply. The dog licked the glass with a big pink tongue.

"What are you, some kind of labradoodle reject, running wild in the woods? Wait until I report you to animal rescue." He thumped against the window again.

Turning away from the sink, he stepped toward the back door and placed a fresh trash liner in the kitchen receptacle. Then he slid both plastic gloves into a plastic bag, which he wrapped closed, tying a knot at the top. Dropping the bag and gloves in the trash can, he released the lid. It fell with a thunk.

That done, The Tool glanced over toward the kitchen window, relieved. *Stupid dog is gone. Good riddance.* There was something about the dog's eagerness and that lick on the window that gave him the creeps. He'd never appreciated open people or friendly dogs.

The Tool hates dogs. Overeager to please. Just stay away, you mangy mutt. As he turned to head back inside the house, he heard a vehicle pull up in the next driveway. Maddox Hall sat behind the wheel of a red Toyota pickup. She waved at him with a smile on her face.

He forced a grin and nodded back, unable to ignore his attraction to her. Mainly because they'd hooked up at the last Time to Tidy conference. It was just one night.

Not memorable at all. I just don't want her to get any ideas that I'll, you know, help her out during this conference. We only have a few days to win and I don't want to compli-

cate things by hooking up again and sleeping with the enemy.

Maddox stepped down from behind the driver's seat. Bruce took the opportunity to spin around and hurry back into his house. He slammed the door shut.

Once inside, he considered his next move. *I need to open more windows. I'll start upstairs.* He prided himself on keeping in shape, so he took two steps at a time, aware of being slightly out of breath when he hit the landing. He checked his watch for his heart rate.

He'd realized early on that part of his brand was to look like an ex military guy, spotless and efficient. Bruce was never in the service, but he went to some trouble, working out at the gym and watching his diet, to maintain his brand.

Standing in the hallway, he glanced at the closest bedroom. Sheets rumpled on the bed, a musty smell of sweat and stale cologne filled his nostrils. He considered bundling all of the linens by shoving them into a plastic trash bag. He could get a head start on the laundry. *Sure is tempting.*

Instead he hurried to the next room. He sniffed. *Probably girls in here. Smells like flowery cologne.* He continued on to the main bedroom. Other than the disarray of sheets falling onto the floor, he didn't detect anything he needed to deal with right away.

He reminded himself with a stern warning, *The Tool has already broken one rule. Better to leave the linens alone. The Tool can open the windows to air the place out overnight and then go downstairs.*

Minutes later he stood by the table in the kitchen. A quick glance out the window facing front told him that Maddox's red truck was still parked in her driveway. To his surprise a knock came at his kitchen door.

If that's Maddox, I'm not going to answer it.

"I know you're in there," called her voice. "Open up, I just want to have a word."

He shrugged. Walking closer, he cracked open the door to peer out. "What do you want?"

"It's okay, I won't bite." Her voice held a sweetness, accompanied by an irresistible dimple at the corner of her mouth. He opened the door wider. Maddox Hall looked well put together. He remembered that she always made a point not to go overboard with frills. His eyes lingered on her breasts pushing against her T-shirt. Bruce appreciated her no-nonsense vibe, especially her light brown hair in a ponytail, no bangs, just a scrunchy.

Unlike the other contestants, she didn't wear a brand T-shirt. A white cotton crew neck, looking ironed and pristine, tucked into her yoga-style black pants. Even her white athletic shoes appeared not too new but not too worn. She managed to keep them very white.

Bruce felt his hands begin to perspire and his heart quicken. *She's good-looking. I may reconsider...* He stood aside as if asking her to enter the cabin.

She didn't move. "I see you're still all muscle," she chuckled. "I hope there are no hard feelings because I didn't return your calls after the spring conference. Just got busy and then I started dating this new guy. Met him online. We're going to a movie together right after the competition." When he didn't say anything, she added, "His name is Rick."

She stared at him. "No hard feelings, right?"

"You must be mistaken. I didn't call you, you know, after we hooked up." His eyes flashed.

"Come on, Tool. Of course you did. Over and over; I blocked your number. Don't pretend that you weren't stalking me." Maddox looked confused and then she shrugged. When he didn't agree or disagree, she said, "Okay then. That's how you want to play it. We both know the truth." She turned to walk away.

*What a b****.* He stopped himself. *The Tool doesn't call women names, even in his own mind. It's probably okay. Everybody knows that a bitch is just a female dog.*

With a shrug he closed the door behind him. Then he stopped, frustration welling up like a bad oyster in his gut. He lifted his arms to flex, appreciating how his toned muscles rippled against his tanned skin.

The Tool deserves to feel mad.

Fists formed in both hands while he growled under his breath.

Calm down, Tool. She doesn't know what she's talking about. You'd never chase a woman.

Then his fear, accompanied by paranoia, crept in. *Did Serenity and Maddox get together and talk about me? Maybe Maddox told Serenity that I kept calling her after our night together.*

That's enough, Tool.

He snatched the keyring off the kitchen table, making his way toward the front door. Time *to stop for a beer at that local pub. Then go back to the main house and settle in for the night. Stay to yourself. Don't give away anything. Maddox and Serenity are pros. They may be plotting right now.*

As the old tires on his van bumped against the gravel road, he found himself reconsidering. Because his thoughts turned once again to Maddie and that well filled out T-shirt. *She's really hot. Maybe The Tool will just sit in the kitchen of the main house after dinner. If I'm there no one will talk about me behind my back.*

25

MADDOX "MADDIE" HALL

One Day Before the Competition Began

Maddox "Maddie" Hall

Little Things Every Day. That's my motto. I knew the first meeting with Bruce would be awkward, but I took charge anyway, just like my therapist advised.

"Even a small act in the right direction will reduce your anxiety," she'd said, her eyes filled with sincerity.

At the time I felt a lump in my gut but then I knew, like usual, she was right.

So I made the first move. The Tool seemed surprised. He ran away. Now that's a sign that I've taken charge. Can't wait to tell Dr. Willis.

Maddie walked up the steps to the porch. The sign next to the front door read Crow's Nest. *Such a cute name. I bet this one rents well.* To the right of the brightly painted yellow door stood a wicker table with two chairs. Recently sprayed white, they were the very definition of inviting. In contrast, the lemon-yellow pillows, plumped and inviting, rested against the back of each chair. *They match the trim.* She looked at her palm. *And the key.*

As soon as she unlocked the door and stepped inside, Maddox inhaled deeply. She dropped her cell and purse on the nearby kitchen table. Rubbing her nose, she inhaled a second time, willing herself to pay attention. Even she had to admit that her sense of smell was not her strong suit. But in this case she felt nearly certain that there was nothing to feel alarmed about.

I'll check the trash to see what's in there.

She popped open the lid by pressing the pedal with her foot. Peering inside, she saw a few crumpled papers.

I am so lucky. The renters followed directions. They emptied their trash before they left. That's good. I won't have to start tomorrow with a huge mess.

She smiled with satisfaction as the trash can lid dropped.

A brief glance at the kitchen sink revealed gleaming porcelain. No used sponge draining in the sink, filled with bacteria and smelling of last night's dinner.

I bet they even put their dishes in the dishwasher. Thank goodness for the rule followers.

Maddox turned to look at the sliding doors leading to the deck. She sniffed again and then laughed aloud.

Come on, Maddie. Stop trying so hard. You know you can't smell.

In the past year Dr. Willis had helped with that too. She'd spent several appointments teaching Maddie how to reframe the negative into something more positive.

"You don't have a gag reflex like your friend Serenity," Dr. Willis had said. "So that's a positive. No scent stuck in your nostrils that lingers. Nothing caught at the back of your throat making you want to throw up."

When Dr. Willis had explained the gag reflex with such detail, Maddie had realized she really was lucky. "I can use my eyes instead of my nose," she told her therapist, bringing a welcome smile.

And that's what she did. If something looked bad, it must smell bad.

Maddie paused, remembering her mom and dad. They were divorced now, living in opposite parts of the country. But when she was small her mother would take old casseroles from the refrigerator and shove them under her dad's nose for a sniff.

Now that man has a great sniffer; more like a beagle than a human.

Maddox felt a tingle of sadness at the recollection. The divorce was hard for her at the time. Even though it had been years, she still felt as if her childhood had been hijacked by arguing adults unable to compromise.

The sound of a low rumble caught her attention. Her phone vibrated against the wood. She reached over to pick it up.

"How's your cabin?" came the familiar voice of Serenity McFee.

"It stinks, but I'm working on it." Maddie knew she exaggerated. *Okay, maybe that's a downright lie.* But she didn't want Serenity to get overly competitive by comparing their cabins right at the start.

"Did The Tool talk to you?" Serenity asked.

"Not at first. But I think I surprised him coming right to the door and knocking. Knocked him off balance."

"That was a smart move. I'm sure he never expected you to be so bold. Did he admit to stalking you after the last conference?"

"He denied it and say that it never happened. The implication being that I am crazy. Gaslighter. But I think I made my point. He must know I can tell Whitney everything if he tries anything sneaky."

Serenity sighed. "Of course he caught me emptying the trash outside."

"You're not supposed to do that!" Her voice and the hand holding the phone trembled. "You know the rules. That may get you disqualified and all of our plans will be tossed out like old garbage."

"Don't worry," Serenity said impatiently. "I put The Tool in his place. I counter-threatened him, implying that I knew his secret. He looked really worried afterward. Turned his back and ended the conversation. I don't think he'll tell Whitney or the Wiz."

"Don't forget we're in this together," Maddie cautioned.

As an introvert and a loner, she was prone to anxiety. As a matter of fact, she'd gone against her better judgment to combine forces with another tidy competitor. So she quickly reminded Serenity of their original plan. "Don't take any more chances by breaking another rule. Remember that one of us is bound to win. Then we'll put the prize money into our new business. With the endorsement of Time to Tidy we can form a dual partnership with a new brand, just like we planned."

Maddie took a deep breath, more words coming in a rush. "Plus we can always tell Whitney that The Tool stalked me last year. Only if he tattles on you, of course. Which I don't think he will. Better to win fair and square."

When Serenity didn't respond she asked, "Everything okay?"

A big sigh came over the phone. "Oh, I think you're right. I don't want to play dirty. It would be best to win because we're good at what we do. The whole point is to get cleaning and then organizing and not get bogged down in petty infighting. I know that. But old habits..."

Listening to Serenity's words gave Maddie a chance to calm down.

Deep breaths. Talk slower.

"I only hope that The Tool feels the same about sticking to the rules." She knew that was most likely overly optimistic as soon as the words left her mouth.

"Only I don't think The Tool feels the same. He'll come at us with any means necessary; playing dirty is what he's good at," Serenity added in a firm voice. "So we'll keep an eye on him just in case."

Maddie felt her chest tighten. Talking about The Tool only activated her fear of being a target. She knew it was time to stop talking and instead take that small step. Her nerves vanished when she'd take back even the smallest bit of control.

Dr. Willis helped her see how her business would be a safe harbor for her anxiety, once she focused on cleaning and organizing instead of what might be waiting for her around the corner. Hadn't she been able to get off her medication with Dr. Willis's help?

Maddie's brand motto, Little Things Every Day, was as much for herself as her followers. Everything in small chunks, taking lots of deep breaths. That's what she told people who attended her online seminars.

Once she said goodbye to Serenity, Maddox glanced up the stairway. The carpet looked fresh, no dust in the corners. No stains across the treads. The neutral beige color with the low risers were a good choice. On closer inspection she noticed a few pine needles, but because of the color choice, they blended in with the carpet.

Maddie walked up the stairs, stopping to pick up the pine needles. Then she did a cursory investigation of all three bedrooms. Feeling very lucky, she concluded aloud, "This place is going to be a snap."

The renters even bundled up their linens. I'll pop them in the laundry when I get here tomorrow and then deep clean the bathroom.

She heard her cell phone buzz. Rushing downstairs, she picked it up. "Hello."

"Settling in alright?" the Wiz asked.

"Yes, I am," she said brightly.

"So I don't mean to throw a wrench in your plans, but I'm going to give you an extra assignment."

"I see." She tapped her chest to push away the immediate sense of panic.

"When I did the pre-inspection of Crow's Nest, I noticed that your cabin was considerably cleaner than the other two. I spoke to Whitney, and in order to make things more fair, we decided to assign an extra bathroom to you. The one that's here in the main house. It's not too dirty, but if you say yes we can avoid complaints from the other contestants."

What he really means is that The Tool will probably complain the loudest.

Instead of resisting, she said, "No problem. I can do two bathrooms easily and I appreciate your fairness."

Could I sound any more cooperative...

The Wiz said, "I must admit I appreciate your attitude.

And I will pass along your decision to Whitney so that she's aware."

Now Maddox smiled.

It was worth it not to sound upset.

"Well I appreciate that you appreciate me. So we're good?"

"Very good. Just one more thing? I do pay attention to who our contestants are, not just how efficient. We want people with integrity on the Tidy Team. Your cooperative attitude matters to Whitney. Whoever she chooses must represent her brand in all the important ways."

"Good to know," Maddie said. "Anything else?" Her eyes wandered to the living room, looking for anything especially dirty.

He's taking up valuable assessment time. I need to get off the phone.

"Not at this time," the Wiz sounded brusque. "See you at dinner. Goodbye."

Once she'd hung up, she took another quick glance at the living room.

I won't even have to shampoo the upholstery on the sofa.

Maddox stepped closer to the sliding doors and glanced outside. The furniture had been covered. She locked the slider.

If I hurry I can stop in town at the market. I need more snacks for my room. Once I get to the main house I can check out the communal bathroom so that I won't be surprised tomorrow. After that I'll still have time to unpack before dinner.

She willed her shoulders to relax, remembering the mantra from Dr. Willis.

Things will always work out.

Stepping outside, she locked the door, taking a minute

to admire the bright yellow painted sign. From the distance a crow cawed. She looked up. He bounced on a tree limb, staring back at her.

He cawed again, this time sounding like a warning. The hair raised on her neck.

"Are you trying to tell me about something?" she asked him. "Don't worry, I've got this."

Dismissing any thought of the crow, a cool breeze brushed past her cheeks as she walked down the driveway.

I like Lily Rock. I feel safe here.

CHAPTER TWENTY-SIX

Janis Jets's face assumed a bland expression. Olivia knew she wasn't buying the Wiz's protestations about the professional relationship between him and his employer.

The next words out of her mouth oozed like honey being dripped in front of a hungry bear. "If you say so. But you wouldn't be the first assistant to have a little on the side with the boss."

"Don't be ridiculous!" A hiss passed his lips. "I resent your implication. Whitney and I are not involved that way." Tears came to his eyes. "It would be unseemly."

Janis scowled. Olivia observed their interaction with fascination, her eyes shifting from one to the next.

She caught the Wiz in a soft spot.

His carefully constructed facade had been stripped away, making him look and sound like that emperor who finally realized he wasn't wearing any clothes.

"Now you wouldn't exactly admit that you two were together," Jets reminded him, as if he were a schoolboy. "I just wanted to see how you'd react when someone made the suggestion and yanked that control out of your vise-like grip.

And now I see that you'll cry. Interesting." Jets leaned toward him. "Aren't we a bit overly protective of our boss?" Her voice taunted, as if daring him to disagree.

"I am the Wiz." He wiped away a tear. "I care deeply for Whitney and don't appreciate your insinuations about our relationship. We are strictly collegial." He crossed his arms over his chest, thrusting his back into the sofa cushion.

Olivia, with her keen discernment of emotional dynamics, felt the energy in the room shift. Trapped in the impasse between Janis and the Wiz, the room fell quiet.

The Wiz's words sounded reasonable, but they also covered up something more. His tears and the pouty bottom lip made it apparent that Janis's questions had unsettled his usual reserve.

Cracked him like a boiled egg.

For the next five minutes Jets barraged the Wiz with more questions. With rapid release, aiming directly at her target, she pulled one arrow, then the next from her quiver. *Zing.* "Describe Whitney Zimmer to me." *Zing.* "Do you sleep together in this house?" *Zing.* "How long have you two been hooking up?" *Zing.* "Maybe I'll arrest you both for the murder."

The Wiz made no attempt to speak. Even when Jets finally paused, he pushed his back further into the sofa cushions with a stunned expression on his face.

Olivia, seeing an opportunity, used her calmest voice. "So Stanley, I heard that each contestant is given the keys to their own house."

He shot her a grateful look. "Along with a list of what requires tidying up and cleaning each day."

"I suppose Whitney inspects the cabins and that's how she concludes who will win the contest." Asking questions he was willing to answer brought the desired response.

Less defensive, he dropped his arms, resting his hands in his lap.

"That's right." His eyes shifted to Janis as if he expected more slings and arrows. When they didn't come he looked back at Olivia. "In case you might be wondering, Maddox's assignment also included the bathroom here at the main house. She decided to finish it up first and then head to her assigned cabin."

"Why did Maddox get extra work?" Jets asked.

"I assessed the three cabins before everyone arrived. Usually there's plenty to do, what with emptying the trash and taking care of dirty linens after the previous renters. We told the contestants they'd face whatever was left, good or bad, as part of the challenge.

"I could see that Maddox's cabin was considerably cleaner than the other two. So I told Whitney. We agreed there was a need to make the contest more equitable. I called Maddox right away to let her know my—I mean, *our* decision. When I asked if she would take on an extra small bathroom, she agreed immediately, knowing that it would even things up."

"She did that willingly?" Jets sounded doubtful.

"I implied that a cooperative attitude would be noticed and appreciated when it came to the final evaluations." He looked down at his lap and then back up. "Maddox really was a nice woman; nicer than the other two by far."

"Okay, so she was nice," Jets muttered. "Doesn't make her any less dead. In fact, that niceness may have gotten her into trouble. So then, Wiz," Jets began, "how about we get the addresses of those cabins. I'd like to have a look around and talk to your two remaining contestants. I have a few more questions for them."

He pulled out his phone and began to text. Janis's cell pinged.

She read his text and nodded. "That's great. I appreciate the photos. They're all in a row. How quaint. Reminds me of Fantasyland at Disney."

"Tourists like that look. We remodeled old A-frame cabins. The floor plans are nearly identical."

"Will I find Serenity and Bruce knee-deep in tidying and organizing?"

The Wiz shook his head. "They're most likely eating lunch."

Jets opened her mouth to speak, but she was interrupted by a *bork* from the entryway.

"Curb your dog," Jets growled at Olivia.

Olivia looked across the room. Mayor Maguire stood in the entryway, her boot hanging from his mouth. With a vigorous wag of his tail, he invited her response.

"Really, M&M? Can't you just leave the boot alone?"

He shook his head vehemently, the boot laces slapping against his face. She glanced away, annoyed at the distraction.

"Bork," he tried again. She watched him with a side-eye, hoping the lack of engagement would get him to drop her boot. Tail down, he shook the boot from side to side a few more times. He looked at her with bright expectant eyes.

The Wiz stood. "If you don't have any more questions, I have work to do."

"You can go," Jets admitted. "You're not under arrest yet. But I could come after you for obstructing justice. At least until you contact your boss and get her in for a chat."

The Wiz walked out of the room, hesitating momentarily to glare at Maguire. With a disgruntled sniff, he disappeared into the kitchen.

Tired of Mayor Maguire's antics, Olivia rose to her feet. "Drop it," she commanded.

Boot still in his mouth, he kept wagging his tail. She came closer. Reaching down, she tugged on the heel. He growled at the back of his throat, clamping his teeth down harder with a yank.

She glared at him, pulling back harder.

The mayor released the boot with a playful jump and crouch.

She picked up her boot and turned around to speak to Jets across the room. "Are we about done here? I need to take the mayor outside. He's getting a bit feisty. Probably could use a good run."

Jets's hand hovered over her iPad. "Sure, go ahead," she said absentmindedly.

"I'm going to send you the cabin addresses. Meet me there in an hour." Jets looked up. "It makes sense to interview the two who most likely had something to gain from Maddie's death. With her out of the way, they only had to fight with each other for the prize."

"So that would be the motive." Olivia walked closer. "But what about opportunity? I assumed everyone was in a big hurry to get to their cabin assignment that morning. If one of them hung around to kill Maddie, they would have been noticed."

"I've thought of that," Jets said thoughtfully. "No one wanted to get behind in their tasks, that's for sure. But I think now is the time to have a chat with The Tool and Serenity. One of them could slip up and then we'd have our answer."

"Okay then." Olivia turned to Maguire. "You're being a pain this morning." She came closer and patted his head. "You must be bored. Maybe we can play outside for just a few minutes." Once she'd retied the frayed laces, she opened the door. The dog bolted outside, running across the driveway toward her car.

Finding a tennis ball under the front seat of her Ford, she held it in front of the dog's eager face. "Mayor Maguire, fetch!"

With a strong overhand throw, the ball sailed through the air into the woods. Instead of running after it, Mayor Maguire watched. His front legs began to tremble, but he didn't move from his spot.

"Go on, you know you want to chase it," Olivia urged. "Come on, Maguire, what's going on with you?"

"Bork," he said, looking longingly toward the trees. Yet he refused to fetch.

She sat down on the driveway right in front of him. Grasping his face in both hands, she looked into his dark eyes. "What's up with you this morning?"

His tongue slipped out of his mouth as he quickly licked her forehead.

"Eew," she said, wiping her sleeve across the wetness. "You have to admit you're acting odd, refusing to chase a tennis ball. I assume you have your reasons. But would you please stay away from my boots." She leaned forward to kiss the top of his nose.

When she stood, Mayor Maguire ran to the passenger side. He waited for her to open the door. Olivia looked toward the woods, still perplexed. She'd never known Maguire to refuse to fetch a tennis ball.

<h1 style="text-align:center">CHAPTER TWENTY-SEVEN</h1>

Back on the main road, Olivia eyed Mayor Maguire as he pressed his nose against the passenger side window. At first she'd thought he regressed to puppy behavior, chewing on her boot. But after refusing to chase the tennis ball, she wondered...

Do I need to take him to the vet for a checkup?

A cell phone ping interrupted her thoughts. She leaned over to hit the green button.

"Hey," she said.

"Driving?" Michael asked.

"Yep."

"So I was wondering. Have you been able to order those moving boxes from down the hill?"

When she hesitated, he hastily added, "I can pick them up later if you'd like."

"I haven't ordered them yet," she admitted. "But I will very soon. I know you're busy. I can do it tomorrow."

"Hot on the trail of your murderer?"

"Janis and I interviewed the Wiz this morning. She really got his back up. Still not sure when we'll get to interview his elusive boss. But now I'm supposed to meet her to look at the row of cabins. That's where the other contestants are working."

"Does the Wiz look guilty?"

"He kinda does. He's hiding something for sure."

"Well then be careful when you're around him."

"Oh, I'm careful," she insisted. "I'm sorry about not ordering the moving boxes. I'll get on it."

"Honey, if I have to carry everything we own on my hands and knees through the dirt, we're gonna get that move done. Boxes be damned."

She laughed. "Okay then, I see that you have a plan B. Talk to you soon."

Mayor Maguire pawed at the window. She looked over. "See a squirrel, buddy?"

The dog pawed again.

Maybe the vet would be a good idea.

* * *

After grabbing a quick lunch at home, Olivia eagerly hopped back into her Ford. Plugging in one cabin's address to her GPS, she backed out of the driveway and followed the directions.

It only took ten minutes before she pulled her car into a spot next to Janis Jets's pickup. She turned the key; her engine sputtered off. Three A-frame cabins sat in the middle of the lot all in a row.

If I were Goldilocks, which would I pick? Olivia got out of her car for a closer view. The colorful paint and identical porches made each cabin look whimsical.

Before she could look any further she caught sight of Janis. Holding up her iPad, she appeared to be taking photos of the lot and the cabins. Olivia walked closer as Jets turned off her tablet's screen.

"Where's the mayor?" Jets asked unexpectedly.

"As soon as I got home to make a sandwich, he took off."

"I guess we're boring him." Jets looked thoughtful.

Olivia added, "Just as well. I doubt if he'd be welcome in the houses now that they're coming close to the deadline for the competition. Dog hair everywhere might be less than desirable."

"True." Jets nodded. "I'm getting a funny vibe from him. He's been by the constabulary more often than usual."

"Since Maddox's death?"

"Mostly to hang out with Roxy. But he comes into my office, plops himself down, and stares at me while I'm working. Like I need an audience?"

"I know. His looks can be unsettling," Olivia admitted.

"Ready to knock on some doors?" Jets asked. She turned back around to stare at the three cabins.

"Which one was Maddie's?" Olivia felt a fleeting sense of sadness at mentioning Maddox's name.

"The one on the right." Jets pointed. "That's The Tool's there, and Serenity's in the middle."

Swallowing the lump in her throat, Olivia said, "Just three days ago Maddox had high hopes that she'd win the competition."

"Caw," came an unexpected call from a crow nearby. Olivia glanced at the uppermost branch of the pine tree and then back at Janis, who glowered.

"Yah, Maddox's gone. It feels wrong that the other two are still cleaning and competing, but I suppose there was no reason for the contest to stop."

"Other than respect and kindness," muttered Olivia.

"Well there is that." Jets looked at the dirt, scuffing it

up with one boot. "But don't forget, one of them is most likely our culprit. If we can find that person, then we might feel a little better. Justice doesn't make the person come back from the dead, but it sure helps. Shall we begin by looking in Maddie's cabin first? It's called Crow's Nest."

"I suppose."

As they walked side by side toward the brightly painted A-frame, Olivia heard two birds exchange caws. *I've read that crows mate for life.* That idea turned her thoughts to Michael. Maybe we're like crows, Michael and I.

Stopping on the front porch, she brushed aside her thoughts.

"Well isn't this cute," muttered Jets.

Olivia took in the bright yellow front door, her eyes traveling to the carefully placed wicker set of two chairs and a table. She sniffed. The smell of fresh paint still lingered. A bright yellow cushion had been plumped up in each chair, making Olivia think of one of those television shows where a decorator fusses over every detail.

The sign beside the door read Crow's Nest. Painted with black lettering that stood out against the bright yellow background.

Olivia stepped up to the front window. She cupped the sides of her face to see inside. "I can't see anyone," she admitted to Jets, and then stepped back.

"These rental vacation places?" Jets said. "Very bright and kind of silly, if you ask me."

"They're not a Bellemare design, that's for sure. And If I remember correctly, Whitney owns all of them; uses the cabins for renters when she's not running a competition," Olivia said.

"Free cleaning. Nice idea." Jets looked thoughtful. "I

wonder if the dead contestant, once it's reported on social media, will besmirch the Time to Tidy brand?"

Olivia felt surprise. She had no idea that Janis paid any attention to branding. "The attention may improve her brand. That's the weird part about social medial. A good murder story, especially one with intrigue, could increase followers," she said.

"Only if she's a dead white girl," Jets muttered.

The front door opened, revealing the Wiz. He looked more composed than earlier. "Do come in, ladies." He pushed the door open farther. Resuming his previous personality, his tone of voice gave no indication of their earlier interview.

He's all calm now that he's back in charge.

In the living room, the Wiz handed Jets three keys. "One for each cabin. They are color coded. Please return them after your inspection. I informed Bruce and Serenity that you'd want to have a word. They both agreed."

"That will save me a warrant," Jets said. She took the keys. "I'll leave these under the Crow's Nest front mat when I'm done."

"That's fine. I have other things to do, so I won't be staying." He walked outside, leaving Janis and Olivia to look over the cabin's interior.

Once he'd gone, Olivia closed the door. She turned to Janis. "The Wiz has a British vibe."

"More like Winnie the Pooh, if you ask me." Jets smiled. Then she became all business. "Assuming no one has cleaned up this place since Maddox's death, it does feel clean. No wonder they assigned our victim an extra bathroom."

Olivia took the few steps to the kitchen. She popped the

trash lid by pressing her foot on the pedal. "Just a few papers in here," she reported.

Jets joined her, opening and closing a row of overhead cupboards. "Nothing unusual up there."

"Look under the sink," Olivia suggested.

Janis opened the two doors. A familiar-looking plastic tote alongside a container of dish soap and dishwasher powder were neatly lined up.

"That's an extra tote, like the ones each contestant was given on the first day," Olivia noted. "But I thought Maddie died before coming to the cabin."

Jets reached into her back pocket. She pulled out latex gloves, slipping them over each hand. Then she retrieved the tote. Placing it on the counter, she inspected four plastic bottles one by one. "So we have bleach, vinegar, glass cleaner, and tile spray."

"They've been labeled?"

"With a label maker."

"Like the one I found in the pantry at the main house," Olivia added.

"I'm gonna have someone pick it up and take it to the lab. The contents need to be analyzed."

"But I'm wondering. What exactly did you find when you had the tote in Maddie's bathroom?"

"I told the guys on the scene to bag and tag all the cleaning bottles along with the tote as soon as we found the body." Jets looked puzzled. "The lab is slow getting back to me with their report. Our assumption is that the combination of bleach and vinegar killed her."

Olivia nodded. "So if Maddox had a tote at the main house, then how did this one get here? Maddie hadn't made it to her cabin yet. She died before she could start cleaning the A-frame."

Janis's jaw tightened as her eyes narrowed. "Very interesting observation, Nancy Drew. I think you're on to something." Jets pulled out her cell phone.

"Brad, call forensics. I need someone to pick up more evidence. I'll text you the address now. And before you hang up? Find out if the toxicology report is back. I need to know the specifics of how someone tampered with those spray bottles." Jets pressed the red End Call button with a scowl.

CHAPTER TWENTY-EIGHT

Finished with Crow's Nest, they walked toward the next cabin. Olivia pondered the recent discovery. She knew that the tote under the sink was an obvious clue.

Olivia stopped in her tracks. "Give me a minute," she called out to Jets. "I have to make a phone call."

I nearly forgot about ordering those packing boxes again.

"Whatever," Jets answered, stepping up to the porch.

Holding her phone to her ear, Olivia could still hear Janis's running commentary. "Well isn't this just adorable," Jets stated in a loud voice. "A green door and a matching cabin sign. Pine Haven. Gag me now." Jets rapped her knuckles against the door.

After a few seconds Bruce Ward appeared. Olivia, having been put on hold, let her eyes fall to the tool belt wrapped around his waist. An odd assortment of screw drivers and hammers bounced in front of his crotch, making her wonder. *Is The Tool trying to draw attention to his privates or is he protecting his manhood with those hammers hanging from his waist?*

Feeling uncomfortable with her own assessment, Olivia

moved her eyes upward to his logo T-shirt. *It may have shrunk in the wash.* But Olivia suspected that he'd deliberately bought the shirt small so that it clung to his broad shoulders and muscled arms.

"This is the Box Store," came a voice on the other end of her cell. "How can I help?"

"I need to order boxes for my move," Olivia said.

"Go ahead," he replied.

Olivia placed her order for the various types of boxes that she'd need.

She tapped her foot in the dirt as the proprietor of the store hemmed and hawed. "It's been my experience, just sayin', that people order boxes and they never get as many as they need. Especially wardrobe ones. So are you sure you don't want more?"

"Okay make that seven cartons to hang clothing. That should do it!" She waited impatiently while the proprietor recited her order back.

Before she could finish the call, she watched Janis Jets disappear inside the cabin. The door closed, making it impossible for her to overhear the conversation with The Tool.

"Fine," she shouted into the phone. Five minutes later she disconnected, having ordered twice as many boxes as she'd intended. *At least I can tell Michael that I followed through. More than enough for our packing needs. After we're done with the interviews I'll drive down the hill and pick them up. Then I can surprise him when we both get home for dinner.* For the first time in a week, she felt less anxious.

Walking up the steps to the porch, Olivia reached for the doorknob. She stepped inside the cabin, hearing voices coming from upstairs. Her initial impression was that Pine

Haven, as the sign outside indicated, was nearly identical to Crow's Nest in design. Following the sound of voices, she walked up the carpeted steps. Feeling a slap against her ankle, she looked down. The lace on her left boot had come undone.

She bent over to tie another knot to connect the broken ends. When she stood back up, she heard Bruce speaking loudly to Janis.

"I wasn't even near Maddox that morning," he explained.

From the hallway she could hear everything they said.

"You came right to your cabin after you left the main house?" Jets asked.

"I already told you that!" The Tool growled.

After a pause, Olivia walked into the room. The Tool loomed over Janis Jets. *He has six inches on her at least.*

His face appeared slightly flushed; the vein at his temple throbbed.

Jets lifted her chin, defiantly glaring back at him. Olivia watched as her right hand inched its way along her belt to the back of her blazer. She knew that move. *She's making sure her weapon is ready in case she needs it.*

The Tool's eyes followed Janis's hand. He may have realized that Jets was armed because he took a step backward, increasing the distance between them. Ducking his head, he looked as if he was concentrating, his lips moving but no words coming out.

Jets didn't give an inch. Her eyes narrowed as she waited for him to speak.

The Tool finally raised his head. This time he looked more calm. The vein at his temple no longer throbbed.

"You knew Maddox from before," Jets stated calmly.

"I'd seen her around. At the Time to Tidy conferences.

We'd didn't know each other very well; not like we were friends or anything," he said.

"And you'd met Serenity before..." Jets prompted.

"I didn't know Serenity except to talk to her in passing." His eyes focused over Janis's head.

"Oh, I see," Jets stated, clearly not seeing at all. "I'm going to interview her next, so I'll ask her."

His eyes came around quickly. "You don't have to do that. We knew each other. I follow both of them on social media. Maddox was always a bit standoffish. Serenity is religious and not really my type, if you know what I mean. They—Serenity and Maddox—knew each other very well," he blurted out. "I heard them talking together the night before in the bedroom next to mine."

Jets shot a quick glance over her shoulder toward Olivia, as if inviting her to ask questions. When she didn't jump in, Jets continued.

"Finally the truth. Took you long enough. So you knew the other competitors. We've established that. But now I want to know about your business. You call it From Tidy to Mighty. An interesting name. Very male-centric if you ask me. The mighty part." Jets held up her arm as if to flex her muscle. "And the tool belt." Jets pointed directly at the large hammer hanging in front of The Tool's crotch.

Olivia pretended to cough, stifling a smirk.

"You have to find your niche," The Tool explained. "There are plenty of feminine women cleaning their houses every day. I wanted to show that it's also a man's work to keep things clean. I push the idea that I come from a line of janitors, my grandfather and my father. Then I show people how to use power tools and products to clean their houses."

"And you sell the tools and the products at what I assume is a considerable profit?" Jets asked.

"I have my own line, if that's what you mean. My tools can be bought from my website and through small brick-and-mortar stores. I have big future plans. I'm in negotiations to have my line brought into bigger stores, like retail home improvement centers."

Jets looked thoughtful. "So then the endorsement from Whitney Zimmer means a lot to you. If you win, of course."

The Tool glanced nervously across the room toward Olivia. Then his eyes came back to Jets. "The more people I can get interested in my brand, the more opportunity for profit. That's just business. So if we're done here, I'd like to get back to my work. I have a contest to win and time is money."

"Now that's an old saying I haven't heard in a long time," Jets said sarcastically.

Olivia saw a muscle twitch on the side of The Tool's neck and his face flushed. He took a deep breath. "My dad taught me everything I know about business. And electric tools," he stated flatly.

Jets looked him over as if she suspected there was more to say. When he didn't add anything, she continued, "Okay, we're nearly done here. Because I say so, not because of your need to win a contest."

She turned to Olivia. "You have any questions for The Tool?"

Olivia smiled brightly. "I noticed that you all have the same totes with the four bottles of products. Did you bring the tote with you that first morning?"

"We weren't allowed to pick them up from the cleaning pantry until then. All three of us were handed a tote. Identical with the same products, according to the Wiz."

"With all the cleaning chemicals carefully labeled?" Olivia asked.

"Yep, I asked earlier how that would go." And then as an afterthought he added, "I wanted to use my brand of cleaning chemicals, the ones I sell in the online store. But I didn't swap them out because I knew if Whitney found out, she'd disqualify me on the spot."

"Sounds like you've thought every aspect of this competition through," Jets mumbled.

"The Tool..." His voice faded. "I mean, I'm happy you think so. But now I really need to get back to work."

When Janis didn't disagree, Olivia stepped away from the door. The Tool moved quickly toward the hallway. She could hear his footsteps as he made his way down the stairs.

CHAPTER TWENTY-NINE

Janis and Olivia stood on the porch. "Only one more interview with Serenity and then we're done for today," Jets told her.

"I have to drive down the hill on an errand," Olivia explained. "Will this take long?"

"I'll make it fast," Jets growled.

"I'm picking up moving boxes," she explained, "so that I can move into my castle, the one Michael designed and built for me." She lifted her chin with a big grin. She hoped making light of her circumstances might make Janis back off her teasing.

"Because you like being a maiden all locked up and taken care of," Jets retorted.

Jets's jab hit its mark. Olivia's fingers curled, her nails digging into her palms. To hide her anger, she turned her head away.

Olivia scrambled down the stairs past Jets. She walked ahead toward the last cabin, reminding herself to take a deep breath. *Don't bite the hook.* Michael told her that's what he said to himself whenever he felt conflicting emotions.

Olivia hesitated at the stairs. When Janis caught up they walked toward the door. She took in the Somewhere Over the Rainbow sign. And then nodding to Jets, she rapped on the door. It opened before she could knock again.

Serenity McFee stood on the other side as if she'd been waiting. *Did someone call ahead to let Serenity know we were coming?*

Serenity McFee wore an apron with gold sparkly letters across the bib that read Cleanliness is Next to Godliness. "Hello," she said brightly. "Do come in."

The overpowering smell of lemon furniture polish hit Olivia as soon as she stepped inside. She turned her head to cough and then glanced around. *Not one cleaning tool in sight. No mops nor brooms.*

"Are you already done?" she asked Serenity. Olivia had to admit the interior of the cabin looked and felt organized. The furniture, not exceptional in any way, suited the A-frame cabin.

Two occasional chairs faced a sofa with a low table in between. Upholstered in a sturdy neutral fabric, everything went together. Fresh pillows, designed with bright yellow sunflowers, connected with the color theme on the porch.

"I've been finished for a while." Serenity closed the door behind them. "Don't tell The Tool. I want him to think I'm struggling to meet the deadline. Actually I've been online with my feet up." She pointed to the kitchen. "Why don't you come and sit down."

Jets didn't need another invitation. She was the first to plop herself into the mid-century metal chair, adding a tired grunt. Once they were all seated Olivia had to admit that

Serenity appeared every bit as calm and collected as her name would imply.

Jets didn't waste any time. "So your business is about cleanliness and godliness." She looked around the kitchen. "Looks like you've finished here. Are you satisfied that everything is as clean as God intended?"

Serenity blinked when Jets said the word God. "Something like that," she said quietly.

Olivia interjected. "You must have been finished for a while. Where's the rest of your cleaning stuff, specifically your tote with the spray bottles?"

"I've put it out of sight," Serenity stated. "Extra cleaning tools don't need to clutter up the space. If you put everything away, you breathe more easily. That's the godliness part, the calm that a well-organized room creates."

Olivia noted the lack of appliances on the kitchen counters. "No toaster or coffeepot?" she asked.

"Oh, I have them in the pantry." Serenity thumb-gestured toward the tall cupboard over her shoulder. "I took my mops and brooms back to the car. And the rest of the cleaning products are under the sink. If you want to look inside the cupboards and pantry you might be surprised. I also reorganized the inner spaces. It's part of my brand."

"I am interested in the cleaning bottles. Not the soup cans," Jets assured her. "I assume you picked up your tote the morning of the first day?"

Dropping her deliberately calm manner, Serenity's voice took on an edge. "Why do you care so much about my tote?"

"Just a routine question," Jets answered smoothly.

"Excuse me." Olivia walked across the kitchen to open one side of the double pantry. All of the cans and jars were lined up. From the tallest in the back, a bottle of red wine vinegar, to the shortest in the front, a jar of mild salsa. "They're very tidy," she said.

"And what do you notice about the labels?" Serenity prodded, no longer annoyed.

Olivia expected to see the cans in alphabetical order. She'd heard about organizers doing that. Then it hit her. "All of the labels are facing forward."

Each label could be easily read from where she stood. "They look very organized even if they're not alphabetical." She turned to grin at Serenity. "I fully assumed you'd be that kind of person, lining up the soup cans in ABC order."

"I don't go that far." Serenity looked more pleased. "But I do organize in terms of size and shape to make the pantry feel calm. When I stand over there by the sink, I can feel if one of those cans is out of place. My head scrambles, like there are bees circling me. As soon as I turn the labels to the front my mind grows calm. That's how I do everything. After cleaning I stop and feel the room and then make adjustments."

Olivia nodded as Serenity warmed to her subject. Sounding like a professor teaching a class, she continued to explain. "If you keep your house clean, your mind will be less cluttered. You'll feel calmer and more peaceful. God wants us to be filled with serenity. So you are closer to Him when you are clean and organized. That's why I compare cleanliness to godliness."

There's something about her voice.

Olivia felt uncomfortable. She loved a clean and tidy environment, that could not be denied. But Serenity's implication that you'll be closer to God if your bottles and cans are organized by size, with the labels facing front?

Feeling a cloud of confusion settle over her brain, she deliberately broke eye contact. The confusion vanished, leaving her with a stronger opinion. *It's not right to imply that God will love people more if they are tidy. At least I don't think so.*

She looked toward the sliding doors leading to the deck. Two chairs and a small bistro-style table had been arranged on an outdoor carpet. They looked inviting as if waiting for people to sit down and have a cup of coffee.

Jets cleared her throat. "I prefer my place all messed up and dirty. It's sexier that way. My boyfriend agrees." Jets turned aside with a smirk, disregarding Serenity's look of incredulity.

"Everyone has their own internal sense of knowing what's right for them," she said brightly with a slightly condescending tone.

"You have a lot of followers," Olivia admitted. "I looked at your social media profile a while back, before I met you. Pretty impressive."

"My followers understand that I'm concerned for their spiritual well-being. It's not about being perfect, it's about making progress and connecting with their higher power. One person at a time. Things get done and people find success in my methods." She eyed Olivia, her face controlled in a contented expression.

Janis Jets spoke louder. "So you must have met Bruce and Maddie before the competition. Did you like them or were they just in your way?"

Serenity did not bat an eyelash. "Bruce and I respect each other. He stopped to talk the afternoon before the contest began. He's okay if you like that sort of man."

A sly expression came over Jets's face. "Who doesn't like a man with muscles, I ask? You gotta be blind not to notice him in a crowd."

"If you say so." Serenity lowered her glance.

"Okay, what about Maddox—did you have a good relationship?" Jets prodded.

"I didn't know her very well. Just saw her in passing. You know, the three of us do tend to show up at the same events. But Maddie kept to herself."

"Is that so." Jets did not look convinced. "Bruce said you knew Maddox pretty well."

"Bruce is not a reliable source when it comes to my relationships," she responded primly.

"One last thing," Jets said, standing. "I haven't forgotten about the tote. I assume you picked it up early that first morning, like everyone else."

"I did," she answered quickly. "We all got the same totes with the same bottles. The contract we signed was very specific about the totes, an entire page devoted to the products and size of containers, how many ounces. Rather tedious. I guess there was some trouble a year or two ago, so Whitney nailed it down with her attorney."

Jets's eyes narrowed. "So I know you had motive to kill Maddox. You wanted to win. Now I'm gathering information about means and opportunity."

Olivia chimed in. "By the way, who handed out the totes that first morning? I imagine it was kind of official with stopwatches and making notes on a clipboard. Did Whitney make last-minute announcements and wish everyone well?"

"Not Whitney nor the Wiz. I didn't see either of them. I picked up my tote right after Bruce. No sign of Maddox. I was there right at seven o'clock. Maybe she got there before Bruce. I have no idea."

"So The Tool is your alibi and he is yours." Jets eyed Serenity. When she didn't say more, Jets stood. "I'm done here."

Olivia led the way out of the kitchen.

Once they were outside, Janis called after her, "Wait a minute. During the interview I got an email, a report from forensics."

Olivia turned around as Janis scrolled on her iPad.

"Not too surprising. According to the report, Maddox Hall died of inhalation poisoning."

"What chemical did she inhale exactly?" Olivia asked.

"Just like we figured, a combination of bleach and vinegar. Common household products."

"So it was just like Cayenne said?"

"Cayenne was exactly right. It's not the products, it's the combination," Jets explained. "People usually use one or the other to clean. But when you combine them and use them in an enclosed space, the chlorine in the bleach mixes with the sodium hypochlorite in the vinegar. That creates chlorine gas. Deadly when inhaled. Says right here." She pointed to her iPad.

"Just from spraying it on the toilet?" Olivia asked in disbelief.

"I guess she could have taken the spray top off and poured the products into the tub and toilet. She was in a hurry, maybe didn't notice the smell right away. And there has to be no ventilation in the room. And the person has to be breathing in and out, ignoring the smell."

Jets closed her iPad. "Maddox went into respiratory failure through the inhalation of toxic chlorine gas. That's what the report says."

CHAPTER THIRTY

Finished with their interviews, Olivia hurried to her car. She knew the Box Store would be closing and she had to get down the hill.

After a quick turn onto the main road, she pressed her foot to the pedal. Though her Ford was more clunky, she still enjoyed driving the winding roads, especially now that she'd gotten used to them.

Her confidence with mountain driving had increased since moving to Lily Rock. Plus whenever she got behind the wheel for more than ten minutes, she thought of Michael. She still couldn't believe how the one-time tail-gater had turned into her best friend and the love of her life.

Then her thoughts would drift to more specifics. How he was great-looking and a sensational spa companion. She felt the heat rise up her neck, thinking of those first weeks, when she'd finally agreed to go out with him. Taking it slow was no longer an option after that.

Used to Mayor Maguire's presence in the passenger seat, she felt a tug over her heart. The vision of him standing at the top of the stairs with her boot in his mouth came next, reminding her that she wanted to take him to the vet.

She blinked. *Wait a minute. There was another time when M&M found a boot. When I was undercover at the music academy, he found a boot in the trash that helped crack the case.* She took another sharp curve in the road, accelerating on the other side.

Before she could follow her thoughts about Maguire, a vehicle pulled closer to her back bumper. She knew that was the universal sign to slow down and let them pass. So she tapped her brakes and took a turnout, bumping over the berm. The car gave a short honk and sped away. *I'm so much better on mountain roads now.* She eased back into the single lane without a mishap.

As the straightaway approached, where the road widened to two lanes going in both directions, she remembered with embarrassment two speeding tickets she'd gotten in the straightaway, right past Thomas Mountain. Those experiences had taught her to pay attention to the speed limit and that even she had a tendency to speed up over the mountain roads.

Driving past an intersection, Olivia noted a familiar vehicle waiting to pull into traffic. As she sped by she realized with a start, *it's the Mercedes SUV!* She lifted her foot from the gas pedal, watching in her rearview mirror.

The SUV turned onto the main road, accelerating toward her. She strained to see who was driving but was unable to get a good look. Not even when the SUV pulled up to her bumper could she identify the driver. Since the vehicle was too high and moving too fast, only the grill was reflected in her rearview mirror.

Olivia held her breath, slowing her car down. Shifting

her eyes straight ahead, she groaned. The setting sun cast a glare on the front of her Ford. She pulled down her visor.

A strong honk from the car behind her made her flinch. She pressed her foot on the accelerator to go faster. To her surprise, the SUV only came closer. A slight tap to her bumper made her gasp. Before she could pull to the side of the road, the vehicle swerved to pass her, heading straight toward another car illegally passing coming from the opposite direction.

Her hands trembled on the steering wheel. She pulled as far to the side as possible, giving the SUV room. With another honk the driver passed her car, barely missing a truck coming the other way and her front bumper. Now in front of her car the SUV accelerated, leaving her behind.

That was close.

She pushed her foot to the pedal. The Ford sputtered at the same speed, not a match for the horsepower of the newer vehicle.

Olivia's jaw tightened. She knew the SUV was deliberately trying to upset her. Twice might have been a coincidence. But not three times...

Lifting her foot from the accelerator, Olivia let go of any hope of catching the SUV. It was then she remembered the boxes. As she approached the town, more and more signs contained advertising, including the one that read "Box Store, left on Temecula Glen." Slowing down, she made a left-hand turn into the strip mall parking lot, all thoughts of the SUV pushed aside.

She locked her car and made her way toward the office. The door creaked open, revealing a long counter that took up nearly all the cramped space.

She stood in front of the counter. A clipboard and a bell lay on the worn surface. When no one appeared, Olivia dropped her palm on the bell. The third ring produced a man from the back.

"I called earlier," she explained.

He reached for his clipboard.

"I'm Olivia Greer."

"Okay then. Sign the waiting list. I take people as they come. Put your name there and when I'm finished filling these other orders I'll get to you."

"Will there be time? Before you close, that is?"

He shoved the clipboard across the counter. "We'll have to see, now won't we."

Olivia sighed. She might be able to convince the guy to stay later, but her dinner plans with Michael would need to be delayed. Leaving the clipboard, she reached for her phone and texted.

> Picking up boxes right now. Might be a bit late. Can you hold dinner until I get home?

He responded right away.

> Of course. Let me know when you're on the road back.

She pocketed her phone and grabbed the pencil attached to the top of the clipboard. One glance at the paper made her eyes open wide. Only one person had come and gone ahead of her, none other than Whitney I. Zimmer, which was written in a bold scrawl.

I just missed her. Shoot!

Olivia signed her name and sat down on the folding chair with a thud. She allowed herself another moment of frustration. Her mind whirled.

Michael is disappointed with me because I've waited until the last minute to pack. Janis is being a big pain with her castle comments. An SUV nearly drove me off the road again. It's probably Whitney Zimmer, I feel it in my gut. And then we've been chasing down that Time to Tidy woman for days and still no sight of her. She continues to stay one step ahead of me.

The sound of shuffling came from behind the back room. The man appeared, dragging flat cardboard pieces under his arm. "I've got your boxes," he huffed. "Why don't you drive around back and I'll help load the car. You can pay now if you want to drive away after loading."

Olivia handed over her debit card. Once he ran it through the machine he handed it right back. She hurried out the front door to her car.

A quick drive around the back of the shop revealed the man already waiting. He'd propped the stack of broken-down boxes against the stucco wall.

Getting out of her car, she helped him load the boxes. "Thanks," she said hastily. Not waiting for a reply, she climbed behind the driver's seat. Pulling the car out of the strip mall, back onto the highway, she felt a little better.

That was pretty efficient really. Can't wait to see Michael's face when I come home with these boxes.

She sniffed. The used boxes filled the car with the smell of old cigarette smoke. She rolled down her window, letting the wind blow her hair away from her face. Taking a deep breath, she turned on her radio.

By the time she arrived home she found Mayor Maguire standing in front of the house. He greeted her.

"Bork." His tongue draped out the side of his mouth in a smile.

Michael walked from the house, looking happier than he had that morning. He came closer to the car. Once she'd pulled the keys out of the ignition, he opened her door.

"I'll unload the boxes," he said, looking over the back seat.

"There's more in the trunk," she said.

"Why don't you go inside and see what I made for dinner," he suggested with a nod.

The smell of fresh garlic bread met her nose. *I hope he made pasta.* She dropped her purse on the table, hearing voices coming from the kitchen. A man's light baritone exclaimed, "Look at her kick those feet. She's a live wire."

The man's voice was followed by Sage's giggle.

Olivia walked through the doorway and discovered Luis Martinez and Sage leaning over the baby. Sage ticked Star's chin as Luis watched.

"Hey, Olivia," Sage called out. "Is it okay if Luis stays for dinner? Michael said he has plenty of steaks for the grill."

Olivia took a sharp breath, aware of her disappointment. *Not Jeff but Luis.* She walked toward the refrigerator.

"Of course he can stay for dinner. I'll start a salad."

When no one answered, she turned to face the table. Star had wrapped her hand around Luis's forefinger. He didn't smile at her, but at Sage. Olivia felt his charm all the way across the room. Hair stood up on her neck.

"Salad is great," he told her, without removing his eyes from Sage.

At that moment Olivia knew what bothered her and why she preferred Jeff over Luis. *Jeff cares about Star and Sage; Luis sees Star as a means to get to Sage.*

By the time Olivia finished tossing the salad, Michael returned to the kitchen. He stood next to her, leaning over to whisper, "Looks like our matchmaking has met an impasse. I think the doc is ahead."

She nodded. "Looks that way."

He chuckled. "I suppose we can give up. But I admit

matchmaking was kinda fun while it lasted. Gave us another mutual interest." He leaned over to kiss her neck as he put his arms around her. "Besides the obvious, of course."

She turned in his arms, looking up at his face. "I thought about you today, driving down the hill."

"Were they good thoughts?"

"Oh, more than good. I thought of our spa right out there in the woods and how much we enjoy looking at the stars at night." She felt the heat come up her neck, as it always did when she thought of Michael.

"Did you now." He made his face a mask, but the twinkle in his eyes gave him away. "Maybe we need to do some stargazing tonight."

She nodded. "And here I thought that was my idea, but you were ahead of me yet again."

"Do you want to go now before dinner?" Michael grinned.

She looked past his shoulder at Sage and Luis. "Let's have dinner first. Star should be asleep by eight. And then it would be wonderful to relax and look at the night sky."

CHAPTER THIRTY-ONE

The ping from a text message woke Olivia with a start. She picked up the phone on her nightstand.

Olivia tossed the phone on her nightstand and got right out of bed.

By the time she'd showered and dressed, she found Michael in the kitchen filling his travel mug with tea.

"Janis and I may get to meet Whitney Zimmer today. She's managed to get a Lily Rock address."

"Good. Ask her why she keeps harassing you with her SUV while you're at it." His jaw hardened.

"I plan on asking her that and more," Olivia admitted.

Michael came closer to give her a quick kiss on the

cheek. "See you later. Keep me posted about Zimmer. I know I won't have your full attention until this case is solved. We've got packing to do." He opened the back door.

And there stood Jeff Grossman on the other side, his hand extended. "You outta here, man?" He stepped back to let Michael pass.

"Got work. See you later." Michael's boots crunched across the gravel path as Jeff closed the door.

Olivia poured him a mug of coffee. "Have a seat," she offered. "I only have a few minutes until I need to leave as well."

Jeff took the mug from her hands.

At first glance Olivia noted a few days of beard growth on Jeff's lean jaw. Dark circles under his eyes accompanied a downcast glance.

"Are you okay?" she asked.

He looked up and cleared his throat. "Not really." He rubbed his fingers over his beard. "I'm preoccupied. Roxy was telling me last night about some things she overheard. Before they found Maddox. I guess she's had a lot of time to think, staying in that cell."

"She told Janis and me a bit of that too. People talking in the pantry before Maddie died," Olivia said.

"Roxy's wondering if Serenity and Maddie were good friends. At least more acquainted than they let on. She assumed, like everyone else, that the contestants had just met each other. But the way they talked, she's thinking Serenity and Maddie were much closer."

"They probably saw each other at any number of conventions over the years," Olivia agreed. "What gave Roxy that impression?"

"The night before. She heard Maddie talking to Serenity in her room. They left the door ajar. She kept going, had to put away fresh sheets in the linen cupboard, but then on the way back she heard more talking. Roxy wasn't snooping," he added hastily. "But she was, you know, curious."

Olivia leaned forward to hear more.

"Especially when she heard that other guy talking. Bruce. He calls himself The Tool." Jeff shook his head. "Anyway that's all she said, that she heard him too. In Serenity's room."

"Has she mentioned this to Janis?"

"I don't know." Jeff's eyes narrowed. "Do you think it's relevant?"

"You never know." When Jeff took a sip of his coffee, Olivia turned back to the sink. She quickly rinsed the dishes, in a hurry to meet up with Janis. "You can stay as long as you want," she told Jeff, drying her hands on a towel.

"I'll finish my coffee. Maybe say hi to Sage and Star." His voice sounded wistful.

Olivia left him in the kitchen and made her way to the front door.

By the time Olivia walked into the constabulary, Brad was nowhere to be found. She pulled out her own security card to trigger the keypad to open the inner security door. She immediately heard murmuring down the hallway, coming from Roxy's cell.

Curious, Olivia stopped to say hello but pulled up short in surprise. Roxy sat on Brad's lap and they both looked very busy.

He had braced his back against the wall, holding Roxy's body close to his chest. Kissing noises, a succession of wet smacks, made Olivia wince. "Hey, you two," she said.

When neither of them looked up, Olivia's eyebrows lifted. "Hello," she called out. When they still didn't stop, she spoke louder. "Hello. I can see you. You know you're in jail, right?"

Brad disconnected his lips from Roxanne's as he glanced around Roxy's shoulder. "Oh hey, Olivia. Didn't hear you come in." He ran his hand self-consciously through his hair, which stood in a jumbled mess.

"Obviously," she muttered. Roxy buried her head into Brad's chest as if to hide her embarrassment. When she didn't turn around, Olivia directed her question to Brad. "Hasn't Janis warned you about fraternizing with arrested people in a cell?"

Brad eased Roxy off his lap onto the bench. She rubbed her face, a sheepish grin on her lips. Her chin was pink, most likely from Brad's beard.

Brad spoke again. "The boss told me. She did. But sometimes I forget." He glanced at Roxy, who was pulling her shirt down to cover the top of her pants.

Before Olivia could say more, Janis Jets came around the corner. She stopped in her tracks as soon as she saw Brad and Roxy. Shoving Olivia aside, she asked, "What's going on here?"

Olivia immediately felt sorry for Brad and Roxy. She began to explain. "I just arrived. I came down the hall and heard voices; I found them both in here."

Jets's face, still flushed from her discovery, directed her next words to Brad. "I asked you to bring Roxy breakfast, not to sit down and play kissy poo."

Olivia ducked her head, wondering if Brad had just lost his job at the constabulary.

"Go get the food now," Jets barked at her assistant. Then she turned to Olivia.

"Let's go see if Whitney Zimmer is at home. I'll drive." Jets opened the door to the cell, waiting for Brad to step out. He walked past her, his head ducked.

"I'll deal with you later," she told him, shoving the cell door closed.

CHAPTER THIRTY-TWO

Whitney Zimmer's house was located in the more expensive section of Lily Rock. Property prices soared in that area because of the view. In the morning sun, Lily Rock shone like an alabaster sculpture. In the evening, people sat outdoors just to catch a glimpse of the glorious sunset sky surrounding the town's namesake.

Olivia remembered that Michael had researched the area as a potential choice for their lot. He'd not chosen this particular section because he thought they were overpriced. He'd explained at the time, "Too many custom-built homes, financed by corporations to house their employees for vacations. Not the best neighborhood for full-time residents like us."

With patience he'd continued his search. Finally discovering a better lot with an even more spectacular view. "Not as prestigious, at least yet," he'd said at the time. "Eventually this neighborhood will expand and then we can stay or I'll build again."

Olivia had agreed, and now she was glad she had. Whitney Zimmer's neighborhood bore enormous homes on three-acre lots, which looked more like hotels. Or as the town's Old Rockers would say, "McMansions."

Expanses of concrete with circular driveways gave easy access to cars and limos. Built for large parties, people could be easily dropped off. Especially in inclement weather. *This is a neighborhood of castles for sure.*

Olivia knew the town council had not approved at first. Oh sure, they appreciated the revenue and the job opportunities. But that didn't matter because the McMansions interfered with a sacred Lily Rock commitment. The trees. Especially the redwoods. Because in order to build the large places, redwood trees needed to be cut down to make way for the construction. Cutting down old trees was a sore point for the Old Rockers.

The potential owners argued that they would use the wood for other projects. And they'd make more firewood free to residents for the cold winters. Even after the council agreed and issued the permits, the grumbling didn't stop. It just went behind closed doors. And then the builders reneged on their promise about the free wood.

Aggravated Lily Rock residents, driving to see the neighborhood, found stacks of lumber, cords and cords of wood, lined up under open-sided sheds. Most of the Lily Rock residents couldn't even afford to buy that much wood, let alone just to have it sit around.

All of this was on Olivia's mind as she waited for Janis.

"Ready for the grilling?" Jets asked, interrupting her thoughts.

"Every one of these places must be five thousand square feet or more," Olivia remarked to Janis as they walked toward the front of the house.

Jets glanced around. "I suppose. Not my style. Do you think your castle is gonna look like one of these?"

"Not on your life," Olivia said. "Michael didn't choose this area for a reason. Our place is different. Much smaller and more intimate. Very Bellemare." She referred to Michael's unique gift, the one he'd received awards for in architectural circles. Glass and metal along with natural elements had gotten him noticed long before they met.

Janis bounced the large brass knocker against the solid wood door to announce their arrival. "I called ahead to make sure Whitney was here."

Stanley "the Wiz" Weyland answered the door. After a slight pause, a look of amusement crossed his face. "You finally found us," he commented dryly. "Why don't you step in."

Once inside, they both stood in the entryway looking up toward the vaulted ceiling. *This place is enormous.* Olivia felt her jaw drop and then snapped it closed. *I don't want to be impressed.* Jets raised an eyebrow at her, adopting a bland expression as if to agree.

Olivia's eyes darted toward the main living area. Designed as an open concept, it was easy to see a woman sitting at the end of an enormous overstuffed sofa. The woman smiled engagingly, her mouth filled with very white, straight teeth. Clothed in black joggers and a cropped top, her shoulder-length blonde hair was carefully arranged. She looked like a photo on a magazine cover.

The woman's hands, folded in her lap, showed manicured red fingernails. A large glittering sapphire surrounded by smaller diamonds adorned the ring finger of her right hand.

As Olivia came closer to greet the woman, she felt a tingle down her spine.

We finally get to meet the elusive Whitney Zimmer.

Her glance fell to the coffee table in front of the sofa.

An array of magazines covered the top. A copy of *Variety* lay closest to where the blonde woman was seated, opened to an advertisement.

When the blonde saw Olivia glance at the magazine, she quickly leaned over to close it, shoving it to the bottom of a stack. "I like to check out the advertisements," she explained.

Jets stepped past Olivia. She pointed to the badge on her shirt. "I'm Officer Janis Jets, senior detective at the Lily Rock constabulary. This is Olivia Greer, my consultant. I assume you are Whitney Zimmer."

The blonde stood, extending her hand. "And I want to thank you for taking the death of one of my contestants in hand so quickly. Have you arrested the murderer yet?"

For a moment Olivia wondered about Whitney's tone. *She's so cordial. I didn't expect that, not from the way everyone spoke about her. Oh, and the way she nearly sideswiped my car...*

Jets gave Whitney a vigorous handshake. "I have been spending a lot of time on this case, but in answer to your question: no. We have not arrested the murderer yet."

Whitney looked puzzled. Her face set in a displeased expression. "Stanley told me that you have a woman in custody. Our caterer. Such an awful situation." Whitney sat back down, demurely holding her knees together, hands folded once again on her lap. "We hired Roxanne Grossman last minute, but I thought she'd been thoroughly vetted," explained Whitney.

Stanley spoke up. "Why don't you two take a seat?"

Janis and Olivia sat across from the sofa in two leather chairs. Jets pulled out her iPad as the Wiz sat down on the opposite end of the sofa.

Jets cleared her throat. "We have reason to suspect that

Roxanne Grossman's confession may have been too hasty. I had no time to read her her rights, so everything she said was technically inadmissible in court."

"I see." Whitney nodded. "So you are looking into other suspects?"

"That's why we're here." Jets glared. "And we're also here because you have been amazingly unavailable since the murder. I've called and texted. We had some trouble coming up with your address. Then I found two addresses for you, one in Palm Springs and the other in Lily Rock."

"I also have a quite lovely home in Malibu Canyon," Whitney added.

Olivia observed the woman as Jets took notes. Nothing about her body language indicated she was remotely nervous. *Maybe she doesn't realize she's a person of interest...*

"Your evasive behavior indicated guilt. Are you aware of that?" Jets spoke firmly.

"Not guilt so much as having other things to do. I expected my assistant to handle the details. I do apologize for the inconvenience."

Olivia knew in her gut that Zimmer's silky voice was meant to soothe any sense of awkwardness. With her casual elegance and contrived communication style, she'd managed to downplay a murder investigation as a mere blip in her otherwise busy day.

Jets scrutinized the woman with a scowl. "So where were you on Monday morning when Maddox Hall was found dead?"

Now that's cutting to the chase.

Olivia kept her eye on Whitney, looking for signs of any possible guilt.

"I was on the phone with Bruce," Whitney said immediately. "I planned on coming to Lily Rock later that day to do the evaluation of the first cleanup."

"Is that common, for the Wiz to start things off without you?" Jets asked.

Olivia saw a slight tremor at the corner of Whitney's mouth.

Here we go. Janis doesn't respond well to privilege. In her book everyone, no matter how entitled, plays by the same rules, especially when it comes to murder.

"Not unusual at all." Whitney finally spoke up. "Stanley handles most of the people interaction part of my business. That's why I hired him." The small smile had disappeared, giving rise to impatience.

She's facile with her emotions, which shows on her face. Yet she doesn't look afraid, just annoyed. Whitney Zimmer would make a good actress.

"But you show up for the first day's assessment?" Jets stated matter-of-factly.

"I usually do. But my plans change. Once you'd discovered a body, I had more pressing things to attend to. I didn't want to get in the way of the police."

"We've been seeing your SUV on the roads." Jets pivoted with an unexpected question.

"Have you now? I'm quite pleased with its performance. It's new..." She looked at Janis. "But you obviously already know that."

Olivia felt the hair stand up on the back of her neck.

Janis Jets's glance shifted to Olivia. *Now's my chance.* She plunged in. "You nearly ran me off the road yesterday. On my way to Hemet."

Whitney blinked as if confused.

Then the Wiz broke in. "Ms. Zimmer has a lot on her mind. Her company, for one, and now the death of one of her carefully vetted contestants. I'm sure she didn't mean to be aggressive."

Whitney glanced at him and then back to Olivia. "Oh, now I remember. I'm so sorry. As Stanley says, I can be easily distracted. It's my creative mind, always working. That can be such a problem. I tend to drive erratically when I'm focused elsewhere."

Having deflected Olivia's statement by making excuses, Whitney resumed her ultra-confident expression. Lips set in a slight smile. Olivia felt her stomach clench. She wanted to push harder. But she didn't say anything more for fear of derailing Janis's objective.

Jets cleared her throat. "So you weren't in Lily Rock the morning of the death, and Stanley can vouch for you?" She looked over at him. He nodded.

"Of course. I am her alibi," he said stoutly. "I was talking to her on my cell most of the morning. There are records."

Olivia watched him closely. A small twitch at the corner of his left eye indicated he was nervous. Especially when it came to questions directed at Whitney's behavior.

"And you weren't dodging my phone calls and texts?" Jets asked. "Like I said, it made you look guilty. At least in my book."

"Oh no. I didn't mean to ignore you. As I said, I thought Stanley was handling all of that for me."

"I did my best," he agreed.

"Okay then..." Jets began typing into her iPad. After a brief note she looked up. "I'll get this report written and I'd like both of you to come down to the constabulary this afternoon. Around four would be convenient for me. You can read and sign the statement at that time. Then I'll have your interview in my records, just in case I have to circle back with any more questions." Janis returned to her typing.

Once again Olivia's eyes fell on the array of magazines on the table. "I haven't seen that many periodicals in such a long time. Do you subscribe to them all or pick them up on occasion?"

The Wiz abruptly rose to his feet. "They do make a big mess." He leaned over to gather them into a stack. Shuffling them with both hands, he placed the stack on the table closer to Whitney. "She loves to thumb through issues while she has coffee in the morning. I make sure she has all the recent ones at her disposal."

"He's thoughtful that way," Whitney murmured.

The Wiz cast another look over the stack of magazines. He frowned. Leaning closer he took the one on top and slipped it underneath the rest. By that time Janis Jets had finished her report.

She shut down her iPad and stood. "See you this afternoon," she told them. "Have a nice day."

CHAPTER THIRTY-THREE

Janis cruised along the main highway as Olivia looked out the passenger window. She played the interview over in her head.

"So what do you make of the Zimmer woman?" Janis interrupted her thoughts.

"She's hiding something," Olivia said. "I can just feel it. She's entirely too smooth. Like she was playing a part."

"The Wiz seemed a bit edgy around her," Janis admitted. "The thing is her alibi is pretty foolproof. We checked the Wiz's phone records."

"Were there texts?" Olivia asked.

"No texting." Jets stared over her steering wheel.

"Then he must have been lying," Olivia said. "He claimed that Whitney texted him right when I was there."

"A small discrepancy," Jet's muttered.

A rebuttal formed on Olivia's lips but she swallowed it back.

Jets continued, "Let's get back to the big issue. They could have hired someone else to kill her. There's no evidence or any fingerprints, that there was another person in the bathroom except for Maddox and Roxy."

"But let's not forget how nervous the Wiz acted today. Makes me wonder about his job security. But tell me more about your background checks."

"Oh you know, besides the forensics and phone evidence, I've been looking into both of them for the usual financial crimes or maybe a juicy murder in the past. If you get away with killing someone once, what's to stop you from doing it again? Or if not murder, something they were accused of that would point to motive."

"Keeping the contest going, even after Maddox's death," Olivia mused, "seems cold-blooded. Whitney could have shut everything down. It's not like she needs the money."

"True," admitted Janis.

"And the Wiz, he must have agreed to keep the competition going. I suppose that goes with his organized personality. Often people like that compartmentalize."

"He's the kind of guy who follows directions. If Zimmer said shut down the competition, he would have done it. But she didn't say that, now did she?" Jets shot Olivia a side-eye. "How about this? What if the Wiz already knew who would win the contest. So he had to finish everything to make that happen..."

"You mean it wasn't a contest at all," Olivia said thoughtfully. "It was made to look like one, but the winner had already been determined."

Jets pulled into her designated parking space behind the constabulary. She shut down the engine. "That would be a good motive for not canceling things." She took a deep breath. "Okay, I can do some more digging, but as you know I'm finding very little on Whitney Zimmer. She's the needle in the haystack. I had a lot of trouble getting that Lily Rock address. Even her photo. I had no idea what she looked like until today.

"And the Wiz is very clean. He doesn't even file his taxes late or have a secret family or drink too much. No arrests. Not even a parking ticket."

Olivia opened the passenger door. "Okay then, see you later."

"Yah, later," muttered Jets.

Olivia left Janis with a puzzled expression, still sitting behind the wheel.

Before getting back into her car, she stopped at Thyme Out. Planning a picnic with Michael was easy when the sandwiches were made by the best baker in town. Ordered ahead, she only had to text and a young girl brought them out to her car.

"Here you go, Olivia," she said.

"Thanks." Olivia took the sack and closed her window.

A quick drive up the hill brought her to the new construction where Michael and his crew worked. Parking in the dirt under a cedar tree, she saw Michael bent over plans, talking to Spike Rocco, his main construction worker. Instead of interrupting, she sat down on their bench. Michael had made the bench out of cedar before they'd even broke ground. "This is where we'll sit and watch the progress," he'd told Olivia at the time.

Instead of unpacking the food, Olivia took a moment to inspect the new house. The front door had been stained in a rich mahogany tint since her last visit. Now her eyes drifted up, past the second story and pitched roof, toward the mountains on the horizon. She inhaled deeply, feeling the familiar tingle of pine in her nose and throat. A crow dipped across the sky, cawing against the wooded backdrop.

Remembering the first time she heard a crow in Lily

Rock, Olivia shuddered. *It was the day I found Marla behind the house.* At the time she'd not known what lay ahead of her, but now she saw the moment as a defining point in her life. When things changed.

Having finished the discussion with Spike, Michael sauntered over, greeting her with a smile. He sat next to her, patting her knee.

"You've really made progress since the last time," she told him.

"I really have." His grin widened. "Like what you see?"

"The stain color came out great on the front door. But more than that, it's unbelievable how a vacant lot became a house that will be our home. At first I had trouble imagining that it was all going to happen just like you planned."

"I can do the imaging for both of us." He looked out toward the house, nodding with confidence.

"Want to show me the inside?" she asked.

He eyed the food basket. "Could we eat first? I'm starving."

"I stopped at Thyme Out on the way out of town." She pulled out the ham sandwich on thick sourdough slices.

Michael took it from her hand. Peeling back the waxed paper, he took a bite. "Before I forget, how did the interview with Whitney Zimmer go?"

Olivia placed her sandwich on her lap. "Whitney was odd. Looked like a movie star. The Wiz seemed really nervous. So Janis is doing more background checking."

"So no one's confessed to you yet?" Michael said.

"Not yet," she said ruefully. "I hope I'm not disappointing Janis."

Once they both finished eating, Michael gathered the trash and shoved it back in the bag. "Come on and see what we've accomplished." He stood, offering her a hand.

As they drew closer to the house Olivia could hear hammering, followed by the whine of a saw. Michael pushed open the solid wood door, inviting her to walk past. Once inside, she looked up and around, appreciating the shiver up her spine. The openness, with the expansive use of glass and rough-hewn timbers, along with the Bellemare style took her breath away.

There had been significant progress inside the house since she'd been there last. Drywall had been put up and taped. The floor-to-ceiling glass doors facing the woods glimmered in the afternoon sun, making the panoramic view of Lily Rock feel close enough to touch.

Everything smelled like fresh lumber, mingled with the scent of pine and cedar. She inhaled deeply, appreciating the view and the accompanying sense of serenity.

"It's just beautiful," she said, turning to him.

He watched her face closely. "I know that look," he said. "The first time you stepped into Marla's house. You were awestruck. Of course you didn't know then that I was the architect."

She walked closer to the glass wall, looking past the deck into the thickly wooded grove. A combination of redwood and pine shaded the back of their lot. She turned to him.

"I remember that moment too. I walked inside from the front door, not expecting much. I mean from the outside it felt like a really nice house. But when I walked forward into the great room, the open concept, how the trees felt as if they grew indoors. I couldn't believe she was lucky enough to live in such an amazing space.

"But it wasn't until this moment that I noticed the similarities. The use of glass makes the forest immediate, as if there's no dividing line between outdoors and in. Just like here. I feel like I'm under the trees. Amazing." She nodded.

He came closer, putting his arm around her shoulders. "This design keeps what we love about Marla's place. I've been listening, you know. I did it to please you. My hope is that you don't feel trapped, like you're a princess in a castle." She could feel the longing in his voice for his creation to meet her expectations. She leaned into the warmth of his body, drawing from his strength.

"All thoughts of medieval maidens have gone away—*poof*. That's because I feel free here. Who wouldn't, staring into the woods with Lily Rock beyond. It's spectacular, Michael. I can't believe I get to live here with you. I guess I'm the lucky one now." She turned to put both arms around his middle, hugging him close.

He pushed her slightly away to lift her chin and gaze into her eyes. "Whenever you visit to look at the house, I feel like a kid bringing home a drawing from grade school. I want you to be proud and hang it up on the refrigerator. This is my *Mona Lisa*."

She chuckled and he continued to explain. "I know that's a lot to ask. But every project is a work of love for me. Otherwise I wouldn't take it on. All the planning I've done is an expression of my love for you. It's taken nearly an entire year. I would hate to dismantle it and build again if you didn't like it."

"I love it," she said without reservation.

"So you won't mind packing up from the other place?" He leaned closer to kiss her ear.

"I do mind, but not because I don't want to live here." Her voice was muffled by the front of his shirt. "I want to live here a lot. With you. It's just..."

"Just what?"

"I'm realizing my misgivings center around Sage, and now Star. I don't want to abandon them. That feeling is holding me back. Not you or the house." She took a step back to look him in the eyes.

He nodded. "I understand. You and Sage just found each other not that long ago. But you're not moving away, Olivia. We're only a short drive from her house."

"I know, but it's not the same as living in the same house. I'm going to work on this," she told him. "I promise."

When he turned to walk toward the windows, she felt her heart sink. *Maybe mentioning Sage and Star was a bad idea.*

"Do you want to show me the kitchen?" she called out.

"Maybe next time," he answered, stepping out on the deck. "I better check in with the guys."

"I can come back tomorrow," she called out.

Michael turned around. "It's okay, Olivia. I can get through this with you. I'll just need a few minutes to wrap my mind around your reluctance."

Then he turned, and the glass door closed behind him.

Once on the winding road, Olivia found it impossible to hold back her tears. *I wish I'd never told him. Why can't I just keep my mouth shut?*

She pulled into a parking place in front of the library. Rubbing her sleeve over her face, she tried to compose herself. When she looked up she found Meadow waving from her window.

Olivia had to admit that Meadow was right. *She told me to pay attention to my feelings of reluctance. This isn't about castles, like Janis said. It's about family.*

She locked her car and walked into the constabulary, finding Brad May sitting at his desk. He looked down at the police ledger without his usual greeting.

Not his usual cheery self.

"Hey, Brad." Even though she felt miserable, she used an upbeat voice for him.

"Hey, Olivia." He sounded listless.

"You seem a little down," she added.

"Janis put me on probation." He shrugged. "I guess I deserve it."

"I didn't realize there was such a thing as constabulary probation, though now that you mention it, you did deserve it. You're lucky you didn't get fired. What made you think making out with a suspect in jail was ever appropriate?"

Brad shook his head. "I guess I just didn't think. Roxy's so cute. And we've been getting to know each other for the past several days and I thought she could use some cheering up."

"How long have you and I known each other—you know, since I moved up to Lily Rock?" Olivia asked.

"I guess we met the first year. Then you went away and came back a year later. About that long."

"Close to three years, but going on four. In that time you've gone from late teen to early twenties. When I first met you, you were scrambling for work. A part-time employee at best. Flitting around from job to job. And now you work full-time at the constabulary as Janis Jets's right-hand man. That's really something, the way you've changed."

His mouth turned up at the side. "I guess that's true. I am Janis's right-hand man. Never thought of it that way."

"So Brad, here's the deal. If you'd have gotten caught making out with a murder suspect three years ago, I'd have said, 'That Brad. He's so immature.' But now that you've become the new and improved Brad, fully employed and Janis's right-hand man, it seems beneath you to make such an impulsive and silly decision."

"Like I'm going backward."

"Right, just like you're going backward. You can learn from old Brad, but you don't have to act like him. Now you're the new and improved smarter Brad. Someone who learns from his mistakes."

"So you really see me as the right-hand man?" He looked

around the room, his eyes stopping on the computer. "And you think Janis really needs me?"

"I do think Officer Jets needs you. And that you've disappointed her with your behavior." Olivia tried to look very firm, but she was having trouble not smiling. *He is irresistible. Just like a puppy, all wiggles and smiles.*

Olivia heard the entrance door scrape against the flooring. Whitney Zimmer and the Wiz walked inside. "We're here to sign the paperwork," the Wiz said.

Brad sat up straight. He reached into his drawer, pulling out a folder. Extracting papers, he said, "I have them right here. Read over them and sign at the bottom. I'll be the witness. You can sit over there by the table."

Olivia heard the shift in the tone of his voice. He'd assumed authority, casting off his previous hangdog look. The Wiz took the offered paperwork. He and Whitney sat together at the table in the corner, heads bent over, reading the forms.

Olivia nodded at Brad. "Would you unlock the inner door for me? I'm here to speak to Officer Jets. I'm not a right-hand man like some people, but she does consult me now and then."

Brad grinned.

The door clicked and slid open. Olivia walked through, making her way down the hall to Janis Jets's office.

CHAPTER THIRTY-FIVE

Wednesday

When Michael left for work early, Olivia stood in her usual spot at the sink in the kitchen. She watched as Mayor Maguire dug vigorously in the garden dirt.

He's industrious this morning.

She filled her mug of coffee when she heard a knock at the back door.

I wonder if that's Jeff?"

To her surprise Bruce "The Tool" Ward stood outside. He had a sheepish smile on his face.

"Hi, Bruce," she said. "What brings you to my house?" Feeling apprehensive, she narrowed the opening in the door. "I thought you'd be busy with the contest." Olivia waited for him to reply, realizing she'd be better off stepping outside to talk.

He seemed to anticipate her move because he barged his way through the space, continuing to speak. Rather than object, Olivia let him go. *He's got the worst manners ever.*

Bruce spoke in a rush. "The cleaning and tidying part are over. We're just waiting for Whitney to announce the winner. That's why, well one reason I came by. Jeff told me you wouldn't mind." He looked around and then added, "I saw him at the constabulary."

He wore his customary jeans and branded T-shirt, which stretched over his fit torso. Without the usual tool belt, his waist appeared trim, emphasizing the expanse of his chest. Short-clipped blonde hair combed back drew more attention to his brown eyes and angled jaw. She smelled aftershave. *Fresh breeze with a tinge of ocean spray.*

Turning to close the door, Mayor Maguire trotted past, making his way toward the pantry. Particles of dirt still clung to the fur on his back.

She shut the door with a huff. "Pour yourself some coffee. I have to wipe the mayor down and feed him breakfast. Then I'll be right with you."

By the time Olivia sat at the table, her curiosity was growing. She opened the conversation.

"I finally met Whitney Zimmer yesterday." She watched his face to see how he'd react.

His eyes grew wide. "So she's in town?"

"In the flesh. Officer Jets and I spoke to her and the Wiz."

"Oh, I knew he was around. We see the Wiz all the time. But Whitney..."

"You didn't expect Whitney to be here to announce the winner of the contest?" Olivia asked.

"I just wasn't sure. In the past I've emailed and received the occasional text. She always gets right back, but she does keep a very low profile."

"Doesn't the low profile thing strike you as unusual?"

He took a sip of coffee and then explained. "Time to Tidy has never been about Whitney's face. She doesn't brand herself; she does brand her ideas and products. You won't find one social media post with her in it. That's why I didn't think it was that unusual not to meet her in person."

"So you've been to other Time to Tidy conferences. Do you mean to say you've never heard her speak or seen her at the event?"

"How can I explain this?" He looked away. Then he looked back. "Her elusiveness makes her more mysterious. Even her classes are taped. Unlike everyone else in the tidy business, who constantly pitch themselves along with their products, she started out being a mystery. The rest of the tidy community looks needy in comparison. Less professional. She makes her absence work for her. Pretty slick, if you ask me."

"I suppose." Olivia felt more confused than ever. "Did you have anything else you wanted to talk about this morning?"

He cleared his throat. "Like I said, I ran into Jeff yesterday when I was visiting Roxy. I was talking to him about Maddie, how sad it was that she died so young. He seemed kinda interested and suggested that I talk to you, since you're a consultant with the constabulary."

"Are you sure you don't want to talk to Officer Jets instead? This is her investigation."

"She's a bit much," he admitted. "Too rough for me. I like women more refined. All business and no pleasure for her. I can't tell her things. She'll eat me up and spit me out and probably put me in jail. No, I don't want to talk to Officer Jets."

Olivia wasn't surprised at his assessment of Janis. She'd

been acting more bristly than usual as of late. *Princess and castle. Please. I get why The Tool is afraid of her.*

At this point Mayor Maguire, having finished his breakfast, inched closer and crouched under the table. He laid his chin on her lap. She patted his head. When he didn't lie down, she kept patting. *We were just getting somewhere in this conversation, but I bet you want to go outside.*

When she caught Bruce staring at the dog, she stood and explained. "Mayor Maguire usually hangs out with us in the morning. He's free range and the mayor in Lily Rock. You might have seen him around..."

"Yeah, I saw him the other day. When I first went to my cabin assignment. He was looking at me through the kitchen window. I was afraid I'd have to call the shelter, but then he went away. Which reminds me, that's one thing I wanted to tell you. I think you and the cop might want to take a closer look at Serenity McFee."

"Why do you think that?" Olivia opened the door for Maguire. He ran outside.

"When I first looked at my cabin she was already emptying the trash. I mean, that's a rule-breaker. If Whitney or the Wiz knew, she'd have been kicked out of the competition for starting early."

When Olivia returned to sit down, he had folded his arms over his chest, an angry set to his jaw.

"Did you tell anyone about that?"

"How could I? Serenity threatened me on the spot. She could invent any story just to make me look bad. So I kept my mouth shut. But when Maddie turned up dead? I wouldn't put it past Serenity. She's capable of anything."

"Because she threatened you?"

"That and she's cutthroat. Her business, Cleanliness is Next to Godliness, is a big front. People like her brand, how she sends them free tidy tips in her introductory newsletters. She even coaches people who want spiritual advice. But behind all that she's not very nice.

"After the first freebies, Serenity jacks up the price, charging big money, especially if you want to take a class or get some coaching. She claims that being tidy isn't about being perfect but about making progress. And that everyone, no matter what your religion, can grow closer to God by tidying up."

He shook his head with a look of disgust. "That's a mixed message, if you ask me. My brand is the opposite. I always tell people if you do it right, you won't have to do it again."

Olivia swallowed hard. *Why would anyone want spiritual coaching from a person on the internet who promotes a cleaning process...*

"You do seem upset by all of this. Is there anything else you'd like to tell me?" she asked in a quiet voice.

"There is, but it's kind of personal." He dropped his arms and leaned forward. "Maddie and I hooked up once at a Time to Tidy conference. It was no big deal. She was okay but not really my type. Anyway I think she kinda had a thing for me. She thought I was stalking her and believe me, that's just not true. But she might have mentioned it to Serenity. And if Serenity tells Whitney or the Wiz, it may be held against me." A slight quiver to his bottom lip and a brush to his eyes made Olivia wonder, *Are those real tears?*

The Tool pushed back his chair and stood. In the same instant, Olivia heard a bark from outside. She got up and opened the back door again. The mayor trotted inside, looked at Bruce, and then instead of ignoring him, swung around, placing himself in front of Olivia in a protective block.

The Tool looked surprised, which only encouraged Maguire to lift himself and lean forward. He bumped his nose directly into The Tool's crotch.

"Hey doggie." The Tool used his hand to protect himself while Olivia held back a smile.

As The Tool backed away toward the door, Maguire followed, his nose prepared for another crotch jab. "Thanks for the coffee. I do feel better now that I've got all of that off my chest. Just in case anyone asks—you know, Officer Jets— you can tell her my story. She'll believe it coming from you."

Bingo! So that's why he stopped by. He hopes I'll tell Jets he's a good guy.

He opened the door and shut it in Maguire's face.

"So he left. Happy?" she asked the dog.

He wagged his tail.

"I have things to do today. Want to come along later when I drive to town?"

"Bork." He scampered to stand in front of the pantry.

"I didn't ask if you wanted a dog treat. You're incorrigible."

He caught the cookie midair.

36

BRUCE "THE TOOL" WARD

Bruce left Olivia's house feeling very good about himself. *Okay, so The Tool nailed that conversation. But The Tool will be out of Lily Rock before Olivia Greer figures it out.*

Once behind the wheel, his nerves returned. Stomach in a knot, he revved up the engine and his inner pep talk. *Calm down, Tool. Only an hour until they announce the winner.* The truth was that even though he'd paid the extra money to win, he didn't feel that confident.

Something could go wrong. Wouldn't be the first time. Not a sure thing until I get that check in my account. His hands gripped the steering wheel.

He reassured himself that the Wiz already told him the prize money would be transferred right after the announcement that he'd won the contest.

Boom. Twenty-five thousand just like that. The Tool can post on social media right away.

No one knew, especially not his dad, that he'd paid so much to win. But in anticipating the influx of cash, Bruce had made a few extra expenditures in the past month. He'd already bottomed out his savings account, investing every last dime into the prototype of his next new tool.

He explained to the Wiz that first day, "It's a pretty cool device, everyone will want one. I'll produce videos that demonstrate all the uses. I call it The Tool's Magic Wand.

"The wand has one long extension pole with ten different attachments. It will clean all of those hard-to-get places, like light fixtures mounted on the ceiling. Or cobwebs in the ceiling corner. Then there is an attachment made for dusting under the bed and sofa. That's where the dust bunnies hide," he told the Wiz.

But then he'd been put off by the Wiz's lack of enthusiasm. Instead of excitement, the Wiz looked like he was trying hard not to laugh.

"You gotta have a catchy name for everything," Bruce explained further, as if the Wiz may have misunderstood.

Bruce knew he had a few things to hide. Especially in the financial department. He hoped that the Time to Tidy audit would not look too closely at his legal problems. The lawsuit about the drill, for example. And the unprecedented return rate of other drills, once people heard about the issues.

He'd covered up much of that by keeping two sets of financial books. It was simple to delete returns at his online store. But The Home Depot. That was a problem. They didn't like returns. Too much paperwork and it cost them more money. The manager had threatened to discontinue the drill and the rest of his items a week before the contest. Bruce had given up returning the numerous calls on his cell phone about the drill. He knew it was only a matter of time.

Once The Tool wins Time to Tidy, all of that will go away.

Whenever he felt anxious he'd reassure himself by

thinking about new sales. *If half of The Tool's followers buy the Wand, then the company will be solvent and back on its feet.*

And then he'd fantasize about how proud his dad would be.

"Well done, son," he'd say, when his dad took him out for a beer.

Back on the road, his gut relaxed. He thought about how well the conversation went with Olivia. *She liked me. Plus The Tool redirected her in one conversation. Nobody doubts The Tool. He's too handsome and convincing. She's probably running to the constabulary right now to tell Officer Jets that Serenity needs to be arrested.*

Bruce drove with one hand on the wheel, reaching over to look at his phone. No text or call from the Wiz or Whitney. When there were no alerts, he dropped it on the seat.

Then to distract himself, he thought more about the conversation with Olivia.

I pointed her to Serenity. She'll tell Officer Jets and they'll get out of my hair. It's a good thing the Wiz told me about Olivia Greer; some kind of town legend, how she works as a consultant with the police to get confessions.

For a moment his thoughts drifted, resting on Maddie. His eyes teared up. *Poor Maddie. She must have been so freaked out at the end. She could have called The Tool on her cell. Except she probably kept his number blocked.*

Shifting gears he slowed his van, driving slower as he approached the town. He pulled into the first available parking space. Once out of the van, he heard laughter coming from the park. He looked over. Mayor Maguire leaped into the air snatching a frisbee. Three young children cheered him on.

That dog mayor is everywhere. Kind of gives me the creeps. People say he's psychic, but that's just stupid.

He rubbed his palm against his forehead, his gut clenching again.

Hey, stop it. No one gets into the head of The Tool. Especially some dog. My mind is like a locked room mystery, where the key has been tossed away and can't be found.

___

37

SERENITY MCFEE

Serenity McFee

Serenity stood on the front porch and yanked the door of her cabin shut. Using her key, she locked the door. She tested the lock by trying to turn the handle. The deliberate steps, noted in her mind, made her feel less anxious.

Good. All secure. Everything's ready for the inspection. I'll come back ahead of time to make sure everything's still the same. I wouldn't put it past The Tool to sabotage my work behind my back. He'd have to break in, of course. I bet he knows how.

Serenity felt tense. She had to admit to herself that she'd gotten no sleep since Maddie's death. She'd begin to doze, then wake up with a start, thinking about Maddie and how she must have felt, clutching at her throat trying to breathe, those last few minutes of consciousness.

We had such a good plan, to share the win and use the profits to start up a new business together.

Walking to the car, Serenity inhaled deeply, the exhale coming out in short gasps. *I can sleep tomorrow,* she told herself. *When all of this is over and I'm down the hill back to my real life, my bank account flush with a win.* She got into her car.

Sitting behind the wheel, she thought more about the prize money. *With some planning I can go ahead and set up the new website, I can tweak the ideas of the new brand, and then with Whitney's affiliation approval, I can draft off of her list of followers to promote and launch. My e-commerce will explode.*

As a child Serenity had learned to pivot and find something good in the most unlikely derailing of a plan. Her stepbrother had taught her that. He'd undermine everything that mattered to her and then she'd have to devise something new to keep out of his reach.

She twisted her key in the ignition. The slight tremble to her hand made it more difficult, but the engine finally turned over. Her mind shifted again.

I'm going to use my GPS to find that labyrinth everyone talks about. Maybe walking slowly in a circle will calm my nerves so that I can get some sleep tonight.

Serenity used everything she could to inspire her followers. In the past she'd posted visits to museum exhibits; she'd take videos and spin her experience to focus on her brand. *Look what you can do once your home is tidy and clean. Take time to nurture your spirit at a museum.*

After she first heard about the labyrinth in Lily Rock, she planned on taking videos of her walk and posting them on Instagram. She and Maddox were supposed to do this together, to introduce their friendship to their followers.

Her engine idled as she opened the music app on her phone.

She selected the acoustic country channel, knowing that it would soothe her frayed nerves. She connected her phone to the bluetooth in the van, then shifted into reverse.

The sound of acoustic guitar filled the car, followed by a familiar voice. John Denver sang with great emotion. To her surprise, she felt emotional, almost ready to tear up.

An unexpected sob escaped from her throat. She swallowed to keep from crying more, but the tears came anyway. John Denver sang as her shoulders shook uncontrollably. Her foot reached for the brake. She pulled to the side of the road.

He described how he walked in the rain with a child. How he held the child's hand, clinging to the warmth. With a quick push she stopped the music, leaning back against the seat.

A memory came to mind.

Before my mom left, she'd sing that same song to me. About walking in the rain. I always imagined I was the one who held her hand.

She rubbed her tears away. Feeling less emotional, she headed toward the main road once again.

Driving past the trees lining the highway, she felt a twinge in her neck. That's what often happened after an emotional outbreak.

Uh-oh, a migraine coming on.

She used her finger to dig into the tight neck muscle, flinching from the pain.

Maybe just a tension headache. I hope that's all it is.

Holding her finger at the tight point, she pushed harder. More pain. She pushed again, and again welcomed the sensation.

When it stopped hurting as much, she dropped her finger.

It feels good to feel bad.

Her eyes strayed toward the side of the road, catching sight of a labyrinth sign.

She turned off the main highway. Looking straight ahead, she was surprised to see a church steeple rising into full view.

The chamber of commerce link didn't mention a church. I hate churches. They remind me of Dad. He'd sit there every week playing the part of a good dad, abandoned by his wife, raising his children by himself.

Parking her car at the far end of the lot, she rubbed her temple. Her thoughts wandered back to winning the contest. *I could use some of my prize money for a spa weekend.*

Visions of lying by a swimming pool, cucumbers covering her eyes, waiting for a deep tissue massage came next.

I wish it were right now.

But then thoughts of Maddie intervened.

We planned to spa together, brainstorming about our new business.

Serenity remembered Maddie's excitement when they'd talk about the future with millions of followers. How they planned together to write up a proposal for a reality TV show on the home improvement network.

A stab of pain in her temple stopped Serenity.

I can't think about that now. Let the past go. Just as soon as I get more sleep, the headache will go away and then I'll be better.

She pulled her cell phone out of her purse. Adjusting the camera setting to video, she pressed the button.

"Hi, Cleanliness is Next to Godliness community. As you can see I'm in the middle of the forest. I want to walk the Lily Rock labyrinth here today, to be in nature and closer to the divine. What's a labyrinth, you ask? Well let me share what I've learned..."

CHAPTER THIRTY-EIGHT

After Bruce left, Olivia rinsed the coffee mugs. She hummed under her breath until she heard voices from the other room. Sage talking to Star in a conversational voice, as if Star would speak right back.

As Olivia swished her hands under the water, she heard another familiar sound, at least it used to be familiar. A familiar tune and the sound of a violin.

Sage is playing for Star.

Olivia lifted her hands from the sink, barely able to contain her excitement.

A violin, bow on strings, scratched out the familiar sound of Sage tuning. Then there was silence. Followed by a few notes and a pause. Olivia closed her eyes picturing all the times she'd been with Sage performing with Sweet Four O'Clock. How every time her sister took up the tune, she'd feel a familiar rush of anticipation.

The notes floated through the air, followed by more confident bowing, which lifted a phrase, then an entire melody.

I know that song.

Olivia dried her hands. As the melody swelled she tried to name the tune just as Sage began to sing the words. Olivia's spirit lifted. She felt a warmth and then the pricking of a memory.

What is that song...

She stood in the kitchen, mesmerized, searching the deep recess of her memory from long ago.

As if beckoned by the Pied Piper, her feet led her out of the kitchen through the great room. She found herself standing at the bedroom door. Instead of interrupting the music, Olivia stood still to watch Sage.

She played with her eyes closed. Next to her was Star, lying on her back in the middle of the bed. The baby kicked her pink-socked feet in the air, a fist shoved in her mouth. Sage continued to play as Star held one hand up. She stared intently, lifting one finger then the next, as if each one fascinated her more than the last.

Olivia inched closer to sit on the edge of the bed. She gently stroked Star's forehead with the tip of her finger. At that instant the tune finally caught hold of her memory.

That's it!

Olivia knew exactly what would come next.

She began to hum along quietly, her eyes on Star then over to Sage, and then to the fiddle. The melody rose up, all of it this time, securing its place from the past to the very present moment.

When Sage opened her eyes, she smiled and then nodded at Olivia. Finishing the last phrase with a flourish, she spoke.

"I didn't hear you come in."

"Heard you from the kitchen," Olivia replied. "Isn't that a John Denver song?"

Sage nodded. "Yes, it is. Found it on my app this

morning and immediately wanted to pick up the violin. It's been a while."

"Mona used to sing that song to me when I was little. Brings back memories. It's 'For Baby (For Bobby)', right?" Olivia looked over at Star.

"That's right. Funny, because Meadow used to sing it for me too." Sage's nose scrunched up. "I hope Mona was a better singer than Mom," she laughed.

As usual, when the conversation turned to their biological mom, Olivia wasn't sure how much to share. Keenly aware that Sage didn't know their mom, having been adopted when she was an infant. *If I talk about Mona it may upset Sage, since she never knew her. But then again Sage may want to hear about the mom she never knew.*

Can I tell her about Mona and her voice? How she sang to me all the time, especially when I felt sad or sleepy. She's been gone so long, her voice is fading in my head.

"Meadow has her own unique voice," Olivia kidded.

It was common knowledge that Meadow liked to sing, even if she wasn't very good at it. "So you never thought of having a mother-daughter band, I assume," Olivia said. "You know, like The Judds?"

Sage put down her violin on a nearby chair. Tugging at the bow hairs that had come unstrung, she snapped them off, dropping them in the nearby trash. "That's better. In answer to your question, I never considered including Meadow in anything musical. Playing fiddle tunes, let alone another instrument. But she is a great baker. You've got to give her that!"

Picking up the violin, she asked, "Want to join me?" She lifted the instrument to her shoulder, plucking at each string, testing the tuning once again.

"I put the autoharp in my closet downstairs. I can go get it..." Olivia explained.

"Just sing," Sage suggested. "Do you know the words?" She began with the first verse, securing the tune and rhythm. Then she nodded for Olivia to join.

Olivia began to hum. And then the words arrived, as if they'd been waiting for an invitation. Not individually, but in complete phrases. Her voice joined, but she hesitated when Star interrupted with a squeal from the bed.

The baby now kicked her feet against the comforter, squealing at the beginning of each new phrase. Sage kept playing, stepping closer to the bed. She dropped her volume and fiddled faster at the bridge, leaning toward the baby, grinning as she danced along.

Star kicked and chortled, her eyes wide. It was as if she knew the song and wanted to join the band. Olivia inhaled quickly and then sang the next phrase. Sage dipped her chin in appreciation, gliding into a line of harmony as Star kicked her feet with delight.

As Olivia's voice lifted, the familiar words came to her tongue without effort. The song felt like an old friend. Baby Star squealed again, singing her part, along with her mother and aunt. Once they circled the chorus for the third time the squeals, voices, and fiddle made a new song. And then Sage ended the tune, sweeping her violin in the air on the last note.

"So I think we have a new band member," Olivia said immediately.

"Star may be our new headliner before we know it." Sage stepped closer to the bed to run her finger under Star's chin.

Olivia frowned. "How will we break it to Meadow that Star's in and she's still out?"

"Oh, I think Meadow will make an exception for her only granddaughter," Sage said. "Especially one who squeals on pitch. She's already on her way."

After lunch Olivia sat across from Janis Jets. They were the only two in the constabulary break room. "So tell me what he said," Janis urged.

Olivia said, "The Tool said it was Jeff's idea to talk to me. That I'd be able to convey the information to you."

"I've got two problems with that," Jets interrupted. "Secondhand information, no matter if it's from a reliable person as yourself, isn't nearly as good as a one-on-one interview. On the other hand there's a problem with the timing. When did he talk to Jeff? They aren't exactly pals, am I right?"

"He said he ran into Jeff when he was visiting Roxy in her cell. Makes sense since Jeff hangs out there a lot to keep her company."

Jets scowled. "It makes sense except that it doesn't. He said he ran into Jeff yesterday?"

Olivia tried to remember exactly what The Tool had told her. "He implied he'd spoken to Jeff recently. That he stopped by the constabulary to see Roxy. To be polite or something..."

"If that's the case, then I have a real problem with him because I sent Roxy down the hill the night before last. I didn't want to make things harder for my assistant, and I thought a change of scenery might be good for her. She's staying at a halfway facility with an ankle bracelet in minimum security."

Olivia felt a tingle up her spine. "So Bruce lied about the timing. He told me he spoke to her yesterday at the constabulary, after she'd already gone."

"Sounds like it," Jets admitted.

Olivia leaned closer to ask, "Did you really move Roxy because of Brad, or was there another reason you're just not saying?"

Jets nodded. "I'm a little worried for her safety. I think Roxy may be innocent. If she isn't guilty, as I'm beginning to suspect, I want to keep her safe until we have the real killer."

Olivia felt relief. "I think Roxy's innocent too."

"Okay, so we agree." Jets smirked. "But that doesn't explain why The Tool had to make a special trip to talk to you, now does it."

"Not really. He basically lied about Roxy and Jeff."

"Which makes me wonder what else he was lying about. I do know one thing from our research. The Tool has an arrest record. Happened in his late teens. He was not charged because of his age." She stopped as if to gauge Olivia's reaction.

"And..." Olivia held her breath.

"He was involved in the assault of an underaged girl. Four guys thought it would be funny to drug her and take advantage. It was a dare thing. Someone interrupted before she was seriously harmed. But she did press charges. The boys got off with a warning. No one wanted to prosecute boys for being boys."

"I hate that!" Olivia felt her cheeks burn.

"Me too," admitted Jets. "Doesn't happen on my watch, I can tell you. I go over to the high school and lecture all those kids a couple times a year. I make sure they know that I can make myself a huge pest in their lives once I sense trouble. But anyway, The Tool is really a tool. At least he used to be." Jets shrugged.

"And looking guiltier by the minute." Olivia nodded.

"You know, between the two of us? I've seen a pattern over and over. People who get away with lying when they're young think they can keep getting away with lying until someone stops them."

Olivia rested her arms on the table. "I may have forgotten something about my conversation with The Tool. Let me tell you word for word, the best I can remember. Maybe we can pick out the lies from the truth together."

Jets took out her iPad. "Start at the top."

"So Mayor Maguire was digging in the vegetable garden." Olivia sat back in her chair.

"Not about the silly mutt. About when The Tool showed up at your back door! Don't you know anything?"

"Got ya," she said with grin. "Okay, enough about the mayor. The Tool..."

CHAPTER THIRTY-NINE

Wednesday

Olivia sat up in bed. Aware that Michael had left earlier without saying goodbye, she knew what she had to do. No more stalling. She lifted her phone to text Sage.

> Could we talk soon? Maybe this afternoon?

When Sage didn't reply immediately, Olivia suspected her sister was still asleep or tending to Star. Either way, she'd made a move in the right direction. She texted Michael next.

> Sent Sage a text. I'm on it. Please cheer up.

She ended with a smiling happy-face emoji.

Once showered and dressed, she walked upstairs to look for her boots in the usual place by the front door. A quick glance told her that one boot was missing. "Mayor Maguire," she called softly. "Do you have my boot?"

She glanced around the great room, hoping to see the dog or the boot or both. "Mayor Maguire!" she called again, this time through gritted teeth. "I have things to do this morning, I don't want to play hide and seek."

Still no sign of his furry self, nor a bork of response.

"Please tell me you have my boot and that it's still in the house," she pleaded.

Turning around, she looked at the great room sofa. This time she didn't call out. She waited and sure enough, a shaggy head appeared, peeking over the back. Mayor Maguire caught her glaring and immediately dipped out of sight. She heard the scratching of his nails against the cushion.

Olivia inched closer. She used a coaxing voice. "M&M, you're not in trouble. Just give me my boot."

His head instantly reappeared. Wagging his tail, he smiled.

Olivia came closer. She lifted her hand to pat his head and to have a look over the cushions. Her boot had been half-heartedly hidden, the toe poking out from under a throw pillow.

Bending over the back of the sofa, she lifted the pillow. Small pieces of leather stuck on the cushion. Half of the sole had fallen away from the left boot. She picked up what was left, shaking it in Mayor Maguire's face.

"Look what you've done," she accused.

Maguire rested his chin on the back of the sofa looking mournful. Bits of leather still stuck to the sides of his mouth.

"You ate my boot?" she scolded. "Why would you do that? I've been telling you for days, you're too old to still be chewing like a puppy."

When Maguire's dark eyes stared at her, she felt a pang of remorse.

I'm scolding his bad behavior instead of rewarding what he does well.

Olivia walked around the sofa. With a deep sigh she told him, "I need to vacuum this mess and find my spare sneakers. Let's go to town together. Better hurry or I'll be late for my meeting with Janis."

Olivia held the pieces of boot in one hand as she reached under the cushion.

I think I have all the pieces.

Looking down at the chewed boot parts in her hand, she realized that half the sole was missing. A quick glance toward the floor revealed more boot remnants. She bent to gather the pieces.

To her surprise a tiny metal disk fell out of the torn piece of sole and bounced across the dark wood floor. The size of her thumbnail, it looked like a watch battery. She picked it up to examine.

"What's this?" She held it in front of Maguire's face. His ears raised as his tail began to thump against the sofa cushion.

He stood to all four paws, bounding across the floor. He turned in circles, making her laugh. "Bork," he commented. She watched as his tail and rear end disappeared into the kitchen.

"I'm not done with you," she called after him. Holding the piece of metal in her palm, Olivia wondered, *Did Maguire know this was in my boot...*

Sliding the disc into her pocket, she picked up the remains of her boots, taking them downstairs. Depositing them on her dresser, she grabbed her sneakers and then hurried back to the front door.

Maguire forgotten, Olivia got behind the wheel. *I have to show that disc to Janis.* Olivia forced calming thoughts into her mind on the rest of the way to the constabulary.

As she circled Lily Rock looking for an open parking space, her phone rang. She picked it up, put it on speaker, resting it on her knee. "I'm here looking for a place to park," she told Janis.

"This is the big reveal day. The Wiz is supposed to announce the winner of the contest at the main house by 10 a.m.," Jets told her.

"And you want me to meet you at the house or the constabulary?" Olivia asked.

"The constabulary," Jets snapped.

The harshness of her voice made Olivia wonder, *Has she gotten some new evidence?*

Jets continued, "I know what you're thinking. Just forget about it. No singing. No autoharps. We'll get this confession the old-fashioned way, by good police work."

"So you know who killed Maddie?"

Jets cleared her throat. "To be truthful, I still have more unanswered questions than answered ones. I do think whoever wins this contest may be so relieved that the truth may slip out by accident."

"Then you think it's Bruce 'The Tool' Ward? He killed Maddie?"

"You don't?"

Olivia paused to consider. "Whoever did it had no trouble switching the spray bottles, creating a toxic mixture that would kill anyone. Especially in a tight space. The bathroom had no window. It could be Bruce or Serenity, or even the Wiz."

"What about ol' Whitney?" Jets asked.

"The Wiz and Whitney Zimmer strike me as holding

back something important. I think they may know who killed Maddie, but they're afraid to besmirch the reputation of Time to Tidy. They aren't as innocent as they seem."

"I agree," Jets said immediately. "So let's say I look in their direction one more time. I have a funny feeling about that Zimmer woman. She feels familiar to me. I need to stop by the newsstand at the market and pick something up. And in answer to your previous question, we have a couple hours before the big announcement. That will give us time to brainstorm who looks the most guilty."

"Just us?"

"I may invite the Wiz and Whitney to drop in. Come to think of it, I wouldn't mind interrupting the whole announcement plan. That would be so me. Uncaring and determined to get to the truth." Before Olivia could tell her about the discovery in her boot, she clicked the phone off.

She finally found a parking space on Main Street near Thyme Out. A man at the mercantile swept in front of his shop. By eight o'clock doors would be opening for early tourist shoppers. The bakery light welcome sign had already been switched on.

People were lined up outside waiting for a seat. Olivia stopped her car to wait for a man pulling out of his parking space. She looked longingly at the people in line.

I don't have time to get a muffin today. Janis expects me.

She checked her phone for other messages.

Neither Michael nor Sage had sent a reply. Feeling pulled in multiple directions, Olivia sighed. Then she checked her pocket to make certain the small disc was still there.

Olivia fingered the disc in her pocket as she entered the constabulary. She felt the impending move and the potential trial of Roxanne Grossman weighing heavily on her heart. So she gave herself a pep talk, knowing that the collision between her personal life and her consultant life were the cause of her anxiety.

We're going to figure this out. It's been nearly a week. Then remembering Michael's sad face from the night before, she sighed.

"Hey, Olivia," Brad greeted her. Before she could say hello, she heard the inner door click open. "The boss is waiting for you."

"Hey, Brad." Olivia walked through the open door.

"I'm back here," came Jets's voice from the break room.

Olivia found her sitting with a mug of coffee and her iPad. Jets took a sip and stared at the document on her device. To Olivia's surprise a familiar magazine lay on the table. *Reading a magazine—that's really casual for Janis.*

"Are you spending time at work browsing *Variety*?" She walked past the table toward the coffee pot. At the counter she filled a mug and returned to sit across from Janis, who had closed her iPad to thumb through the magazine.

Jets's head hovered as she inspected one particular page. She leaned closer and then raised her head. Shoving the open magazine across the table, she said, "Take a look. See if you recognize anyone."

Olivia put down her coffee mug. Before glancing at the page, she turned to the front to check out the cover.

Just like the one Whitney Zimmer had on her coffee table.

Olivia thumbed through the pages. The waft of a flowery perfume met her nose. Johnny Depp, looking handsome and rugged, posed for the ad.

She held up the page for a sniff.

"Are you air-kissing Depp or doing a scratch and sniff? Just go to the page," Jets said.

Olivia deliberately ignored her, taking another sniff. *I'm obsessed with this smell. Maybe I can get some for Michael on his next birthday. Probably would cost a fortune. I wonder if he'd wear it?*

Thumbing past an ad for a celebrity favorite handbag, Olivia paused to look at the model. *Jennifer Aniston for Tom Ford. She never ages.* Then Jets interrupted again.

"Keep flipping pages. Stop at the advertisement for Century Real Estate."

Finally Olivia did as she was told.

"Good. Now take a closer look," Jets instructed. "Pretend it's an Easter egg hunt hand your life depends on finding a golden egg." Jets's voice raised in her excitement.

Olivia stared more closely at the glossy page, determined to discover what Jets already knew. Her eyes drifted over the entire ad, returning to the woman who posed provocatively next to the Sold sign. She wore a formfitting black pantsuit. Red hair waved to her shoulders. Trendy sunglasses covered her eyes. Her arm rested against the signpost in an alluring way, as if she were waiting to be picked up for a Saturday night date.

Olivia ran a finger over the page.

I'm not seeing anything of interest here.

She blinked to try again. Taking a closer look at the advertisement, she read the sign. Century Real Estate. She knew that was a well-known Los Angeles company. Underneath the logo was a webpage link and a phone number.

Jets's fingers tapped impatiently on the table.

I'll take a closer look at the models.

An unremarkable couple stood in the background on a grassy knoll. They held hands. Looking more like brother and sister, both with dark hair, slim builds, dressed in jeans and button-up shirts, they smiled into the camera. A black and white dog on a leash also looked into the camera. He looked so perfect, he seemed computer generated.

"So a happy family advertisement?" Olivia's forehead wrinkled. "Am I supposed to be surprised?"

"Take another look. At the realtor this time." Jets's eyes narrowed. She tapped her finger on her iPad impatiently.

Olivia glanced down at the magazine ad once again.

The redheaded realtor pointed to the Sold sign. She looked young and professional. Olivia's eyes ran down her body to her shoes. Three-inch black high heels. Her pencil skirt had been hemmed to touch the top of her knees, making her legs look long and slim.

"Am I supposed to be checking out her outfit?" Olivia asked Jets. She glanced more closely at the realtor's white blouse, which peeked through the front of the jacket. The collar had been neatly arranged over the lapel.

"Don't be ridiculous. Look at her face," Jets snapped.

Olivia's eyes traveled up from the blazer to inspect the realtor's face. Though the hair wasn't particularly distinctive, her smile felt familiar. Big white teeth, obviously straightened and bleached at some point, stretched across her mouth.

Hey, wait a minute!

Olivia looked closer at the photo again. This time her eyes focused on the one hand resting against her skirt. Bright red nail polish shone from four fingers; the thumb had been tucked beneath the palm. A large ring, a gigantic sapphire set with diamonds all around, glittered in the sunlight.

I know where I've seen that ring before.

Aware of the resemblance, Olivia only needed to look at the woman's face again. The hair was different, probably a wig. But the smile and the facial structure and nose belonged to none other than Whitney Zimmer.

Jets scoffed. "You see it now?"

"It's got to be her. Plus how many women have that huge ring?"

"Take the wig off and replace it with a blonde one with long wavy hair, and you'll know for sure," Jets advised.

Olivia inhaled sharply. "Got it. Whitney Zimmer, the one and only—"

Jets interrupted. "Once you see it, you can't unsee it, right? So I called around. Had to connect with Century first. They told me to call the talent agency where they found the model. Century wanted to sell me a house, but I told them I already had one. Not a castle like some people but good enough. Anyway after that they were happy to answer my questions.

"So that real estate woman in the advertisement? She's an actress, hired by Century. Her name is not Zimmer.

She's Jennifer Lansbury, part-time actress and part-time advertising model."

Olivia felt a ripple of excitement travel up her spine. "So do you think the Wiz hired Jennifer to play the part of Whitney Zimmer? No wonder she and the Wiz kept trying to hide that magazine when we were interviewing her the other day."

"She was probably checking out her photo shoot when we got there," Jets said. "I don't know why the Wiz needed to hire a stand-in, but I'd sure like to hear him explain." Her phone pinged, indicating a text. Jets held it out for Olivia to read the screen. It came from Brad.

Stanley Weyland is here.

Olivia heard the door down the hall open. She and Janis stared at each other listening to the footsteps coming closer.

"I've arrived on time, I hope?" The Wiz stood in the doorway, a smile on his lips.

"Where's Whitney. I wanted her to come too," Janis stated briskly.

"She had to leave Lily Rock. Urgent business. A problem she had to attend to in the desert. Unless you want to detain her specifically, I can answer any of your questions."

Jets stood. She looked Stanley over from head to foot, taking her time in sizing him up. "I got your number, Wiz. I know what you're up to. The problem is I need you to explain why. Hear it in your own words." When he didn't flinch, she continued.

"Why would you want to hire some model to play the role of Whitney Zimmer? Unless of course you're protecting your employer, maybe sent her out of the country because she killed Maddox Hall."

The smile on the Wiz's face vanished. His skin, drained of color, defined the wrinkles around his mouth and eyes. Then his hand clutched at his throat.

"Have a seat and start explaining." Jets pulled out a chair. "Before I arrest you for obstructing justice and accessory to murder."

CHAPTER FORTY-ONE

The Wiz looked at Olivia, then back at Janis. "I can explain."

Jets opened her iPad. "So get on with it. I don't have all day."

Olivia reached into her pocket. Finally connecting the small disc from her boot with the man who sat at the table. She slid the disc across the table to Janis. "Mayor Maguire found this in my boot. I think it might be a tracker and that he," she pointed to the Wiz, "put it there the morning of the murder. Remember that first day, how we had to take off our shoes and line them up against the wall..."

Jets held up the disc to have a closer view. "Yep, looks like a tracker. You can buy these off the internet now." She glared at the Wiz. "So Wiz, why were you so intent on tracking Olivia Greer?"

"I'm not saying a word without my attorney being present," he said, a note of defiance coming to his voice.

"Is that so." Jets picked up her cell phone. "Brad, come escort this guy to a cell. I'm done playing games." She clicked off her phone. Then she nodded at Olivia. "You might as well find something else to do. I think I've just solved this case."

Olivia was surprised. Before she could ask, her cell phone vibrated on the table. A quick glance told her it was a text from Cayenne.

> Could you come up to the labyrinth as soon as possible? I need your help.

> Be there shortly.

CHAPTER FORTY-TWO

Driving up the hill as fast as her Ford could go, Olivia arrived in the labyrinth parking lot. Walking hurriedly from her parked car, she pulled up short, surprised at what she saw.

Cayenne sat on the visitors' bench with none other than Serenity McFee.

Serenity looked very upset. Her body slumped over, face buried in her hands. Olivia's stomach tightened. Before coming closer she looked at Cayenne.

Her large hand rested on the back of the bench. She nodded to Olivia.

Edging closer, Olivia stopped a foot away from the bench. She waited for Serenity to look up. When she didn't, Olivia opened the conversation from that distance. "I haven't seen you in days. So you found the labyrinth..."

Her voice sound like a genuine greeting, as if she'd just happened upon an old friend. But even that did not draw a response from Serenity.

I wonder what's going on here?

"Serenity and I have been talking for quite a while. She's

walked the labyrinth and I think she has something she wants to get off her chest. I suggested you'd be the person to speak to." Cayenne spoke calmly.

Olivia nodded. She pointed to the end of the bench. "Mind if I sit down?"

With head still bowed, Serenity's hands kneaded in her lap. This time Olivia didn't wait for an invitation. She sat down anyway. Inhaling deeply, Olivia waited. Willing herself to be open to whatever Serenity had to say.

For several minutes no one spoke. Cayenne stepped away from the bench. She didn't say goodbye, but she quietly disengaged. Standing close enough to hear the conversation, but not close enough to feel intrusive.

Olivia, aware of her breath, remained silent. Her heart began to warm, a sign of her willingness to listen.

Finally Serenity detached her hands. Laying them on her thighs, she straightened her back and then cleared her throat. Turning partially toward Olivia, she nodded, acknowledging her presence.

Her quiet voice began to speak. "I'd heard that Lily Rock had an outdoor labyrinth and I've always been interested. I heard from a friend. She doesn't live here or anything. Just a weekend visitor. Anyway she explained to me how taking slow intentional steps helped clear her mind, making her feel closer to God." Her voice grew stronger as she spoke.

"So I was getting antsy waiting for Whitney to announce the contest winner and I decided to come up and see the labyrinth for myself." She pointed to her cell phone. "Plus I wanted to shoot a video for my followers. Since no one was here, I just started walking really slow. I made it to the middle. Well, here. You can see on the video I just posted."

Holding up her phone, Serenity pushed Play.

Olivia watched. In the video, Serenity held her phone aloft as she walked. Extended on a selfie stick, the path, outlined by rock, was visible in the background. She spoke at each step but then grew quiet. Only the sound of crows cawing in the distance were audible. Then the phone began to shake, right before the camera focused on Serenity's crying face.

She sobbed into the camera, tears streaming, her nose moist. There was no attempt to hide her emotions from the camera.

Taking the phone back, Serenity shut off the video.

"So you can see something just clicked inside me. It was as if my heart was going to break. I started to cry. I never cry. Well maybe I used to, but I stopped when I was young. It never did any good."

"But you kept filming?"

"My followers like it when I show them my feelings." Her voice sounded defensive and brittle.

Olivia shifted the conversation. "What do you mean it never did any good?"

"I would cry when I was younger, but it didn't stop my brother. We were raised by my dad after Mom abandoned us. He'd be at work all day. My brother would be in charge when we'd get home from school. He was five years older and made my life a living hell."

"Older brothers do tease," Olivia said softly.

"It wasn't just him." Her voice rose. "His friends too. When he invited guys over he'd lock me in my room before they got there. They'd kick my door and terrorize me. Threaten to come in and do things to me. I had no idea what they meant at first. But my imagination went wild."

Olivia knew the horrors of her own imagination. When

she was overly tired especially. And then the dreams. She had no trouble relating to the young Serenity being afraid of the older boys. "Did you tell your father about the boys?"

"He didn't care. You've got to understand, once Dad got over my mom running away, he'd go to work and then come home for as little time as possible. Then he'd go out at night. Mostly to drink. To the bar. He didn't want us to wake up and go look for him so he put locks on our doors. On the outside so that he could keep us in.

"He always said it was to keep us safe. I didn't mind so much if Craig was also locked in his room. But then when Dad was at work, Craig would make a game of shoving me in my room. He'd open and close the door, pretending to let me out but then slam it in my face. After I got really upset, he'd just lock me in. I'd be there for hours. Sometimes missing dinner. He'd only open the door when he heard Dad's car in the garage."

"So your dad didn't even talk to Craig?"

"He didn't do anything. By the time he'd had a few drinks, all he cared about was that we were there when he got home. I tried to tell him. 'Boys will be boys,' he'd say. I hate that expression!" Her voice hissed with resentment. "No matter how much I cried and yelled, it didn't do any good."

Olivia watched Serenity's hands clench and unclench. "Those must be horrible memories. I am sorry."

"No, I got over that!" Serenity snapped. "I went from weak to strong. It took me a while to figure things out, but I changed. I stopped crying, for one. And then instead of cowering in my closet, I started figuring out ways to get back at Craig. It took some time, but I snuck a baseball bat into my room when he wasn't looking. Just knowing it was there, under my bed, made me feel bold. At least I had a plan just in case they broke down the door and tried to hurt me for real."

The words tumbled out of Serenity's mouth. She continued to speak with a fierce intensity. "When I stopped acting afraid, Craig stopped tormenting me. Oh, he'd still lock me in every afternoon, but I didn't care. I stored some snacks on my closet shelf. I had my defense weapon under the bed. My grades at school started to improve because I used the time for homework.

"And then one day, when I'd finished my homework, I started looking around for something to do. My room was a mess. Clothes on the floor. Stuff falling out of drawers. My desk was sticky from the candy I left half eaten. And then because I had nothing else to do, I decided that I'd make a game of cleaning up.

"The tidying made me forget that I was trapped." She nodded. "After that I made a plan to tidy every day. I began organizing my closet, you know, throwing clothes on my bed and sorting. I'd put stuff in bags for the trash, old games and stuff. I forgot about Craig. I forgot about being angry and helpless. I started looking forward to keeping my stuff organized.

"And then I blew Craig's mind because right after school I'd voluntarily go in my room and stay there with the door closed. I'd always find something that needed to be cleaned or sorted. Eventually he stopped locking my door."

"I always wondered what drew tidy people to be who they were," Olivia said. "I mean, I'm pretty organized because my mom taught me how important it was to discard and keep things simple." She paused and then added, "Your story is sad but also inspirational."

Serenity agreed. "Once I decided not to be afraid, everything just fell into place. I haven't been afraid since."

Olivia doubted the truth of that statement. The woman she found on the bench looked anything but unafraid. Terrified would be a more apt description of her spirit.

She seems okay now, but when I walked up she was barely aware of me. And Cayenne texted for a reason. There's more going on here.

"So that was your way out. You stopped thinking about the abuse and occupied yourself with things you could accomplish." Olivia coaxed her to keep talking.

Serenity looked over her shoulder toward Cayenne. Then she cleared her throat. "Now I clean whenever I feel upset. I keep myself really busy with my work and extra tidying at home. Until this week..." Her voice dropped. "This week everything fell apart."

CHAPTER FORTY-THREE

"So what happened this week?" Olivia prompted.

Serenity picked up where she'd left off. "As soon as the competitors were announced for this year's Time to Tidy competition, Maddie called me. We got together and hatched a plan.

"Both of us were a bit bored with our companies. We wanted to do another start-up, this time both of us collaborating. It's exhausting to be posting all the time and running a business. We wanted some free time and thought being partners would make it easier.

"Plus there was the Time to Tidy cash prize. We felt pretty sure that one of us would beat The Tool. And since he was known to be sneaky and undermine other competitors, we figured we would watch each other's back."

"Sounds like a great plan," Olivia said hesitantly.

"Until the night before the competition kicked off," Serenity said. "Maddie waited until the last minute to tell me that she didn't want to partner up with me."

Olivia felt her gut clench. "That must have hurt."

"You have no idea. I was enraged that she was backing

out at the last minute. And I suspected why. She'd changed her mind and decided to collaborate with The Tool instead. He must have offered her a better deal. A bigger percentage of the profits once they collaborated. Like I said, he was known to be really sneaky.

"I kind of knew something was up even before we got to the competition. Maddie started refusing to call me back and she ignored my texts. Then we arrived in Lily Rock and she forced me out the night before the competition began. She claimed our plan was only tentative and that I must have gotten the wrong idea. And then I was stuck, with no one to help me."

Olivia felt queasy. The angry tone in Serenity's voice alerted her that there was more to the story.

Serenity continued, "So after huddling in my room and feeling helpless, I woke up at two in the morning. I knew what to do. Maddie thought she could get away with stringing me along, opening and closing the promise of a partnership in my face. She knew no one would listen to me when I tried to complain. I'd been there before.

"I knew that the Wiz, just like Dad, wouldn't help. If I told him our original plan he'd just ignore me or most likely disqualify me. Maddie could claim that I'd made up the whole thing. The Wiz would believe her over me."

"So you decided to get revenge?" Olivia said.

"I went to the janitor's pantry really early. Before the sun rose. Everyone else was asleep. All I had to do was make an extra tote; I filled the bottles with bleach and vinegar, leaving out the other two chemicals. Then I made a duplicate label with Maddie's name. I knew once she began to spray in the bathroom, she'd mix the chemicals."

"What did you do with the original tote?" Olivia asked.

"I took it back to my room. That way I could keep it

with me. Originally I planned to leave it in the bathroom and take away the other one before Maddie was found."

Olivia felt a triple rush of fear run down her spine. "So you didn't plan on killing her?"

"No, I just wanted to make her sick. She told me before that she had trouble smelling things. So I figured she'd do a lot of spraying and pouring before she'd feel the effects. By the time she inhaled the toxic mixture, she'd be sick and have to drop out of the competition."

"Did you know there wasn't a window in that bathroom?"

"I'd been in there earlier. I did know there was no window." Serenity's hands began to knead in her lap again. She gazed at the dirt in front of her without blinking.

"I didn't want Maddie to die at first, that came later. I only wanted her to feel what I felt when she pretended we never had a plan. Afraid. Alone. Angry.

"So that morning, right at six o'clock, I took both totes and went to my cabin. The Tool saw me right away. He was my alibi. Kind of ironic, don't you think?" Serenity smiled, looking satisfied.

Olivia remembered the crime scene, how the door had been locked from the inside. She knew there was something more to the story. "Why didn't Maddie run out as soon as she realized she was having trouble breathing?"

"Right after The Tool said hi, he went into his cabin to get to work. I took that time to circle back to the main house. I figured he was too busy cleaning to see me go."

"So I assume you brought the original tote with you, to exchange with the other one?"

"Nope. I forgot. I was in a hurry." Serenity's eyes narrowed. "That was a mistake, I guess. Anyway...

"When I got back to the house I parked out of sight. I

came in the front door to avoid the caterer. Once inside I heard Roxy humming in the kitchen, I sprinted upstairs. When I poked my head into the bathroom I saw Maddie working. She didn't know I was there because she was coughing and cleaning the floor. I ducked back out and shut the door. She must have heard me because the knob began to turn. I didn't think, really. I just held onto the knob from the other side. She was at my mercy. I'm pretty strong, you know. All the yelling and inhaling only made it worse. The poisonous gas sucked into her lungs. For once, I was the one in charge."

To Olivia's horror, Serenity smiled as if remembering something pleasant.

"I got to be my brother for once. The one in control on the other side of the door," Serenity said with satisfaction.

"After a while there was one last moan. Once she was quiet I opened the door and looked inside. I decided then and there I wanted to confuse whoever found her. Maybe get people to think she'd committed suicide. So I locked the door from the inside before closing it again."

"Did you check to see if she was dead?"

"Nope. I didn't care. Once she stopped resisting I was done. Plus I had my own work to do back at my cabin. I was already behind The Tool. I had to get going."

"So you didn't feel any remorse?" Olivia's heart thumped against her chest.

"Not really. Maddox tricked me." A half smile came to her lips. Then she added, "Until I started to walk that labyrinth. I hadn't even thought about Maddie. Once Roxy confessed I figured I was in the clear."

"What exactly happened as you were walking the labyrinth, besides the emotional display on your video?" Olivia's jaw tightened with anger.

I'm sitting next to a cold-blooded killer.

"It all came flooding back. How I switched the cleaning chemicals and how I held the door shut. And finally how I didn't even check to see if Maddox was dead. I couldn't take those slow steps on the path that everyone talks about. I walked faster and faster, talking at first, then crying. Within minutes over two thousand people sent me a thumbs-up. Then I collapsed when I reached the center. I couldn't even move until that tall woman found me. She brought me to the bench and called you."

Serenity glanced around. "She's gone. What's her name? I don't know why she called you. But I'm glad the whole story is out. At least I can breathe a bit better." She held her hand over her chest, inhaling deeply.

Olivia eased her phone out of her purse, explaining in a calm voice, "I'm going to call Officer Jets right now. I think she'll want to hear your story. She'll also want to read you your rights. Do you know an attorney?"

Serenity stared straight ahead as if she'd not heard a word.

Olivia texted Janis.

> Serenity McFee just confessed to murdering Maddox.

> Where are you?

> At the labyrinth.

> Be right there.

Olivia double-clicked and tapped a thumbs-up emoji on Janis's final text. Putting her phone away, she sat in silence with Serenity. Her nerves prickled like ants scooting over her arms and legs. Yet she didn't move from her spot.

I hope Cay is close by.

Olivia took a deep breath. To her relief she heard someone approach from behind the bench. She turned slightly to look over her shoulder. Cayenne held her finger to her lips. Close enough, she placed her strong hands on both of Olivia's shoulders as if to offer comfort.

Warmth traveled down her body, pushing away her fear. Olivia heard a vehicle approach. Janis Jets's truck pulled into the parking lot.

Cayenne squeezed her fingers but did not remove her hands. As Janis approached the bench, she held her hand to the back of her blazer. Within earshot, Jets got right to the point.

"Serenity McFee, you're under arrest. I am going to read you your rights. Then I will put cuffs on you. And then we'll take a ride to the constabulary."

Serenity stared at the dirt, her fingers working against the fabric of her T-shirt.

Olivia stood, her legs trembling underneath her.

"You have the right to remain silent..." Jets began.

CHAPTER FORTY-FOUR

Olivia sat in Janis Jets's empty office. She closed her eyes, trying to recall everything that Serenity had confessed. When she heard the door open behind her, she braced herself as Janis strode into the room.

"So Serenity is in custody." Jets pulled out her chair to sit down on the other side of the desk. She looked satisfied.

Probably happy she's got Serenity behind bars.

When Olivia didn't say anything, Jets smiled. "Okay, Nancy Drew. Tell me what you've got and I'll tell you if it matters." She eased back in her desk chair.

"Okay, to be clear, Serenity confessed that she murdered Maddox," Olivia began. "That's the bottom line. As far the details go, I'm still reeling because her account was so bone-chilling. How she held the door so that Maddie was trapped inside. I can't believe she did that, listening to Maddie struggle." Olivia's eyes glistened with tears.

"And then," she continued, "Serenity had a plan all along. She switched out the totes to conceal how she'd put the vinegar and bleach in the bottles."

"So that's premeditated murder." Jets scowled.

"She said something about just wanting to make Maddox sick, but I didn't believe it for a second. Even after she held the door, she just walked away. She said she didn't even think about what she'd done until the labyrinth." Olivia shook her head.

"That's just bizarre," Jets said. "Serenity seems so calm whenever I speak to her. Talk about compartmentalizing. She's an expert."

"I don't know if Serenity will tell you what she told me, but I'm still processing how her confession made me feel. She was so detached." Olivia shuddered. "How awful and also frightening for Maddie. Imagine the terror she must have felt in those last minutes."

Jets laced her fingers behind her head, leaning back in her chair. A thoughtful expression came over her face. "I arrested Serenity and put her into a cell. That's obviously where she belongs."

"Will she tell you what she told me?" Olivia asked.

"She didn't say a word as soon as I slapped the cuffs on her. Clammed right up. Maybe she'll be more responsive later. Jail does that to people. But I probably should call Doc Martinez to have a look at her. Just to make sure she isn't, you know, what's the word we use for it now? I know. Disassociating." Jets scoffed.

"Don't make fun of her," Olivia objected. "I could feel her terrorized spirit, right or wrong. She believed she was deliberately persecuted and lied to by Maddox."

"I'm not making fun of her," Jets said. "This isn't easy for me either, you know. Humor is how I maintain my sanity and detach emotionally from murderous ways." Jets looked up, then back at Olivia. "Okay, I guess I was making fun of her. Sorry not sorry."

Jets dropped her arms, placing her hands on the desk.

"The truth is that I don't get to decide who is justified in killing another human being. It's a good thing too. I'd find everyone guilty." She glowered. "Either way, according to what you heard, Serenity had a premeditated plan to make Maddie ill and push her out of the competition. And then when she had a chance to call 911, she closed the door and held it shut.

"I have to accept your report of the confession until she starts talking." A slight smile came to the corner of Jets's mouth. "But between us, I am not exactly relying on what she told you."

Olivia was surprised by that. "Why's that?"

"I have some evidence that just came in." Jets turned to her desk computer. She clicked and then read, "According to this, Serenity's fingerprints were not on the totes, they'd been wiped clean. But she forgot something. They found prints on the labels and the label maker. The one in the janitor's pantry in the kitchen."

"Will that be enough to convict her?" Olivia asked.

"I'd prefer her confession. But that evidence is enough to arrest her and keep her behind bars for now." Jets clicked to put the computer into sleep mode. "The rest is up to attorneys and judges."

Olivia felt her stomach flip-flop. "I have to admit I'm relieved. I wanted to make a recording of her confession, but it was so quick and unexpected."

"Did Cayenne happen to overhear?" Jets asked. "She could corroborate your testimony if it comes to that."

Olivia shook her head. "I don't know for sure. I think Cay may have been hovering close by. She came right out as soon as Serenity went quiet." Olivia remembered the sense of calm that came over her as soon as Cayenne put her hands on her shoulders.

"I'll ask her later," Jets said. Olivia watched as Janis typed into her iPad.

"I do have my own confession," Olivia interrupted.

Jets put down her device. "What's that?"

"I thought the Wiz was our murderer. He put that tracker in my boot and he hired an actor to play Whitney Zimmer."

The corner of Jets's mouth turned up. "He fooled me too. I talked to him in his cell after you left in such a hurry. He showed me what I missed. She pulled a paper and pen out of her desk. "It was surprisingly simple what he was hiding, and I'm a bit embarrassed I didn't notice it," Jets explained as she scribbled.

"If you write this name, Whitney Isabella Zimmer, on a paper, and then circle her initials? What do you have?" She slid the paper toward Olivia.

Olivia felt her heart skip a beat. "It's W.I.Z. Her initials are..."

"An acronym. Yep, the Wiz is Whitney Isabella Zimmer. He made her up and then pretended she existed for his brand."

"So she never was the boss. It was the Wiz the whole time? I never put that together!" Olivia exclaimed.

"He worked so hard to hide that fact. When it came right down to it he enjoyed pulling the wool over our eyes." Jets shook her head. "I always thought calling himself the Wiz was a bit much."

Olivia smirked. "Think about it. Right under our noses.

.Jets burst out laughing. "So we were both fooled."

"But what I'm wondering is what about the tracker he put in my boot? I'm still confused why he felt the need to do that."

"He told me that he'd heard about your reputation as a

police consultant. He didn't want to be found out, so he put the tracker in your boot to make sure he knew where you were and could keep an eye out. He wanted to stop you from asking a lot of nosey questions."

Olivia sighed. "I saw him on that first day in the SUV. He has a pattern of driving fast and passing other vehicles, barely missing oncoming traffic. I thought Whitney Zimmer was in the vehicle."

"He told me that he drove past you that first day just to distract the police. In case we'd wonder where Whitney had gone. If you remember, I did ask him right away. He started deflecting right away too."

"He was kind of breathless when he answered the door that morning," Olivia said. "He must have driven around and come back to the house from a back road." She looked thoughtful.

"And then I saw the SUV at the labyrinth." Her eyes grew wide. "I kind of recognized it. But then he showed up unexpectedly at the helipad and," she laughed, "again at the Box Store. He made sure to keep me distracted with his fast driving and swerving into traffic. Gave me such a fright each time. Eventually I thought it was Whitney following me in that SUV, only I could never identify who was behind the wheel. The Wiz did a good job of keeping me off balance, I'll give him that." Olivia paused in thought. "But what about that woman we tried to follow at the Refuge?"

Jets explained. "The Wiz finally admitted to me that he dressed as a woman wearing a wig. He knew you'd be there because of the tracker. Apparently he had a wig and some clothes that he'd wear when necessary to keep up the charade. Once he figured out where you were heading, he figured he could put you off for good. So he donned his disguise and then slipped in the side door to sit at the bar.

The fact that I was there with Cookie only made things better. He could distract both of us with one appearance."

"That Wiz is clever," Olivia admitted. "But not the murderer."

"He was just protecting his brand," Jets said.

"No wonder no one could say they'd met Whitney face-to-face," Olivia added. Jets looked glum. "Don't tell anyone we were so dense, okay?"

Olivia giggled. "Our secret is safe with me." She looked at her phone. "So is the announcement ceremony still going forward?"

"That's what Stanley told me. The winner is obvious, but the show must go on."

Olivia sat forward in her chair. "Well, if we're done here, I have to get home." She stood to leave.

"How's the packing coming along?" Jets asked.

"I have the boxes. I'm hoping to talk to Sage."

"Sounds complicated. You can stop talking now. I don't want to be part of your family drama." Jets rolled her eyes. "I've got my own problems. I've been on edge about this baby thing and Cooks is tired of my attitude. That's what he told me this morning."

Olivia couldn't believe what she was hearing. Janis rarely spoke about her personal issues. "I noticed you were more crabby than usual," she admitted.

"Yah, that's because Cookie is all over me about having a family. Now he thinks adoption is the answer. Imagine me. With a kid. Playing all nice." Janis shrugged. She turned to her computer, effectively ending the conversation.

Olivia did not let Janis's dismissal stop her. "For what it's worth, I think you and Cookie would make very good parents. Adopting isn't a terrible idea. There are lots of kids who need a good home."

"Whatever," mumbled Janis.

Olivia left her office feeling proud of herself. She let her thoughts go to Janis Jets.

On the one hand I need to stand up to Janis more. On the other hand I need to disregard her opinions about my personal life.

Like Michael building me a castle. Please.

THE NEXT DAY

"Hey, you two are packing." Michael stood in the doorway to the office. Sage, bent over a box, waved her hand in the air by way of a greeting. Olivia glanced up.

"Sage is helping. She has time since the baby is napping." The television blared in the background, a man announcing the weather.

Michael's eyebrows raised at Olivia "Can you take a quick break? I'd like to talk to you for a minute." He walked out of the door, giving her a chance to put one more book in the box before following him.

"I'll be right back," she told Sage, speaking loudly over the television.

Michael waited on the other side of the office door, leaning his back against the wall. "Do I assume that you and Sage talked and she's on board for our move?" His voice sounded more hopeful than it had in days.

Olivia smirked. "I am happy to share that I've recovered from my damsel-in-distress, captive-in-a-castle, need-to-let-down-my-hair nightmare." She was careful to sound playful, in an attempt to match his good mood.

"Good. I'm happy about that. But tell me more. How did the conversation go?"

"I got home late last night. After deconstructing Serenity McFee's confession with Janis. I found Sage waiting up for me."

"The news that Janis got the killer is already around town, at least at the hardware store," Michael admitted.

"Yep. Serenity confessed to me. Long story. It involved Cayenne too." Olivia watched his eyebrows raise again.

"I didn't hear that part at the hardware store," he said.

"Anyway, after Janis locked up Serenity McFee, I had this kind of insight."

"About..."

"How I don't need to take Janis so seriously all the time. Especially when it comes to my personal life. She's the expert in all things concerning the constabulary and her job, but she's not the boss of my personal life."

"Which means?" He looked puzzled.

"Janis's nonsense about the castle and all of that? Well it isn't my opinion. I love our new home," she said with a smile.

The look of relief on Michael's face made her heart melt. "But that's not all," she said. "On the drive home I realized that I am not the boss of Sage and Star. And maybe my fears aren't about them at all.

"So when I found Sage waiting up for me, I knew it was time for my long-postponed talk. It seems she's also wanted to talk to me about the move. Only it's been hard to work around the baby's schedule.

"We really don't get much of a chance to hang out anymore," Olivia added and then continued. "First we set up a band rehearsal schedule for the spring. That felt so good."

"That sounds great," Michael said, "And then..."

"I asked her right out if she felt unhappy with our move."

"Was she upset?" A look of apprehension returned to his face. Olivia realized with a start, *He doesn't want to upset Sage either.*

"She looked more surprised than upset. So I told her how I felt terrible leaving her alone. And then I talked about growing up with a single mom and how people kind of talked behind my back and gossiped. I told her that's how Marla and I met. We were both the girls without fathers."

"And..."

Olivia's expression changed. She felt her happiness overwhelm her, to the point tears filled her eyes. "So I got it rather wrong, it turns out." She swiped at her eyes. "I assumed Sage, having been raised by a single mother, would not want to raise her baby by herself. I just assumed she felt the same as I did growing up."

"Keep going..." Michael looked intrigued as Olivia wiped away another tear.

"It turns out that Sage always loved being raised by Meadow. She never worried about not having her father around. In fact she was never even teased. No one in Lily Rock thought anything of it, that she and Meadow lived together without a man in the house.

"In Sage's opinion, the entire town helped raise her. The 'it takes a village' idea. She's so okay with raising Star on her own. Oh sure, she still has moments over Beats's death. But for the most part, since the birth, she's not looked back."

Michael instantly reached for Olivia, pulling her closer for an embrace. "Well okay then," he said in her ear. "You got Sage's blessing."

She buried her face in his chest.

They held each other for a moment, Olivia aware of the steady heartbeat beneath his soft flannel shirt. Then she leaned back in his arms. "Not only did I get her blessing, but Sage is helping me pack."

Michael bent his head forward to kiss her mouth. "I'm sorry I've been so overly sensitive lately. Your feelings about Sage, well you only just found each other recently. I can't imagine how that would feel. I didn't want to interfere with the sister thing."

She wrapped her arms around his middle, giving him a big hug. "I felt awful when I hurt your feelings." She buried her face in his chest again, inhaling the clean shirt smell, appreciating the tinge of soap and musky aftershave.

"Hey, you gotta see this," Sage shouted from inside the office. Olivia planted a quick kiss to his chin and hurried back into the room. The first thing she heard was a familiar name broadcast over the television.

"They're talking about Time to Tidy," she called to Michael.

All three of them stood in front of the screen to watch as the Wiz held out an oversized check in front of the camera.

"We're happy to announce this year's Time to Tidy winner, a man who is no stranger to social media. Bruce 'The Tool' Ward!" The Wiz waited for people to stop applauding. Then he stepped back to reveal Bruce "The Tool" Ward's big smile.

"On behalf of Whitney Zimmer and the Time to Tidy organization, we look forward to working with you in the very near future." The Wiz nodded to Bruce and then clapped him on the shoulder.

They both smiled toward the cameras. It was the Wiz's turn to step back, giving the winner his chance to preen before the audience.

The Tool looked particularly pleased with himself, holding the check above his head with buffed and tanned arms.

Olivia grabbed the remote to switch off the television. "I can't believe there was one dead contestant and another person arrested for the murder and that he got the prize after all."

"I, for one, am glad that investigation is over." Michael pointed to the stack of boxes. "How about I tape more boxes before I go. Then you guys can keep on packing."

A baby's wail began to rev up, as Olivia smiled.

"I have to feed Star," Sage said, dropping a book into the box. She stepped around Olivia and then stopped. "So are you two still babysitting tonight? I have that date with Luis, you remember."

"Yes, we are," Olivia answered immediately. "So tell me... You and Luis seem to be getting along really well lately."

Michael grinned at her and then assumed a look of nonchalance.

"Oh, Luis isn't the only one," Sage replied. "I'm also seeing Jeff. He's great with Star and so conveniently located." She nodded toward the window where his cabin could be seen.

"Once we're out of here you could consider having a roommate. Are you thinking of renting the room or inviting a live-in to stay?" Michael asked.

Sage's face drew a blank. "Never thought of that. I might. Depends on Star and her schedule. I have to be careful who gets close to her. In fact, I'm not that interested in anything serious until she's a bit older. I do love my privacy. Gotta go." She put down a book, heading toward the sound of Star's cry.

Once Sage left, Michael took Olivia by the hand. "Could I interrupt one more time?"

"I have to keep packing." She playfully tried to tug her hand away, which made him hold on harder. "So do I assume we are no longer on matchmaker duty?"

"Looks like Sage can handle her own life without me." Olivia sounded only slightly apologetic.

"Are you upset?" He leaned closer.

"Actually no. I'm very excited about our move and the new house. I mean, what a spectacular place, where we get to live. You are the best boyfriend ever!"

He pulled her closer. "Now that's the woman I've been missing. The full-on let's-be-happy, go-take-on-the-day Olivia. And I've missed that smile." He bent to kiss her with great enthusiasm, not stopping until she pulled away with a laugh.

"But I do have one little problem," he said.

"What's that?" she asked, feeling his warm breath against her ear.

"I want you to put a hold on all this confessing and consulting with the constabulary, at least until we're in the house for a few months. And please do not, under any circumstances, find a dead body at my new construction site."

Olivia chuckled. "I can take a break from my consulting work for sure. As for not finding any more bodies? I don't think I can make that promise, not even to you."

Between the Sheets
Redondo and Rose Neighbors in Crime Book Two

Chapter One
Vivienne Rose

"Take a look at him." Rex Redondo pointed. "He's just a toddler and really good on that tricycle." A young boy pedaled down the middle of the street, his chubby legs pumping.

Rex's hand gripped her shoulder. "Oh oh!" The small boy's bike leaned to the left as he narrowly missed running down the orange cone. Several had been placed in the street, serving as an obstacle course.

An older man stood nearby on the grass. "Keep going, Josh. Look out for the next one!" He waved at Rex and Viv, a look of pride in his wide smile. "Isn't he great? Just like Ross Chastain," the man shouted.

"Who's that?" Viv called out.

"You know," the man explained, "like the NASCAR driver. My grandson. He's something else."

The sound of a blaring horn made the hair stand on Viv's neck. A sleek gray Porsche slid around the corner. Driving past the residential speed limit, the car headed straight toward the little boy.

Viv gasped as brakes squealed.

Rex shouted in alarm, "Look out!"

The grandfather froze, his eyes wide with horror.

The trike hit a cone which fell over as the boy tipped off the seat collapsing onto the pavement. The sound of an electric car engine whirred away as the child's piercing wail met Viv's ears.

She darted into the street toward the child. Bending closer, her eyes traveled over his body. "It's okay, sweetie. You'll be fine," she assured him. The little boy sat up, tears streaming down his face.

Smoothing back the hair on his forehead, Viv's trained fingers gently probed his small arm. *Nothing broken.* A cut on his chin oozed blood. She reached into her pocket, pulling out a wad of tissues. Dabbing at the wound, she smiled into his eyes. Her mind continuing to assess. *The wound can be cleaned, might need a stitch.* The next glance affirmed her opinion. Dirt from the road covered both of his knees. *A little skinned up.*

"Is he okay?" The grandfather bent over Viv, his hand reaching for the child.

The child thrust his arms over his head. "Grandpa," he cried. The grandfather reached down and scooped the boy into his arms. Viv watched the child cling to the chest of the older man.

The man spoke over the boy's shoulder. "My wife is going to be furious. She's always telling me not to let him play in the street." He bent his head to whisper assurances. "It's okay, buddy. I've got you. You're going to be right as rain." The child buried his face further into his grandfather's shirt. But the tears had stopped.

Viv stood. "I'd take him to the ER to have him checked out. Just in case."

Perspiration beaded down the side of the older man's face. "Good idea," he said with a nod. "I'm going to take him right now. And thank you." His voice choked with emotion.

Once the man left, Rex turned to Viv. "Are you okay?"

"What, about that?" She pointed to the trike lying in the street. The handlebars tilted backward, an orange cone trapped underneath the front wheel.

When Rex raised an eyebrow she answered his question. "I was really scared." She brushed her hands against her slacks. "I'm going to pick this up," she pointed to the trike again, "and then drag those cones out of the road."

"Why don't you let me help at least." Rex lifted the trike in one hand. Viv grabbed a cone and made her way to the sidewalk. In a matter of minutes Rex had stacked the others, leaving them on the grass.

"The car didn't even stop." Rex looked toward the community exit.

Viv's eyes narrowed. "Isn't that just what we wanted to talk to the board about? Kids playing in the streets, how dangerous that is. And now there's been an actual accident.

"I think he's going to be fine, only scrapes and bruises. Mostly, he was just frightened," Viv added, more to reassure herself and to calm down.

"Did you see who was driving the Porsche?" Rex asked.

"A guy with a shaved head. Probably mid forties. He gunned that engine and didn't even stop to see if the child was okay." Viv shook her head in disappointment. "I only have first aid training. I do hope the boy is alright," she said again, feeling as if she should have insisted more strongly about having the child checked out by a doctor.

"So we'll bring that up at our first meeting," Rex assured her. "At the homeowner's meeting. We're still going, right?"

"I want to go more than ever," she stated firmly. "A fifty-five-plus neighborhood is not supposed to have children playing in the middle of the main road. Why do people think it's okay to treat the street like their backyard?"

He placed his hand on her elbow. "So we're a bit late. But let's take that indignation and put it to good use. Our first HOA meeting."

His voice sounded reassuring, but Viv still felt mad. But she did agree with Rex that the best course would be to take this up with the board. The list of community rules was quite long, but it didn't matter if there was no one to make sure they were enforced.

GET A FREE SHORT STORY

Along with contests, discounts, giveaways, and events, I'll send you *Meadow's Hat,* a free

short story download.

Signup on bonniehardywrites.com/newsletter

For a full list please go to <u>bonniehardywrites.com/Books</u>

The Lily Rock Mystery Books

Olivia Greer's trip to the mountain town of Lily Rock turns out quite differently than the getaway she expected. Her friend is found dead and she ends up being the prime suspect in the murder. With the help of Mayor Maguire, the town's labradoodle, and Michael Bellemare, the famous hunky architect, she comes to discover deep connections to the town that she could never have anticipated. Love. Laughter. Whodunit. Join Olivia as she begins her journey of self discovery.

The Welcome to Lily Rock

Holiday Cozy Mystery Novellas

As an homage to the holiday classic film, *It's a Wonderful Life,* Bonnie Hardy contemplates what the small town of Lily Rock was like before the arrival of Olivia Greer. In this prequel spin-off series, you'll enjoy fresh adventures with holiday themes and learn the backstories of the characters you've come to know and love.

Redondo and Rose Neighbors in Crime

Cozy Mystery Series

HE'S A MENTALIST. SHE'S A DOULA. THEY ARE NEIGHBOR'S IN CRIME.

In this new series by Bonnie Hardy, Neighbors Rex Redondo and
Vivienne Rose are entangled in the investigation of who murdered
the woman floating in Viv's swimming pool. Playing Bogart to her
Bacall, Rex and Viv solve the mystery and explore their mid-life
romance in a setting reminiscent of Old Hollywood.

NOTE FROM THE AUTHOR

A Very Tidy Death was inspired by an incident in my childhood, the day when I realized the satisfaction and calm that came to me from tidying up my closet.

I was eight years old living in a less than functional home, wondering what to do with my life. That sounds quite odd as I read these words aloud. I mean who at eight thinks about their life purpose?

I did. Mostly because people left me alone. Not always in a bad way. My parents and brother had their own lives. I was cared for and loved but not spoken to that often. This left me in my room with lots of spare time.

So I read constantly, one book to the next. And I sang songs from a funny little edition of children's music. And I imagined lots of stories. I had crayons for drawing but was never terribly artistic in that sense. It wasn't until I opened my closet and stood back to declare, "This is a mess," that I realized it was within my power to clean things up.

I started by removing everything from the closet. Then I threw some stuff away. I dusted and vacuumed the interior and put things back in an orderly fashion. I still remember how satisfying that felt to my eight year old self. Such control. From that moment and throughout my life I've found myself tidying up whenever I feel anxious or need a break from my routine.

Over the years I've had many opportunities to use my tidying skills. Of course before and after every military move. And then with my children and their rooms. I've worked at a number of churches where I tore through back closets and reorganized, in-between writing sermons and leading bible study. I figured that the military might move me away but at least I'd leave the church with clean closets.

And now some important recognition. Thanks to my author team, led by Christie Stratos at Proof Positive and Ebook Launch who draws original cover art for each book.

And thanks to you dear readers. I hope you love Olivia and Michael and the gang as much as I do. If you want more details on the next book in the series, please join my newsletter at bonniehardywrites.com

Until then, be one with the mystery!

Bonnie

ABOUT THE AUTHOR

Born and raised in Los Angeles, Bonnie Hardy is an educator, curriculum writer, musician, and preacher. A lover of libraries and literacy, Bonnie also directed a literacy center in her home town, Carlsbad, CA.

A retired military spouse, she's lived and worked in Washington DC, No. Virginia, and Maryland. After two years in Twentynine Palms, Bonnie decided it was time to writes books that she loved to read.

Bonnie has published in *Christian Century, Presence: An International Journal for Spiritual Direction,* and with *Pilgrim Press.*

When not planting flowers and baking cookies, she's sitting at her computer plotting her next cozy mystery.

facebook.com/bonniehardywrites.com

instagram.com/bonniehardywrites

bookbub.com/authors/bonnie-hardy

goodreads.com/bonniehardy

9 781954 995178